P9-CRI-957

By Danielle Steel

HAPPINESS • PALAZZO • THE WEDDING PLANNER
WORTHY OPPONENTS • WITHOUT A TRACE • THE WHITTIERS
THE HIGH NOTES • THE CHALLENGE • SUSPECTS • BEAUTIFUL
HIGH STAKES • INVISIBLE • FLYING ANGELS • THE BUTLER
COMPLICATIONS • NINE LIVES • FINDING ASHLEY • THE AFFAIR
NEIGHBORS • ALL THAT GLITTERS • ROYAL • DADDY'S GIRLS
THE WEDDING DRESS • THE NUMBERS GAME • MORAL COMPASS
SPY • CHILD'S PLAY • THE DARK SIDE • LOST AND FOUND
BLESSING IN DISGUISE • SILENT NIGHT • TURNING POINT
BEAUCHAMP HALL • IN HIS FATHER'S FOOTSTEPS • THE GOOD FIGHT
THE CAST • ACCIDENTAL HEROES • FALL FROM GRACE
PAST PERFECT • FAIRYTALE • THE RIGHT TIME • THE DUCHESS
AGAINST ALL ODDS • DANGEROUS GAMES • THE MISTRESS
THE AWARD • RUSHING WATERS • MAGIC • THE APARTMENT
PROPERTY OF A NOBLEWOMAN • BLUE • PRECIOUS GIFTS
UNDERCOVER • COUNTRY • PRODIGAL SON • PEGASUS
A PERFECT LIFE • POWER PLAY • WINNERS • FIRST SIGHT
UNTIL THE END OF TIME • THE SINS OF THE MOTHER
FRIENDS FOREVER • BETRAYAL • HOTEL VENDÔME
HAPPY BIRTHDAY • 44 CHARLES STREET • LEGACY • FAMILY TIES
BIG GIRL • SOUTHERN LIGHTS • MATTERS OF THE HEART
ONE DAY AT A TIME • A GOOD WOMAN • ROGUE • HONOR THYSELF
AMAZING GRACE • BUNGALOW 2 • SISTERS • H.R.H. • COMING OUT
THE HOUSE • TOXIC BACHELORS • MIRACLE • IMPOSSIBLE • ECHOES
SECOND CHANCE • RANSOM • SAFE HARBOUR • JOHNNY ANGEL
DATING GAME • ANSWERED PRAYERS • SUNSET IN ST. TROPEZ
THE COTTAGE • THE KISS • LEAP OF FAITH • LONE EAGLE • JOURNEY
THE HOUSE ON HOPE STREET • THE WEDDING
IRRESISTIBLE FORCES • GRANNY DAN • BITTERSWEET
MIRROR IMAGE • THE KLONE AND I • THE LONG ROAD HOME
THE GHOST • SPECIAL DELIVERY • THE RANCH • SILENT HONOR
MALICE • FIVE DAYS IN PARIS • LIGHTNING • WINGS • THE GIFT
ACCIDENT • VANISHED • MIXED BLESSINGS • JEWELS
NO GREATER LOVE • HEARTBEAT • MESSAGE FROM NAM • DADDY
STAR • ZOYA • KALEIDOSCOPE • FINE THINGS • WANDERLUST
SECRETS • FAMILY ALBUM • FULL CIRCLE • CHANGES
THURSTON HOUSE • CROSSINGS • ONCE IN A LIFETIME
A PERFECT STRANGER • REMEMBRANCE • PALOMINO • LOVE: *POEMS*
THE RING • LOVING • TO LOVE AGAIN • SUMMER'S END
SEASON OF PASSION • THE PROMISE • NOW AND FOREVER
PASSION'S PROMISE • GOING HOME

Nonfiction
PURE JOY: *The Dogs We Love*
A GIFT OF HOPE: *Helping the Homeless*
HIS BRIGHT LIGHT: *The Story of Nick Traina*

For Children
PRETTY MINNIE IN PARIS
PRETTY MINNIE IN HOLLYWOOD

THE WHITTIERS

DANIELLE STEEL

THE WHITTIERS

A Novel

Dell
New York

2023 Dell Mass Market Edition

Published in the United States by Dell,
an imprint of Random House, a division of
Penguin Random House LLC, New York.

DELL and the D colophon are registered trademarks of
Penguin Random House LLC.

Originally published in hardcover in the United States
by Delacorte Press, an imprint of Random House, a division of
Penguin Random House LLC, in 2022.

This book contains an excerpt from the forthcoming book
Second Act by Danielle Steel. This excerpt has been set for
this edition only and may not reflect the final content
of the forthcoming edition.

ISBN 978-1-9848-2185-0
Ebook ISBN 978-1-9848-2184-3

Cover design: Lisa Amoroso
Cover images: © Spiroview Inc/Shutterstock (mansion),
© gremlin/Getty Images (people in the window),
© Olga Krämer/Alamy (snow), © P. Spiro/Alamy (door)

Printed in the United States of America

randomhousebooks.com

4 6 8 9 7 5

Dell mass market edition: September 2023

To my wonderful children,
Beatie, Trevor, Todd, Nick,
Samantha, Victoria, Vanessa,
Maxx, and Zara,

May you treasure and honor each other
and all the beautiful memories we share forever.
With all my heart and love.

I love you all.

Mom/d.s.

THE WHITTIERS

Chapter 1

Three weeks after Christmas every year, Preston and Constance Whittier left their home in New York and took a vacation. When the children were younger, their beloved German housekeeper, Frieda, and one of a revolving door of nannies would take care of their six children. They would come home energized and refreshed after a romantic two- or three-week interlude alone. They both loved to ski, and a favorite spot for their holiday was one of the Three Valleys in the French Alps. They went to Courchevel, Val d'Isère, or Megève in France, Zermatt and St. Moritz in Switzerland. Occasionally they skied in Aspen or Vail in Colorado, but with their kids grown, they preferred to take their annual child-free vacation in Europe rather than in the States.

They often took the children skiing with them

when they went to Aspen, during their winter break from school. Their ski trips in Europe were a special treat for Connie and Preston. They usually ended the trip with a weekend in Paris or London before heading back to New York to resume their family life. As the children got older, they teased their parents about the trip, and called it their Wintermoon.

They all summered on Shelter Island, in a big family house they had eventually sold, when the children stopped spending summers with them and the house had become more of a burden than a joy. Connie and Preston had begun to streamline their life in recent years, cutting down on unnecessary expenses, and avoiding projects that were too much work for them. In the summers, they rented a house in Maine now, or in the Hamptons, or on Cape Cod, large enough so that the children who wanted to could come and go for a few days or a weekend visit. Renting was easier than owning, and the headache of maintaining a summer home was someone else's problem, not theirs. The children never came at the same time, so they didn't need an enormous house. Preston and Connie still clung to the tradition of their Wintermoon, which they called it now too. It was important to them, and they looked forward to it all year. After forty-three years of marriage, it still felt like a honeymoon to them. Constance was sixty-five years old and the time had flown. She couldn't believe how old her children were, all adults now. Even their "baby" Annabelle, a late surprise, had just turned twenty-one.

Their oldest, Lyle, was forty-two, married, with two children of his own, a son and daughter, Tommy, ten, and Devon, seven. His wife, Amanda, had been a disappointment to them all. Lyle had been enjoying his bachelorhood and burgeoning career in land development and commercial real estate ten years ago when the girl he was dating none too seriously had gotten pregnant and he had married her. She had never warmed to his family, nor they to her. She was socially ambitious. Constance thought her greedy, although Preston's attitude was more charitable. She was bright and lively and fun and sexy, and knew how to turn the charm on for Lyle, but within a short time after they married, Connie didn't think Lyle looked happy. But Lyle never complained. He was loyal to a fault and wanted to make the marriage work once he'd agreed to marry Amanda.

Amanda never worked after they were married. She had strong desires for expensive things, made heavy demands of him, and gave little in exchange, in Connie's opinion, but Connie loved her grandchildren, and enjoyed spending time with them. Both Annabelle, now twenty-one, and Benjie, twenty-eight, Preston and Connie's two youngest children, still lived at home with them. Connie loved having the last of her children still near at hand. Their other children, all on determined ca-

reer paths, had moved out years before. Gloria,
next after Lyle, had a big job on Wall Street in finance, and was generous with business advice to
her brothers and sisters, whether they asked for it
or not. She had bought an apartment on the Upper
West Side, which she loved. She visited her parents'
home often, but was happiest living alone, even
now at thirty-nine.

The twins, Caroline and Charlie, had bought an
apartment together in SoHo. At thirty-three, they
worked brutally hard on their steadily growing
fashion brand of women's clothes. They spent every
waking hour working, and had transformed a loft
in an old warehouse into a living space they loved.
Inseparable as children and growing up, they had
opted to live and build a business together as
adults. It worked well for both of them.

Lyle was the only one of the six siblings who
was married. Gloria, Charlie, and Caroline were
busy with their careers and there was no hint of
marriage on the horizon or even serious romantic
relationships for any of them in their fast-moving
worlds. Benjie needed his parents' help, and at
twenty-one, Annabelle was still too young for marriage, and had no interest in it. But she was eager
to have an apartment of her own, and was in nego-
tiation with her parents to allow her to get one.
Independence from parental supervision was her
only current goal. She had recently dropped out of
college, which her parents weren't pleased about,

and moved back in with them. This had stalled her ability to convince them that more freedom was what she needed most now. So the prospect of moving to her own apartment was currently on hold. And Benjie was delighted to have her back at home with him.

Connie and Preston had met for the first time at her debut in New York, when she was presented to society, in an antiquated social rite her family still clung to. Preston was ten years older and didn't pay attention to her. She was just one of twenty-five eighteen-year-old girls in pretty white dresses who curtsied to the assembled company and had escorts their own age. They met again at Connie's first job, after she'd graduated from Vassar. She was a junior editor at a publishing house, where Preston was already a respected senior editor. He noticed her immediately and found her intelligent and beautiful. They married the following summer and started their family immediately.

Connie gave up her job to raise the children they planned to have. Eventually Preston became the publisher, and held the job for the rest of his career. Now seventy-five, he had been retired for ten years. They loved having more time to spend together. He had enjoyed a distinguished career, and they had similar interests. They never tired of being together, and there was still a spark of romance between them, which grew into a steady blaze during their Wintermoons in Europe.

They came from similar backgrounds. Preston's family had had a great fortune from steel and copper at the turn of the twentieth century. The Crash of '29 had taken a heavy toll, as had time, but hadn't wiped them out entirely, as it had others. The family just had less than before, and had to live more carefully. But neither Preston nor Connie had a taste for luxury. Although Preston's fortune had diminished over the years, they had enough money to live well. Preston had made wise investments, and he made a respectable salary. They could comfortably afford their six children, and a solid, stable lifestyle, without extravagance. While their children had been well educated and would inherit a modest amount one day, they would never be "rich" as his family had once been. The value of the house and Preston's investments made them vulnerable to estate taxes, and what was left would be divided six ways. What they inherited would help them buy homes, educate their own children, and start businesses. With their inheritances, they would be comfortable, but none of them would be very wealthy from what their parents left them.

Their mother, Connie, had inherited a small amount from her aristocratic parents and grandparents, but their fortune had never equaled Preston's, and what she'd inherited had dwindled to very little over the years. But Preston supported them well.

The most valuable asset they had to leave their children was the house they had lived in since before Lyle was born. It was an old once-grand mansion they had bought for a ridiculously small sum in a foreclosure auction Connie had read about. No one wanted a house that size, so they bought it for a price they were able to afford at the time. It was in the East Seventies between Fifth and Madison Avenues, at a very impressive address. It had once been an extremely elegant home. They had turned it into a family home, despite its size and history. Its location made it valuable, and they expected their children to sell it one day for the substantial price it would bring. It had been an incredible opportunity when they bought it. Preston had been afraid it was too big when Connie found it, but with the six children they eventually had, it had proven to be perfect for them. It had beautiful moldings, magnificent high ceilings, graceful French windows, and several wood-paneled rooms. Connie and Preston maintained it well, but with some modernization and restoration, its grandeur could be easily refreshed by new owners willing and able to spend the money. It could bring a fortune from the right buyer. It had turned out to be their best investment, and was worth far more than they had paid for it forty-two years before.

There was no way that their six children would

want to live there together again as adults, particularly once they married and had children of their own. It would have to be sold, as they had both stipulated in their wills. The children were all deeply attached to their family home, but selling it would add handsomely to the money Connie and Preston would be able to leave them, which was what they envisioned for their children's future after they were gone. Now, with only their two youngest children living there with them, they had far more space than they needed. Only Lyle was married and had children, but once the others had families of their own, they wouldn't want the house anyway. It wouldn't be practical for them, and their parents couldn't imagine any one of them being able to buy the others out of their individual shares of the house.

Lyle was the most successful of their children, had the opportunity to make real money, and was doing well. And Gloria made a big salary and commissions. But the house made no sense for Lyle and Amanda as a couple with two children, and they had a beautiful apartment a little farther uptown on the East Side. The house made no sense for Gloria either, still single at thirty-nine, after a series of dead-end relationships and a broken engagement just shy of the altar at twenty-three. She insisted now that marriage wasn't for her, and had put all her energy into her career. Connie doubted that she'd ever marry, or might do so very late. And Glo-

ria loved her apartment on the West Side in a famous old building with a view of the park. Charles
and Caroline were struggling to make a success of
their fashion business and loved their loft together
in SoHo. They lived and worked together.

And after Annabelle dropped out of college as a
senior because she said she was "bored," her parents wanted her to go back to school and graduate
or get a job before they got her a small studio apartment. She couldn't afford rent at the moment, so
she was living at home. Benjie would be staying
with them, although he was older than Annabelle,
but happy at home.

So there was no question in Connie and Preston's minds, the house would have to be sold one
day. They hoped to stay there until it became too
much for them to manage. But for now, they were
in good health, and happy to still be living there.
They loved their big old home, and had no intention of selling it in the foreseeable future. They had
no reason to for now. They could still afford it, with
some deferred maintenance. They only repaired
what was pressing.

Frieda, their old housekeeper, was still with
them. She was sixty-eight now. There was also a
young man they hired occasionally when they had
heavy jobs that Preston couldn't do on his own. He
loved puttering around the house and keeping it in
good repair, handling the small projects himself

with ingenuity. But he couldn't do electrical or plumbing.

Preston played golf with his friends who had retired, and Connie still played tennis once a week with a group of women friends. Once in a while, they went skiing in Vermont for a weekend. They were both fit and skiing was a sport they still loved. They had a very pleasant life, and were proud of their children, although Annabelle was worrying them at the moment. She needed to go back to school or get a job, and for now, she was doing neither. Her parents thought she was a little too involved in the nightlife of New York, going to parties and hanging out with her friends. The others had all had more direction at her age. Lyle had graduated from Yale and had gone to business school at Columbia. Gloria had gone to Harvard, both undergraduate and business school. The twins had gone to Parsons School of Design, and had been in love with the fashion industry since their teens. They had started their business when they graduated. Caroline was the designer, and Charlie was the CFO and handled the financial end, and had a strong fashion sense too. Benjie had a job he loved at a pet shelter and he was devoted to it. Only Annabelle had no definite direction at the moment, but she was still very young. Her mother kept a watchful eye on her, and on Benjie too. Preston was happy to leave the child rearing to Connie now. He had been more involved with the older four, but at seventy-five he felt past the age of scolding Annabelle for how late she stayed out, or for sleeping until noon, or about who her friends were. Connie was better at it and still enjoyed being on the front lines of motherhood, and close to her children. Preston was happy to give his adult children his advice, if they asked him for it, but he no longer wanted to police them, and the older ones didn't need that from him and hadn't in years. He enjoyed a mutually respectful adult relationship with them now.

For two or three blissful weeks every January, Connie and Preston didn't think about any of it. The children weren't children anymore, and could manage without them while their parents played and enjoyed each other. It was one of the benefits of their mature years, which they both reveled in. This year was no different, and so far the skiing had been superb, and the meals excellent, in Courchevel. They were staying at a family-style hotel they had enjoyed for years. It wasn't extravagant, but cozy and comfortable and romantic. The children hadn't heard from them since they arrived, and didn't expect to. They were old enough now to leave their parents alone to enjoy their Wintermoon. And the older ones checked in with Annabelle and Benjie to make sure they were all right. Charlie dropped by to see Benjie regularly and Caroline called Annabelle, who didn't appreciate her calls.

* * *

When Lyle woke up on Saturday morning, he found a note from Amanda in the kitchen of their apartment. It said only that she might be back late and was meeting friends. She had left him the time and location of Tommy's soccer game, which meant that she wouldn't be home to take him there. Lyle didn't mind taking Tommy to the game in the park. He enjoyed it. He worked hard during the week, and liked spending time with his children on the weekends. Amanda often went shopping with her girlfriends on Saturdays. It wasn't an unusual occurrence, although he would have preferred her being at home with them. Amanda frequently considered Saturdays her "day off" because Lyle was home and could be with the children, so she felt she didn't have to. She preferred being with her friends.

Lyle got the kids up, saw to it that they got dressed, and made them breakfast. Later, in plenty of time for Tommy's game, he made lunch for Tommy and Devon and sat down with them at the kitchen table while they told him what they'd done all week. He liked being a hands-on dad. Tommy liked it when his father came to his soccer games, and Devon never complained about going with them. She wanted to be on a girls' soccer team next year when she turned eight. She liked sports and looked up to her big brother. Most of the time, they got along, although Tommy was three years older. He was in fifth grade and Devon was in second.

It was cold when they left the apartment, bundled up against the January weather. Lyle made Devon put on an extra sweater under her puffy pink down jacket. The game was due to start at two, and he knew they would be in the park until about four. He had made a thermos of hot chocolate for them to drink at the game, and brought cookies with him. They walked to the garage, and he drove them to the field where they played on the west side of Central Park. Several of the mothers turned and noticed him as they walked toward the bleachers. Tommy took off his jacket and joined the team and the coach. Lyle had made him put on thermals under his heavy uniform, with his name on the back of his sweatshirt. Lyle sat down in the bleachers and Devon cuddled up next to him and he put an arm around her. She had on a pink knitted cap with matching mittens, and earmuffs and fleece-lined boots so she wouldn't get cold during the game. Devon looked a lot like him, with dark hair and big brown eyes.

Tommy was fair, with blond hair and blue eyes, like his mother. "Hi, Lyle," one of the mothers said to him. She was an attractive blonde with her own daughter in tow, and he was a familiar figure there. He brought his kids to the games often. "Where's Amanda?" she asked him.

"Busy today," he said simply, not offering a rea-

son for her absence. He didn't see why he needed
to. He paid no attention to the mothers who looked
at him admiringly. He waved to one of the fathers
he knew who came over to talk to him and sat
down on the bleachers next to him, while Devon
stayed close on his other side. The two men chatted
until the game started and then paid close attention to their sons playing. The mothers were more
engaged in talking to each other, while their daugh-
ters or younger sons played in the area around
them.

Lyle watched when one of the boys scored a
goal, and Tommy missed one, and he waved and
shouted encouragement.

In the end, Tommy's team won, although he
hadn't scored any goals himself. He had played a
respectable game, and Lyle never put any pressure
on him about winning, as some of the other fathers
did. Two other mothers had come to chat with him
in the course of the game. He was friendly with
everyone but never flirted with the women. He was
tall with dark brown hair, as his father's had been,
and warm brown eyes. He and Amanda made a
handsome couple. She took good care of herself
and went to the gym three or four times a week.
She had a terrific figure and didn't look her age.
She was thirty-seven and could have passed for ten
years younger.

They had a housekeeper who doubled as a babysitter, and was reliable, which gave Amanda plenty

of free time. She spent most of her time shopping and having lunch with her girlfriends, or at yoga classes or the gym. Molly drove the kids to school and picked them up, Amanda didn't. She always had something on her agenda, and she often came home after they were back from school. It would have been easier for Lyle if she got on better with his family, particularly his sisters, but she had never made any great effort in that direction, and she knew what they thought of her. They still thought she had trapped Lyle into the marriage, but he had been a willing participant, as he pointed out to his parents and siblings in her defense.

"She didn't force me into marrying her," he reminded them when the subject came up, which it still did from time to time, much to his chagrin. "I wanted to. It was a choice I made. It was the right thing to do." His closest sister, Gloria, was the most outspoken about it, and called Amanda a gold digger to the others. Lyle always pointed out, to be fair, that he would have married her anyway eventually, but his family wasn't as sure. He'd had a roving eye in those days, while they were just dating, but he no longer did. Women's gazes followed him often for his good looks, and he always pretended not to notice, out of respect for Amanda. He had suggested marriage to her when she had found out she was pregnant, and he didn't hesitate. He felt it was only right. He had been careless about protection on a number of occasions, and she had let him.

So, he manned up when she got pregnant and paid the price. He didn't regret it, because of their children, although the heat of his passion for her had waned early, and for the past few years had been nonexistent for both of them.

Amanda made no effort to make love to him either. Their hunger for each other had long since disappeared. They had nothing in common. She loved the lifestyle he offered her, and the fact that she didn't have to work, but she didn't melt at the sight of him as she had when she first met him. She could barely remember how that felt anymore, and he had gotten used to living without affection or a gentle touch. In fact, the sex used to be better after they argued, which they did often.

But they weren't as close as Lyle had hoped they would be. Amanda wasn't a warm person, with him or their children. But she was his wife, and like his parents, he believed that marriage was a lifetime commitment, so he made the best of what he had, which wasn't much. She had no interest in intellectual pursuits, didn't like family life, which was all-important to him. She had no interest in his business, and they hardly spoke to each other now. She avoided spending time with him.

After the game, he was home with the children by five o'clock. They went to their rooms to watch videos until dinnertime. Lyle assumed that Amanda would be home by then, and he worked on his computer while he waited. It was twenty to seven when she got home, which was later than usual, and she'd been gone since eight o'clock that morning, long before she could do any shopping.

She'd been to a friend's home for an exercise class, and then they had showered and dressed and gone out. And they had stopped at the Plaza for a martini after shopping, which accounted for the late hour of her return. She loved being out with her girlfriends and found her home life with Lyle dreary.

"Where the hell have you been?" he asked her, looking annoyed by the time she got back. He tried to give her time to herself, but it irked him when she did it on weekends.

"I was just out, shopping. We stopped for a drink before I came home."

"The kids missed you today," he said simply. "So did most of the fathers. Everyone asked me where you were." He envied the couples who did things together, like his parents. Amanda had always been independent, even when they were first married. Her parents had divorced when she was young and she had no role models for marriage.

And she let the housekeeper do things with the children that he thought Amanda should do herself, since she didn't work. She had turned out not to have strong maternal instincts. She'd rather go to the gym or spend time with her friends.

"And what did you say?" she asked him.

"What I always say when you don't go to Tommy's games. That you're busy." He wondered as he said it if she was having an affair, but he didn't think so. She just wasn't interested in him anymore. She was much more interested in what he could buy her. He had always been generous with her, and didn't hold it against her that they had to get married. He had lived up to his side of the bargain. She was his family now. He was a profoundly nice guy, even though their marriage had been a disappointment to both of them. He never forced his own family on her. Amanda and his sister Gloria had clashed early on, when his sister had begged him not to marry her. Amanda was too different from the women Lyle had dated before. She hadn't gone to college and had no career goals. She had worked as a model occasionally, at a restaurant at other times. She had been estranged from her family since she was sixteen, and it was obvious that she wanted to marry a man with money. Gloria had suggested that he pay her support for the child, but not marry her, which didn't feel right to him, no matter what her background was. And he was thrilled the moment he saw Tommy. In recent years, fatherhood had come to mean more to him, and been more satisfying, than marriage. He had suggested the second baby to her, which seemed like a normal progression to him as part of marriage. Amanda wasn't enthusiastic about it, but she thought a second child would cement the deal between them even more, and make his family accept her. It hadn't. She was just as unacceptable to them with two children as she had been with one. All the second baby had done was convince his family that he would never leave her, and Lyle loved Devon as much as he did Tommy. His physical attraction to Amanda had waned after Devon was born, even though she got back in shape quickly, and was still beautiful and young. She had no interest at all in family life. Having grown up in a family where her father beat her alcoholic mother and eventually left her, she had gone out on her own when her mother died of cirrhosis when she was sixteen. She had no idea where her father was, or if he was still alive. Lyle felt sorry for her. She had grown up with none of the advantages he'd had, with a loving family, stable parents, an education, and enough money. He respected what she had survived, but it had hardened her.

She had expensive taste, and however much he made, it was never enough for her. She spent his money lavishly, mostly on things for herself. She had come home that day with several shopping bags filled to the brim with what she'd bought at the expensive stores where she shopped. She never apologized for what she spent, and acted as though he owed it to her. She had a strong feeling of entitlement, and gratitude wasn't part of it. She went to her dressing room to put her purchases away, while Lyle tried not to get angry at her. He went to find her to ask her what they were doing for dinner.

He didn't want to fight with her, with the children near at hand.

"Let's order in," she said blithely. Molly, their housekeeper, didn't work on the weekends. Amanda never made the effort to cook on weekends. Lyle cooked occasionally on Sunday nights. She never did. "I'm tired," she said simply. He nodded and went to ask the kids what they wanted. They both requested pizza and he went to order it. Amanda said she'd make herself a salad, and he decided to eat pizza with the kids. She set the table. When the pizza came, Tommy told her they had won the game, and she looked at Tommy blankly. He knew she didn't care about soccer, or who won, but he always sought her approval and wanted to impress her. The look on his face cut Lyle to the quick. She didn't even try to fake it. Lyle was still annoyed at her when the kids left the table after dinner.

"You could at least pretend you care that his team won," he said, as he threw the rest of the pizza away and put the dishes in the sink with a clatter. "It matters to him." Tommy was always struggling for her attention, as Lyle had for years, but Lyle no longer bothered. He had always been sure there was a warm woman in there somewhere, behind her walls, and knew now that there wasn't. Tommy didn't know that yet. The abuse she'd experienced as a child had left her cold and empty.

She looked at Lyle coldly. "He knows I don't like sports." There was nothing she cared about except

herself, her shopping, and her friends. She and Lyle
had never liked the same people. She liked rougher
people, diamonds in the rough, more like her. After
ten years of marriage, she thought Lyle was dull
and square. She had never adapted to the more
conservative style he had grown up with. He had
been racier when he was younger, when they met,
but had settled down quickly. Amanda knew now
that she would never measure up to his family, so
she no longer tried. She hated them. Lyle was the
bridge between two warring camps, trapped in the
middle. Amanda liked sexy clothes that were short
and tight, with cleavage whenever possible, that
showed off her figure, and he never criticized her
for it, although his sister Gloria said she looked
cheap. Lyle was tolerant and a respecter of people.
He had asked Amanda several times to tone down
what she wore when they saw his family, but she
did what she wanted, which was to defy them, and
remind them every chance she got that she had
won ten years before when he married her, three
months pregnant. She didn't need to rub it in by
looking cheap, to prove the point. But she did
whenever possible, with total disregard for how
Lyle felt about it, or how awkward it was for him.
His parents never commented on it, but his sisters
did.

Amanda made no effort to fit in. She had what
she wanted, a man to pay her bills. The children
were just accessories to her, leverage she could use

with him to get whatever else she wanted. And he knew now, and had for several years, that he couldn't make her into something she wasn't. She was never going to fit his vision of a wife and mother, and had no desire to try. She didn't have to. She thought his family were boring snobs, and she hated them. Lyle knew now that she was never going to be anything like his mother, or any of his sisters, or even his friends' wives, and no amount of pressure or reasoning with her was going to change her, so he accepted her as she was, and made the best of it. She liked showing off and looking sexy and cheap. He had long since made his peace with it, although they fought a lot. He no longer tried to change her. She had no empathy for him or their children. She wanted a jazzier social life with people more like her, which Lyle refused to engage in.

He watched a movie with the children after dinner, and tucked Devon into bed afterwards, and then stuck his head into Tommy's room later to say good night. He was watching a favorite show on TV as Lyle quietly closed the door, and went back to his bedroom, where Amanda was watching a reality TV show.

"You need to spend more time with the kids," he said softly. It was a familiar refrain between them that she didn't want to hear. She increased the volume on the TV to drown him out. "You were gone all day. You could at least have spent some time with them this evening."

"Why?" she answered without looking at him. "I'm with them all week. They have you on weekends. Saturday and Sunday should be my days off." But their babysitter spent more time with them during the week than she did.

"We don't get 'days off,' and Molly is with them all week, you're not. You're never here when they get home from school."

"No one was at home for me as a kid, it didn't kill me. Besides, I have my yoga class then," she said, annoyed. He was always hounding her to spend more time with the children.

"We've got two kids. I'm asking you to spend more time with them. That's not a lot to ask. My mother was always there when we got home from school," he said, his voice growing taut.

"Mine was always at the corner bar getting drunk, or passed out," she said coldly. She got up and left the room then, and he followed her to her dressing room, chock full of everything she bought, thanks to him. He never reminded her about that.

"If you don't care about me, Amanda, I can live with it. But you need to at least pretend for them. They need more from their mother than you give them. I know you had a hard time as a kid. But our kids need you," he said, as gently as he could, trying to get through to her, with no success.

"They're fine," she said, stone-faced, as a muscle tightened in Lyle's jaw.

"They are now. But maybe one day they won't

be." And he didn't want them turning out like her, hard, cold, bitter, self-centered, and greedy. They were sweet kids, and he didn't want them damaged and deprived by an unfeeling mother.

"You judge everything by your family's standards," she accused him. "They're pathetic and dependent on each other. The twins live together at thirty-three. Gloria hasn't had a serious relationship in ten years, and hangs out with your parents half the time. You're on the phone with them every time I turn around. Benjie lives at home like a child instead of being placed somewhere with others like him. And Annabelle is turning into a slut, and your family is so blind they don't even notice. You all think you're so saintly and lily pure, and none of you know a damn thing about real life." He was well aware of how hard Amanda's youth had been, but he was deeply offended by her description of his family. Their values and strong bond meant nothing to her.

"I know you hate them, and they've been tough on you at times. We got off to a bad start with them. But you're not fair. And what you said about Benjie isn't correct. He does well at home, he has a job, and my mother is terrific with him. He does really well at the pet shelter. He's worked there for five years now, and they love him. He's doing fine," Lyle said firmly, quick to protect his brother.

"If he were from a normal family, they'd have sent him away years ago. He can't live on his own.

And what's going to happen to that when your parents are gone? Don't count on bringing him here. I'm not running a group home for your brother," she said harshly, and Lyle's eyes blazed as he looked at her. She could be cruel at times, and heartless. He adored his brother Benjie, who had a high IQ and was at the higher end of the ever-changing autism spectrum. He exhibited some symptoms of Asperger's in his social skills, but was pretty capable in other ways, and a bright, loving young man.

"He manages very well, and he's a wonderful person. He doesn't need a group home, and don't worry, I would never move him in with us. You can't even be decent with your own kids, you're so frozen from your own damaged history. You barely have it in you to be a mother to your children, let alone be loving to my brother. And I will *never* send him away to live, as long as I'm alive. He's smarter than any of us sometimes, even if he's socially awkward at times. Watch your mouth, Amanda. You're crossing some dangerous lines. I put up with a lot from you. Stay off the subject of my family if you expect me to keep doing it." She glanced up at him and didn't acknowledge what he'd said, but she had heard it. She didn't like his telling her to spend more time with their kids. She spent as much time with them as she wanted to, which wasn't much. She was making up for everything she hadn't had, not thinking about her own children. Amanda interpreted the amount of money spent on her as love. It was all she understood.

"If your parents had any sense, they'd sell that white elephant of a house of theirs and divide up the money between you, so you could all live better now. Why should you have to wait until they die? They don't need a house that size. Annabelle will move out in the next five minutes, so it'll just be them and Benjie."

"That's up to them. They have the right to live however they want to. It's their money and their house, not ours. I'm not sitting here waiting breathlessly for their money. We have more than enough with what I earn. And I'm happy we still have my parents." He thought what she was suggesting was disgusting, but she had said it all before, not often, but enough.

He knew how she felt about him, his family, how they functioned as a tight unit, and what he stood to inherit.

"You could have a lot more now, if they sold the house," she insisted doggedly. Money was everything to her, her main interest in him, and why she stayed in the marriage.

"It's their home, and where we all grew up. To you, it's just money." Her greed knew no limits. She had no sentiment about what was important to all of them. Their parents, their siblings, and their home, which meant nothing to her.

"You're like the Addams family. You give me the

creeps sometimes," she said harshly. The creeps and a lifestyle she wouldn't have had otherwise, which she didn't even appreciate. She wanted more money to spend and felt deprived.

"I think you'd be smart to stay off the subject of my family," Lyle said, fuming, and slammed the door of her dressing room when he left. He put on his running shoes and heavy down jacket and went for a run in the cold, so as not to lose his temper with her.

Amanda was asleep when he got back. He took a shower and climbed into his side of the bed, and lay awake for a long time, thinking about his marriage. He knew he had done the right thing ten years before when he married her, and there was comfort in that, but the effects of that decision were becoming harder to live with, more and more with each passing year, and sometimes he wondered where it would lead them. She was treading on a minefield now and one day it would explode. His family was sacred to him, and that's where Amanda liked to hurt him. It reminded him of who she was, as though he needed a reminder. Even her own children meant little to her, and her husband even less, except that he provided a lifestyle she felt was her due. She was on dangerous ground now. He had been loyal and loving to Amanda for ten years, which was more than he got from her. His family meant everything to him, his parents, his siblings, and his children. In the end, they were all

Whittiers, and Amanda wasn't. She had chosen to remain outside the circle of the family, and she would pay the price for it one day if she pushed him too far. She knew it too, and pushed him anyway. He had almost reached his breaking point with her.

Sometimes he wondered if that was what she wanted, to finally push him over the edge, and then what?

Chapter 2

Phones were ringing off the hook, people were running, deliveries were being made, a cluster of models were chatting in the corner of a large room. Charlie and Caroline Whittier had bought an old factory on the Lower East Side when they'd graduated from Parsons eleven years before, and started their own fashion brand. They made elegant, stylish women's clothing with beautiful fabrics from France and Italy. They showed their line in a fashion show during ready-to-wear Fashion Week in New York twice a year, in February and September. They had raised their prices a few years before, and their clothes were sold in some of the best stores in the country. They were proud of what they did and how far they'd come in eleven years.

Most of the time they worked day and night, and Caroline had a small studio area set aside in the loft where they lived in SoHo, so she could work at home if she was inspired. She worked most nights and weekends. She was the designer and fashion director of their brand, but Charlie's contributions were valuable too. He had a head for finance, and a strong sense of design. Caro always showed him her drawings, and he often added some small detail and tweaked them in a way that made them even better. He had a good eye for design.

Caro knew he could have been the designer if he wanted to, but he preferred to be their CFO and handle the business end. They had started the business on a shoestring, with money their father had loaned them and money from investors, and they were now a respected brand. The company was called CCW, and their logo showed a large W at the center of the design with a smaller C on either side, for Charles and Caroline Whittier. They had made a mark on the fashion world and eleven years had flown by, with their dedication to their business. They weren't afraid of hard work, and the business took precedence above all else, for both of them. As twins, they had always been extremely close. Before they could talk, they had had their own language, and as they grew up, they had an instinctive sense of each other, as though each knew what the other was thinking. When Caroline had doubts about something, she always found that Charlie had them too, and together they found the solution. Sometimes Caroline felt as though they were each half of the same person, and she was sure that it was because they were twins. They looked very much alike, both of them very blond with blue eyes like their mother, and they had her fine features.

Their determination to make a success of their business and the amount of time they put into it had kept them both from forming long-term romantic attachments. Their work was always the priority, and potential romantic partners always found it tedious and somewhat insulting to take second place to their business. Both Caro and Charlie felt young enough at thirty-three to invest time in the brand they were building, and dedicate themselves to serious relationships later. Neither of them was in a hurry to marry and have children. The business was their baby.

Their fashion show was ten days away, and as usual the fabrics from Italy had been late. Then the fabric shipment got stuck in customs and now the sewers were frantically trying to catch up. They had a group of fit models waiting to try on samples. The real models would try them a day or two before the show, and their seamstresses would make the necessary adjustments. Prunella Clark, the well-known British stylist they used for their shows, had already chosen the accessories for each look, from among Caroline's designs. There were sketches and drawings all over Caro's office, and she looked possessed as her twin flew past her and stopped for a minute to chat. Her long blond hair was tangled in a knot on top of her head with half a dozen pencils stuck through it. She was wearing a T-shirt and torn jeans and looked like a model herself. So did her brother. He was strikingly handsome. They had both modeled a few times while still in design school, but it was the production end of fashion and having a voice in the trends of the day that interested them. They wanted to be a major brand one day, not just a small one. They both knew that would take a large infusion of money, from a bigger brand like Kering or LVMH, but they didn't want to be owned by anyone. So far, they only had private investors, who had a small share of the business. Caroline was particularly vehement on the subject. Charlie was more realistic and knew that they'd eventually have to give up more in order to become major players. They had already invested eleven years in their brand and Caro refused to sell a bigger share to anyone. But there was no other way to do it, and Charlie worked on her regularly to convince her. So far he hadn't, but he hoped he would one day soon so they could go to the next level.

"You look halfway to insane." He grinned at her, with half a box of pencils in her hair, a smudge of the charcoal she drew with on her cheek, and a pincushion on a strap on her wrist.

"I'm already there," she said, with a desperate look. "They shorted us on one of the fabrics from Milan. The one for the green evening gown."

"Change the design," he suggested rapidly.

"That's what I'm doing. They sent us so little we'll be lucky if it doesn't turn out to be hot pants and a halter top, or a bikini."

"You can do it, Caro." He always encouraged her. He had her back and she had his.

"I know, but they do it to us every time, and Customs sat on it, so I didn't know till this morning that I don't have enough to make the dress. I may have to make it in a green satin I bought for something else, and I'll use the green chiffon for number twelve." She was half talking to herself and half to him.

"You'll figure it out, you always do."

"One of my fit models is sick, but," she said with a huge grin, "Nicola Wickham got in a fight with the designer at Herrera, and she's walking the show for us," she said victoriously.

Nicola was the biggest model in New York at the moment, and having her in the show was a major coup. "She's coming in for a runway fitting at two." Charlie knew there would be a thousand minor and major victories, tragedies, and cliffhanging moments in the next ten days until the final dramatic moments of the show. They lived on the edge of an abyss constantly, and for them every moment in the fashion business was a life-or-death situation. Caro was as thin as their models and barely ate while they were working on a show. Charlie was fiercely protective of her. They both cared passionately about the reviews they got for each show, which would affect the quantities of their orders from major stores.

The ready-to-wear shows of Fashion Week took place so that the best stores in the country could place their wholesale orders months in advance. Fashion editors from every magazine also came to see the shows to get an advance view of new trends and see which designers were the most talented. Caro and Charlie worked a year in advance, and the day after the show, Caro would start working on the next collection, with sketches of what she already had in her head. Her brother thought she was a genius, and even the critics said she had immense talent. Charlie's gift for design had taken a backseat to hers, and she was the star of their brand, while he remained in the background, which he preferred. And he had financial knowledge she didn't.

At night, they went home to the loft they had bought together in order to save money, but also because they loved living together. As long as they were both single, there was no reason not to share an apartment. Their parents were very supportive of their business and proud of them, although their mother worried about the lack of personal life for both of them. Their father was impressed by how hard they worked, and by Charlie's head for finance. The fashion press called them "the Super-Talented Whittier Twins," and usually gave them rave reviews. But each show was a moment that could make or break them, and that was how it felt each time, as though their careers were on the line.

"Eat something," Charlie reminded her, as he sped away for a meeting. She went back to her drawing board, working on adjustments to the green evening gown. It had to be changed now to accommodate the different fabric, which wouldn't drape in the same way as the fabric they now had too little of. Every day was a crisis leading up to the show. She still had to oversee the final casting of the models and make sure the samples were finished, which they usually weren't until two hours or less before the show. The fittings had to be impeccable. Every last detail had to be right. She was a perfectionist, and Charlie was equally so. He had just gotten to his office for his meeting when Caro handed off all her changes for the green dress to their patternmaker, who had to cut the pattern again.

The phone on Charlie's desk rang. It was Gloria, their older sister, just checking in. She knew what a madhouse and how stressful it was for them before a show. She was six years older, at thirty-nine, and loved her job on Wall Street in finance and investments. Charlie often sought her advice. She was highly respected in her field.

"How's it going, as crazy as ever before a show?" she asked with a sympathetic tone. She admired how hard they worked.

"Poor Caro is going insane, but it always works out in the end."

"That's because you work your asses off. I have no idea how you do it. I have six black suits and two charcoal gray ones, and I can't figure out what to wear to work every day, let alone start a fashion trend and dictate what the whole country should wear six months from now." Gloria was as dark as they were fair. She was a handsome woman. She wasn't as obviously beautiful as they and Lyle and Annabelle were, but she had an aristocratic face and looked like their father. She was tall and slim like him, extremely disciplined, and went to the gym every day at five A.M. before work. She got to the office at seven every morning. She had an instinct for finance as the twins did about fashion, and worked just as hard as they did, in a more orderly way in a saner world. Charlie was always grateful for her financial advice.

"I was going to call you after the show. I still want to talk to some potential investors, to see if any of them might feel like a fit for Caro without asking us to give up too much."

"That's a tall order. Big, solid investors are going to want a chunk of your business and to have control."

"Caro will never agree to that," Charlie said.

"She may have to if you two want to get as big as you say. Let's face it, this isn't a cottage industry now. Fashion is in the big leagues. It can be a billion-dollar business. If that's where you want to go or think you're headed, you'll have to play by major-league rules, or stay in the minors."

"I want the major leagues and so does Caro, she just can't stand the idea of giving anything up to get there."

"I'll check around and see if I can come up with someone who's in love with fashion, and willing to play by your rules. I'll let you know what I find." She was always serious about business and had helped them get the investors they had. "How's everything else?"

Charlie laughed. "There is no everything else before a show, or most of the time in this business."

"Yeah, me too." Their older sister grinned. "Let's have dinner sometime after the show."

"Caro will be working on the next show by then, but we'll make time. Maybe we can all have dinner together when Mom and Dad get back from Europe."

"It's a good thing Mom can't get pregnant or there would be fifteen of us by now. It always amazes me that they're still in love after forty-three years, and go on a honeymoon every year. I haven't had a date in two years and I'm not even sure I want one, and they're still acting like lovebirds." All six of Connie and Preston's children admired them for it. They were a role model for all of them. "Mom says they want to renew their vows for their fiftieth. She wants us to make her dress. Caro already has sketches for it."

"Good for them!" Gloria said. She'd had her share of disagreements with their parents, as they'd all had, over minor things. But for the most part, she respected them profoundly and was grateful for the love they all shared. Only Lyle had upset his parents deeply when he married Amanda, but they had accepted it by now, and loved the grandkids. "Have you heard from them?" she asked Charlie.

"Of course not." He laughed. "I think they forget we exist for these three weeks every year."

"Who can blame them? Frieda says that Annabelle is out till all hours every night. Mom will have to deal with her when she gets back. I'm glad I don't have to. I could never handle kids. I think being single is the right choice for me," she said seriously.

"Don't give up yet," Charlie told her. "You never know who you'll meet."

"Yeah, well, since I've dated Frankenstein and Dracula, and all their Transylvanian cousins, and was engaged to a sociopath and nearly married him, I think I'm fine as I am. I'll quit while I'm ahead." She wasn't bitter, she was just leery of the men she met, and Gloria wasn't easy. She was smart, tough, and had a sharp tongue and a mind of her own and wasn't afraid to express it. Her brother knew she had a kind heart and a brilliant mind, but she scared most men to death. The rare times men asked her out, it was unusual for her to hear from them again. She wasn't sorry when she didn't. They didn't pass muster for her either. She kept the bar very high, for herself and others, and didn't hesitate to say so. Charlie was sorry that she was alone, but she didn't seem unhappy. And like him and Caro, she was a workaholic. It seemed to be a family trait. Their father had worked hard too, though maybe not as hard as they did, in a less crazy publishing world, at a more gentlemanly time. The modern world moved at a much faster pace. Computers and the internet had changed everything, for all of them. Their father often said he was glad he wasn't working now.

Gloria wished Charlie luck with the show, and they hung up a few minutes later. She'd promised to keep her eye out for an investor for them. Charlie agreed with Gloria. Caro would have to compromise some of her ideas about the percentage of the business she was willing to give up. But for now, only the show was on her mind, and the look and fit of the clothes, and the "story" of the show. All the clothes had to work together. To Caro, it was pure art. Charlie was more practical, since he handled the finances of the business, and more realistic.

Before Charlie and Gloria hung up, he told her he was going to take Benjie to his gym. Benjie loved going with his older brother. They were only five years apart, and Benjie worshipped him. Of all the siblings, Charlie paid the most attention to Benjie, and it touched Gloria but didn't surprise her.

"You're a good man," she said to Charlie, but that wasn't news to her either. Charlie left the office at five o'clock, to take the subway uptown to meet Benjie at his job. He was planning to come back downtown afterwards to lend Caroline support, but seeing Benjie and spending time with him was important. He never let him down.

Their parents had taught them to take care of each other, and they'd all taken it seriously and lived accordingly.

Charlie arrived at the pet shelter where Benjie worked on York Avenue, near the river in the Eighties. It would have taken him an hour by cab. He walked into the shelter in his gym clothes with a big duffle coat over them, and asked for Benjie at the front desk. The minute he asked for him, the veterinary tech at the desk smiled at him.

"You're his brother, right?" Charlie nodded, with a smile. "We love him. He's so great with the animals. He's upstairs with the dogs that are waiting to be adopted." He pointed to the stairs and Charlie headed to the adoption department to find his brother.

The shelter provided numerous services, including adoption and caring for injured dogs they found abandoned on the streets and nursing them back to health before they found new owners for them.

When Charlie opened the door to the adoption section marked "Dogs/Medical" he saw his baby brother immediately. He was a tall, good-looking dark-haired boy with big blue eyes and a sweet face who looked about sixteen, not his chronological age of twenty-eight, and he was holding a small shaggy dog of mixed breed with a bandage over its head and half its face, and gently stroking it, making cooing sounds as you would to a baby. He looked up and saw Charlie and beamed.

"Hi. He got hit by a car and hurt his eye and his head." The dog had one leg in a cast and looked truly pathetic as Benjie gently set him down in a soft, fluffy bed in an enclosed area. "He's going to be okay, but he's sad. He likes me to hold him. He's scared." Benjie really had a gift with the animals, and worked there diligently for eight hours every day, doing whatever they needed him to do. Their mother had found him the job five years before. The shelter was run by a charity she contributed to, and the job had been magical for him. He had a purpose and a useful way to spend his time that helped the people at the shelter as well. All the animals loved him.

"Do you still want to go to the gym?" Charlie asked him, and Benjie threw his arms around his brother and hugged him. He was taller and more powerfully built than Charlie, but was infinitely gentle with him. He seemed young for his age at times, but he was entirely rational and capable of intelligent conversation, and very bright. There was no apparent reason for his differences, but parental age when he had been conceived might have been an issue, although their mother had only been thirty-seven when he was born, and their father ten years older. And they were both even older when Annabelle was born, but anomalies were unpredictable. And there were no precise reasons known for either Asperger's or autism. Both were common albeit unanswered mysteries of the age. But with structure and family support, Benjie managed extremely well. His mother was involved in his daily life and he lived at home. He frequently went for long walks with his father, and liked talking to him. Both his brothers were close to him. Charlie spent the most time with him.

They walked to the gym Benjie liked to go to. He walked on the treadmill and rode an exercise bike with a stiff uphill setting. He was in very good shape, and many people who spoke to him weren't aware of his differences. He was socially awkward at times and smooth at others. Asperger's had become harder and harder to diagnose as the official definitions changed and were reevaluated. He was a combination of skills and naïveté, which made him appealing as a person and full of charm. He loved going to the gym with Charlie, and after an hour, they left, and Charlie dropped him off at home, where Frieda was waiting for him and cooked him dinner every night while his parents were away. She stayed up until he went to bed. She had been doing it all his life when Connie was busy, out for the evening, which was rare, or away as she was now on their annual trip. Benjie was discreetly supervised and protected. He took a cab to the shelter on his own on most days. He managed surprisingly well. After Charlie took him home, Benjie gave him a bear hug and thanked him.

Charlie went back downtown to his office then, and found Caro still working hard at seven-thirty. There were still fit models waiting for fittings, and a dozen people poised to ask her questions. Charlie could tell from the scene around her that she'd be there until two A.M., and he headed to his own office to do some work. He usually tried to stay as late as his sister did, so they could go home together. He felt guilty if he left her there on her own, while he went home to rest, and he didn't mind doing some work of his own while he waited. There was always a mountain piled up on his desk, and he never seemed to catch up no matter how long he worked or how late it got.

After Benjie ate dinner, he went upstairs, showered, and got into his pajamas. Then he went to his room and turned on the TV. He liked to watch his favorite shows. Several of them had dogs in them. He liked those best, and some comedies. He didn't like scary shows where people hurt each other.

Around ten o'clock he got hungry. As he went down to the kitchen to get something to eat, he passed his younger sister, Annabelle, coming out of her room. She was wearing a slinky silver dress and towering high heels, which made her almost as tall as he was. She had a fabulous body and nearly jet-black hair and green eyes, and was carrying a black fur coat of their mother's, which Benjie didn't recognize. He looked surprised when he saw her, and smiled as soon as he did.

"Where are you going? Are you going out?"

She hesitated, and then nodded. "I'm just going to see some friends," she answered vaguely, holding the coat a little closer. She was going to put it back before their mother came home from her trip, so she wouldn't know, and Annabelle didn't want him to tell her.

"Are you going to sleep there?" he asked her directly, and she shook her head.

"No, of course not," she said. "I'll come home."

"Did you sleep at your friend's last night?" he asked her, and she squirmed.

"Why would you ask me that? Of course I didn't."

"I saw you come home when I got up to have breakfast. You were just coming in at six o'clock." He was very literal and precise about details and remembered them all.

"That's ridiculous. I was home hours before that," she said. "You must have read the time wrong."

"No, I didn't." He extended his arm with the watch on his wrist. "I never make a mistake telling time. It was 6:02."

"Well, stop spying on me," she said sharply.

"I won't tell," he said gently. "I won't tell Frieda or Mom. I promise. Are you going to a party?" He looked interested, and though she knew the questions were innocent, they were unnerving anyway. She never knew when he'd share some piece of information he shouldn't, and she didn't want their mother to know about the hours she was keeping in her parents' absence. She'd been out late every night since they'd been gone. She was twenty-one, old enough to do what she wanted.

"Sort of," she answered vaguely. She was in fact going to a party at a nightclub with a group of people she had recently met, some of whom were less savory than her parents would have liked. She had total freedom while they were away. "You should go back to bed," she told her brother.

"I'm going to get some cookies. Then I'll go to bed," he said, and she walked past him and waved as he walked into the kitchen and the door closed behind him. She hoped he wouldn't tell Frieda in the morning what time she had gone out. It was nearly ten-thirty by then, and she knew the housekeeper wouldn't have approved, would have scolded her for it, and would tell her parents when they got back. She hated it when they treated her like a child.

She walked to the corner of Madison Avenue, hailed a cab, and headed downtown to the bar in the Meatpacking District where she'd gone for the last few nights. She was the youngest person in the group, although she looked considerably older. She looked more like twenty-five than twenty-one. Her long dark hair cascaded down her back and looked sexy. She was wearing bright red lipstick, and dark eye makeup, and the sexy high heels Charlie and Caro had given her for Christmas. She didn't mind being taller than some of the men. They assumed she was a model. She looked like one.

As soon as she walked into the bar, she saw them, the same group she'd already met up with several times that week. There was one particularly handsome man. He was Brazilian and the sexiest man she'd ever seen. She had lied and told him she was twenty-six. He had shared some cocaine with her the night before, and she liked it. She'd had sex with him in the bathroom after that. He had said he'd bring more tonight. She knew she'd have to stop when her parents came home. But for now, she could do what she wanted. She'd had cocaine once before, when she was in college. She hadn't gotten hooked and wouldn't this time either. She felt incredibly grown up just being there.

The Brazilian, Joao, wanted to go to her place, but she said she had roommates so they couldn't.

He was staying with friends and couldn't take her to where he was staying either. His friends had children and a dog, and he was sleeping on their couch. He was going back to Sao Paulo in about a week, so the fun would end anyway, around the time her parents came home. Being with him was exciting and a little scary all at once. She had never met anyone like him.

The phone rang in Lyle's apartment at five A.M. It woke him before it woke Amanda, and he reached for it, still half asleep, and answered. He couldn't imagine who it was at that hour. Probably a wrong number, but he answered anyway. The caller asked for him by name, and had an accent. Suddenly Lyle was awake as he sat up at the side of the bed and a chill ran down his spine.

"Yes, this is Lyle Whittier," he confirmed. The caller identified himself as a member of the French gendarmerie in Courchevel, France, where his parents were. The gendarme cleared his throat and, as compassionately as he could, informed Lyle that his parents had gone for an early morning ski run, and were the first skiers on the mountain, in spite of avalanche warnings for that morning. An avalanche had come almost as soon as they began skiing down, close together. Witnesses had seen it from the lift. They had been instantly swept away and buried half a mile from where they'd started. The ski patrol had found their bodies an hour before. They had been identified by the manager of the hotel, who knew them. Lyle's number was in their passports as next of kin to call in an emergency. Both of them had been killed instantly. It was presumed that they had died from suffocation and internal injuries on impact. The gendarme offered his sincere condolences and said that the French authorities would remain at his disposal to make arrangements, and Lyle would need to contact the U.S. Embassy to help them deal with the technicalities and red tape to release their bodies. He added that in spite of the force of the avalanche, their bodies had been found close together. He said he was truly sorry. Lyle jotted down the number of the gendarmerie on the pad next to his bed. After he hung up, he sat staring at the wall in front of him, seeing nothing, hearing the Frenchman's words in his head. It was inconceivable, unimaginable. It wasn't possible. His parents were dead. Lyle couldn't imagine a world without them in it with their steady, stabilizing influence for his entire lifetime. Somehow, he had expected them to live forever, or to a great age, together, always strong for their children and each other, perhaps frail one day, but not killed in an avalanche on one of their yearly trips.

Lyle got up, walked silently out of his bedroom, and stood looking out his living room window. He hoped that death had been swift, and they hadn't suffered, as the gendarme had said. All he could think of, as he watched snowflakes begin to fall in New York on a January morning, was that they had died as they would have wanted to, together, doing something they loved, still in great form. It had been foolish of them to go out so early, and dangerous, and they were experienced enough to know it, but had risked it anyway. He was sure that they had assumed nothing would happen. Instead, the worst had happened, and all Lyle could think of was what were he and his brothers and sisters going to do without them? How was he going to tell the others? He suddenly felt like a child again and couldn't imagine his life without his parents. Even more frightening, he was the head of the family now. His mother and father were gone forever. Tears rolled down his cheeks as he thought of them, and his shoulders shook with silent sobs as Amanda watched him from the doorway of their bedroom. She didn't approach him. She knew something terrible had happened, but didn't dare ask him, and she tiptoed softly back to their bedroom and closed the door behind her. Lyle stood alone, crying, mourning his parents. He had never felt so grown up in his life, as he realized he was an orphan and cried like a child.

Chapter 3

Half an hour after he got the call from France, Lyle sent a text to his brothers and sisters. It was nearly noon in France by then, and not quite six A.M. in New York. Charlie saw the text before Caro did. She had gone to bed at three and was dead to the world, but Charlie was a light sleeper and heard the text come in. The text didn't tell them why, but asked them to meet Lyle at the house at nine o'clock that morning. Lyle needed the time before that to compose himself and speak to the authorities in France and at the embassy in Paris. He would have to break the news to his siblings when he saw them. He dreaded every moment of what lay ahead of him.

He had spoken to all the pertinent authorities by seven-thirty, and had seen Amanda by then. She had overheard some of the conversations and knew what had happened.

"I'm sorry," she said softly, and handed him a cup of coffee. He nodded with tears in his eyes.

"I know you never got along with them, but this is going to be a shock for the whole family. There will be so many decisions to make, so much to take care of," and as his parents' executor, much of it would fall on his shoulders. He had texted his office to tell them he wouldn't be in that morning. He had called his parents' lawyer, Patrick McCarthy, an old family friend they all knew, and had asked him to come to the house at ten-thirty, to give him time to break the news to the others. There were things they needed to know as soon as possible. He was still dealing with the formalities of getting his parents' bodies returned to the United States, and the embassy in Paris was helping him. "You're going to have a lot to do," Amanda said, but didn't offer to help him. She assumed that the others would object if she was involved. There were six of them to do whatever was necessary. And they needed to take some responsibility for Benjie now, and Annabelle. Benjie would need some help and Annabelle supervision. Lyle sent Charlie a text asking him to make sure Benjie was at the meeting. He didn't want to alarm Benjie by sending him a text. Benjie was astute sometimes at sensing that something was wrong, and Lyle didn't want to scare him. He had sent texts to all the others.

Charlie woke Caro at seven-thirty, to give her time to dress and for them to get uptown to the house. He told her that he didn't know why Lyle had called the meeting, but they both assumed that it was serious, and looked worried. They feared that one of their parents had fallen ill or had an accident and was seriously hurt. It didn't occur to either twin that one or both of them were dead.

Gloria got Lyle's text at seven A.M. when she was about to leave for the office, decided not to go, and texted her assistant instead.

Lyle dressed in a dark suit, white shirt, and tie, which seemed suitable, and headed to the house. He was walking up the front steps at eight when Annabelle got out of a cab, still in the silver dress and high heels, wearing her mother's black mink coat, with her eye makeup smudged all over her face. She looked drunk to Lyle, who was shocked to see her looking as she did.

He stared at her for a minute as they met at the front door, and she cringed, and seemed slightly unsteady in the high heels.

"I don't know where you've been or what you've been up to, but the party is over. Sober up. Get cleaned up. We're having a family meeting in an hour, and I expect you to be there in decent condition," he said, and opened the door for her. She'd been fumbling to find her key in her purse. She slithered through the front door like a ghost and ran up the stairs to her room. Benjie was just coming out of his room to have breakfast. Annabelle didn't give him time to comment and ran past him. He headed for the kitchen, where Frieda was waiting for him. Lyle didn't go to look for him and closed himself into his father's study. He didn't want to tell Benjie before the others, nor Frieda, who would be devastated and give it away. He wanted to tell his siblings all together. He was going to tell his own children after he told his brothers and sisters. They had the right to know first. Amanda had agreed not to say anything to Tommy and Devon before they left for school.

Gloria was there before the others and went looking for her older brother. She found him in her father's study, and as soon as she saw her brother's face, she knew what had happened. Her legs were shaking and she sat down in one of the big leather chairs.

"Which one of them is it?" she asked in a choked voice, and tears filled Lyle's eyes again. He sat down in the chair next to hers.

He couldn't speak for a minute and then he told her. "Both of them." Her eyes flew open wide as she stared at him. All she could think of was that their plane must have gone down, since she didn't know the exact date of their return. But she hadn't heard anything about a plane crash on the morning news. "They got caught in an avalanche. They were the first on the mountain for the morning run. It hadn't been cleared yet, but they went anyway. I know it sounds

awful, but after I heard, in a weird way, I thought
that this is what they would have wanted, to go together. Neither of them had to survive without the
other. They were still in great shape and doing what
they loved best. It's kind of perfect in a way, except
that it's much too soon for us." They both started to
cry then, and hugged each other. Ten minutes later
Charlie and Caroline walked in, and Annabelle right
behind them, deathly pale, in an old sweater and
torn jeans, with no makeup on, but she looked sober.

Lyle asked her to go get Benjie. He was still eating breakfast in the kitchen with Frieda. A few minutes later, they were all together in their father's
study. The scent of his cologne was still faint in the
room, mixed with the leather of the furniture that
had been in the room all their lives.

"I don't even know where to start," Lyle said, trying to get control of his voice. "There was an accident in Courchevel this morning. There was an
avalanche. Mom and Dad were in it, going for an
early morning run," he said, letting the words sink
in. The twins looked shocked.

"Oh my God, how bad is it? Are they hurt?" Caro
asked him, as she and Charlie held hands. Lyle shook
his head, and looked at all of them.

"They were killed instantly. The authorities
called me at five A.M. They had just found them."
There were sounds of agony in the room, of crying,
murmurs of grief, as they sobbed in each other's
arms and held each other. Benjie looked at Charlie.

He knew that something bad had happened but he wasn't sure what.

"What happened to Mom and Dad?" Benjie asked Charlie, and he explained it to him in simple terms. Benjie stared at him and was in shock, and finally spoke up. "Who am I going to live with?" he asked the room in general, and Charlie put an arm around his brother's shoulders, to comfort him. He looked agitated.

"You can live with me and Caro," he said, and she nodded. Lyle remembered what Amanda had said only recently about Benjie not living with them.

"I can't," Benjie said. "Your apartment is too small, and you don't have a bed for me."

"We'll get one, or we'll move if we have to," Charlie said, trying to reassure him.

"Do I have to move now?" Benjie looked at Lyle for an answer.

"No, Benjie, you don't. We all have to make some decisions, but there's no hurry. This is your home."

"I'll come and stay here with you," Charlie volunteered immediately and Caroline nodded approval. Someone had to be at the house for Benjie and Annabelle. They both needed supervision, now that their parents couldn't be there to provide it for them.

"Are Mom and Dad ever coming back?" Benjie asked them, struggling to understand, and one by one, they all shook their heads, grappling with the truth themselves.

For the next hour they alternately cried and talked, with no final answers. Lyle didn't know when their bodies would be returned or precisely when the funeral would be. They had to make decisions about the house, but they didn't want to talk about that yet, or upset Benjie unduly. From one instant to the next their lives had changed forever, and the life they had known had ended with an avalanche in Courchevel.

They were still talking and crying, when Patrick McCarthy, their father's attorney, knocked on the door and entered the room. They all stared at him, and Lyle explained that he had called him. They needed to know their parents' final wishes, even just for the funeral, and their interment, awful as that was to think about.

Patrick was a few years older than their father but hadn't retired, and handed each of them copies of both their parents' wills. Lyle glanced through his copies and there were no secrets there. Connie and Preston had explained it all to them beforehand. They had tried to be very fair. Lyle was executor of the estate, as he knew he would be. He and Gloria were Benjie's trustees for financial matters, and Charlie and Caroline were the guardians of his person. All of them agreed that their parents had chosen wisely and used their respective talents and strengths. Gloria was not a nurturing person, but Caro and Charlie were, and Lyle and Gloria were both extremely astute and responsible with money, even more so than the twins.

The attorney talked about their parents' wishes for the house, and their intentions. They had always planned for their heirs to sell the house and split the money. They had each been left a bequest, which would allow them to buy modest homes, or start businesses, or live reasonably, but it was what they would get from the sale of the house that would make a real difference to them, after inheritance taxes and dividing the estate in six parts. Financially, it was a necessity for them to sell the house, although they weren't desperate. None of them needed a home that size, nor could they afford it. It made no sense for them. They didn't have to sell it immediately, but the attorney advised them to do it soon, and Lyle and Gloria agreed with him. Charlie was the showstopper after they said it. He looked around the room at his siblings.

"I won't agree to sell the house. Mom and Dad managed it. I want to keep it." And Caro seconded it.

"That doesn't make good financial sense," Lyle countered what Charlie said.

"I don't care. Everything in life isn't about money. We love this house. We grew up here. We just lost our parents. We don't have to lose our home too."

"You don't live here," Benjie said, being literal and practical. "I do. I don't want to sell the house

either," he said clearly. He turned to look at Annabelle then. She looked shell-shocked by everything
she'd heard in the past two hours, and she wasn't
fully sober, although Lyle's announcement had cut
through the haze of alcohol and drugs.

"I don't care what you do. I'm going to move out
soon anyway," she told them. "Mom and Dad said I
could. We were going to look for an apartment."

"I don't think that's a good idea," Gloria said. Lyle
had told her about Annabelle arriving at the house
when he did, in a state of total disarray.

"This is all too fresh," Lyle said sensibly. The attorney had left by then, to leave them to figure it
out themselves. "We need to think about all of it.
We have time." And they were all still too shocked
to make good decisions or think clearly.

"So do I have to move out?" Benjie asked them
all again, anxious to know what was going to happen.

"No," Charlie said softly. "We're not doing anything in a hurry. I'm going to move in here with you
and Annabelle," he said, glancing at them both. Annabelle did not look happy about it, but Benjie did.
He was smiling when they all stood up to leave. It
was nearly noon by then. They had a lot to think
about and digest, and decisions to make, especially
about the house. Lyle had papers to file, and he and
Gloria were going to study their parents' investment portfolios together. There wasn't an enormous amount of money there, but their parents

had been responsible and cautious, and they had left a decent amount to each of their children, which would prove useful over time. Once they sold the house, which they had to do, they would each have considerably more. They couldn't keep the house out of sentiment, just for Benjie to live in. Annabelle didn't want to stay anyway. She wanted to spread her wings and fly on her own, with no supervision now. She had no guardian of her person. She was twenty-one. She would have total freedom, and from what Lyle had seen that morning, he could tell she was going to abuse it. Benjie was another case entirely. They had to protect him. But for now, Charlie would be with him, until they decided where he would live after they sold the house. They needed to consider that carefully for Benjie, so he would feel comfortable and have the structure he'd need to feel secure.

They all left at noon, and Benjie asked Charlie to drop him off at the shelter. He wanted to go to work and take care of the injured dogs. He said they needed him. He didn't seem to fully understand that their parents weren't coming back, but he knew something very bad had happened. He could tell from his siblings' reactions.

Lyle stayed after they all left, to explain to Frieda what had happened, and that they still needed her for Benjie, and would, even after they sold the house, but that they had no immediate plans to sell.

After he left, she went to her room and sobbed. She had loved her employers for more than forty years, and couldn't imagine what it would be like now without them. She loved their children, but it wouldn't be the same. She went to church that afternoon to pray for their souls, and promised them to take good care of the children, as she always had. And she had a special affection for Benjie because he still needed her, more than ever now without his parents. She had been with the family since Lyle was born. And their parents were more than just employers to her. Lyle told her that they had left her a small bequest, which made her cry more. They were like family to her.

With considerable help from the embassy, it took the siblings a week to get their parents' bodies back from France. With hideous timing, they landed the day before Charlie and Caro's show. Lyle took care of all the paperwork and arrangements, and Charlie and Caroline had promised to plan the funeral. They just had to get through their fashion show, which added more stress and turmoil to an already frantic time. Charlie was staying at the house with Benjie now, which annoyed Annabelle as much as it comforted her brother. None of the others had realized how much their mother did for Benjie, and it was going to take some organizing to replace all that she had provided for him and maintain the same level of support. She had done it so quietly that they didn't know. Benjie explained it to them day by day, and Charlie began to realize that keeping Benjie on track took time and organization and dedication. And Annabelle needed policing, more like an adolescent than an adult. She had been spoiled and indulged by her parents, since she was their youngest child. She regularly accused Charlie of being a spy when she ran into him in the hall at night, when she was on her way out and he questioned her about it. "Why are you here?" she shouted at him. "For Benjie, or just to report to the others about me? It's none of your business what I do, who I see, or where I go. I'm twenty-one years old, not fourteen."

"Then act like it," he said calmly. "You stay out almost every night."

"So what if I do?"

"Who are you hanging out with?"

"I don't have to tell you anything."

"No, but you're going to get into some kind of trouble if you go wild." She ignored him whenever possible, and slammed the door when she left the house, and came back in the morning on most nights. Joao was going back to Brazil soon, and there was another boy she liked too, her ex-boyfriend. They had broken up for a while, but he was back and leaving for Italy for a semester abroad in a few weeks. She was seeing both of them and it was very confusing. And the drugs and alcohol Joao was giving her didn't help. She was heading for disaster and refused to see it. And losing her parents had shaken her more than she would admit. She was drunk every night.

Caro's show went off smoothly in spite of everything she was dealing with at the same time. She was overwhelmed with grief over her parents. But the sewers finished their work on time. The models they had booked showed up. The show was spectacular and the reviews were excellent. And somehow the twins got through it. The day after, she and Charlie made all the arrangements for their parents' funeral. Lyle had written the obituaries and they appeared with a wonderful article about their father in *The New York Times*.

The morning of the funeral, Amanda dressed in a black leather miniskirt and a black Chanel jacket, with high-heeled thigh-high boots and a very stylish hat, and Lyle looked at her, surprised.

"Something wrong?" she asked him. She had dressed the children in navy blue, and Lyle was wearing a black suit, and suddenly looked and felt much older than he was, with the responsibility for the entire family on his shoulders.

"You look beautiful," he said cautiously, "but I think you should probably wear something a little more serious to my parents' funeral. My sisters might get upset." She looked sexy, which didn't seem appropriate even to him, and he was very tolerant of what she wore, to avoid unnecessary fights.

"Do they set the dress code for me now?" she snapped at him.

"No, but it's a funeral, not a party." There was a reception afterwards at the house, which Charlie and Caroline had arranged. They were expecting at least two hundred guests, maybe more. Lyle's secretary had called their parents' closest friends to invite them.

"I hope you've all agreed to sell that mausoleum of a house. You can't keep it just for Benjie, and you can all use the money. I hope they left you a decent amount." He hadn't said a word to her about it so far, and she had picked the wrong morning to be insulting about it. She took off her stylish hat, and tossed it on a chair, but the short leather skirt and high-heeled black suede boots were a statement of their own, and he could guess what his sisters would say. Amanda's mouth was set in a thin, angry line when they left for the church. She didn't like Lyle criticizing what she had worn. She wore a short black fur jacket with her outfit. And she didn't care what his sisters thought, or what he did.

When they got to the church, there were white orchids everywhere, arranged by Charlie and Caro. Seeing the two caskets side by side, covered by blankets of lily of the valley, nearly broke the fami-

ly's hearts. It was a deeply emotional service. Each
of the Whittier children except Benjie did a short
reading from the Bible. Benjie felt too shy to do it,
so they didn't insist. The minister had known Preston and Connie for all of their adult lives and gave
a beautiful eulogy. The funeral was elegant, traditional, and respectful, and a fitting tribute to them.
Charlie and Caro held Benjie's hands. Lyle was
flanked by his children, and Gloria looked daggers
at Amanda whenever she got the chance. Annabelle stood next to her siblings, looking lost. It had
finally hit her that she had lost both her parents,
and she cried through the entire service. The church
was full to bursting, and nearly three hundred people showed up at the house afterwards. It was an
exhausting, emotionally draining day, and all seven
of them, including Amanda, sat together after everyone had left, staring into space for a minute.
Thanks to Caro and Charlie, it had been beautifully
done, elegant and serious, and touching.

"Mom and Dad would have loved it," Gloria said
quietly, and Lyle nodded.

Amanda helped herself to another drink. The
children had gone back to their apartment with
Molly. Benjie looked handsome and very stylish
and adult in the black suit Charlie had bought for
him.

Lyle and Amanda were the first to leave, and
Gloria shortly after. Caroline decided to spend the

night in her old room, to be with Charlie and Benjie, and once the others had gone, Annabelle
showed up in a short black skirt and high heels,
ready to go out.

"Where are you going?" Caro looked at her, surprised.

"Why are you all always checking on me?" Annabelle asked angrily. "Why can't you leave me
alone?" The twins exchanged a look and nothing
more was said, and a few minutes later, they heard
the front door close.

Charlie looked at his twin and spoke quietly.
"She's up to no good." It was obvious to both of
them.

"You're probably right," Caro said with a sigh,
"but I'm not her mom."

"She doesn't come home at night," Benjie said
matter-of-factly, and went upstairs to change. The
three of them met a little while later in the kitchen
for something to eat, and then went to bed. Caroline fell asleep as soon as her head hit the pillow,
she was totally drained and exhausted after her
show and the funeral. Charlie was reading in his
own room, unable to sleep, when he heard a knock
on the door and Benjie walked in, in his pajamas,
with a worried expression.

"I can't sleep," he said.

Charlie nodded and patted a spot on his bed to
invite his brother to sit down.

"I can't either. It was the hardest day of our lives, for all of us. It doesn't get much worse than this."

"Am I going to have to move? Is Lyle going to sell the house? I heard Amanda talking to him, and she told him he should. Do you think he'll listen to her?" Benjie was panicked, afraid he was about to lose his home.

"She has no say in this, Benjie. It's up to us," Charlie told him. "Caro and I don't want to sell it. And whatever we do, it won't happen for a long time. Houses don't sell just like that in a few days, and this will be a hard house to sell. It's bigger than most people want. If we do sell, you can come to live with Caro and me. We'll get a bigger apartment," he reassured him, since he knew Benjie was concerned about the logistics.

"This is my home," Benjie said. "Don't I get a vote too? The others don't live here. Annabelle and I do. And she doesn't sleep here anymore," he commented with his usual unfiltered honesty.

"She's supposed to sleep here," Charlie said with a smile, touched by Benjie's earnest wish to protect his home. Charlie felt that way about it too. They had too many memories there to give it up. "Caro and I want to keep the house. But it's expensive to take care of a house like this. That's what Lyle and Gloria are worried about. They're trying to figure out what we should do."

"Should I get a better job? I love the shelter, but they don't pay me very much." He got a small salary, which he couldn't have lived on, but he didn't have to.

"Don't worry about it," Charlie said, wanting the best solution for Benjie, whatever that was. It seemed simplest and kindest to keep him in the home they all loved, and not uproot him, but it tied up an enormous asset. Charlie understood that too. "I promise you we'll find a good solution. We won't sell the house if we don't have to. And you can keep your job." Benjie looked relieved, and Charlie walked him back to his room and tucked him into bed.

"I'm glad you're here," Benjie said, with his head on the pillow, looking up at his brother.

"So am I." In an odd way, it was nice being home again. It was like returning to the past, and the place where they had been so happy and felt so safe growing up. He could almost feel their parents there with them.

"I think Mom and Dad are here," Benjie said quietly, as though reading his brother's mind.

"So do I. Now go to sleep. You've got work in the morning, and all those dogs to take care of."

"I want to be a vet someday," he said dreamily, suddenly sleepy, and Charlie looked at him with tears in his eyes, knowing that he never would be a vet, which took years of study. This was as good as it was going to get for him. It made Charlie realize that he had a sacred mission to fulfill for his parents now, to keep Benjie happy, loved, respected, and safe from harm, with a fulfilling life, within the parameters he was comfortable with.

"Sleep tight," Charlie whispered, kissed his forehead, and turned off the light.

Benjie was already asleep by the time he left the room.

Chapter 4

The days after the funeral were painful for all six of the Whittier siblings. They were still in shock over what had happened to their parents. They had stressful lives and demanding jobs, except for Annabelle and Benjie. They had important decisions to make that didn't have to be resolved immediately, but they had to come to some conclusion about the house that they all agreed to, and move ahead with selling it if possible. As large as it was, it wouldn't be easy to sell. And they were deeply attached to it, and would want a buyer who would care about it as they did. And one who could pay a fair price for it if they sold. But with only Benjie living there, it made no sense to keep it, and the others had their own homes. They couldn't afford to keep the house.

Lyle was sitting at the breakfast table a few days

later, lost in thought, when Amanda came into the room, and poured each of them a cup of coffee. She set Lyle's down in front of him and he woke from his reverie. He hadn't touched his morning paper yet. Molly had taken the children to school as usual. He had a thousand things on his mind, and all the financial work to prepare for the estate. His parents had had an insurance policy to help pay for the estate taxes, which was a relief, but there were so many other details to handle. Gloria was helping him with it all. They had been on the phone discussing it for hours the night before, and he looked as tired as he felt. The decisions and tasks ahead seemed overwhelming, and emotionally upsetting.

"Have you called a realtor to put the house on the market yet?" Amanda asked him after his first sip of coffee. She hadn't lost any time getting to what she considered the most important issue, but there were other things Lyle had to deal with first as the executor.

"No. We have inheritance taxes to pay. Gloria and I are just starting to sort it all out. And the house is in a trust for all of us, so it doesn't get stuck in probate." Their father's tax attorney and accountant wanted to meet with them. As the trustee of the estate, Lyle had a fiduciary duty to all of his siblings. He was almost sorry his father hadn't chosen someone else to do it. He felt responsible to all his siblings to do things right, and didn't want to make any mistakes.

"I would think the first thing you'd want to do is get the house off your hands. You ought to get a small fortune for it," she said, smiling. The look on her face upset him. Greed lit up her eyes. "That'll be a nice windfall for us," she said. "We need a bigger apartment. I want to start looking soon." His parents were barely cold in their graves, and in her mind, she already had their house sold, and knew what she wanted to do with the money. It wasn't as simple as that for him. As always, he had to set her straight.

"We haven't decided what to do about the house yet," he said clearly. "It's not just my decision."

"What does that mean?" She stared at him and set down her coffee cup.

"Just what I said. They didn't leave the house to me, they left it to all six of us. Everyone has a voice in what we decide to do."

"Not Benjie, I assume," she said in a sarcastic tone.

"We haven't decided on that yet either. It's his home. He still lives there, and Annabelle. The rest of us don't. They all have a voice in it too, even Benjie. It's not just a financial decision for any of us. It's a very emotional issue. It's the house where we grew up. We have a strong attachment to it."

"And a lot of money tied up in that house, money you could all put to better use." Her eyes bore into his, and he was quiet for a minute.

"That's for each of us to decide, and as the executor and a trustee, I have to abide by their decisions. It's a felony if I don't. There are criminal charges that can be levied against trustees who don't follow the rules. I think the house should be sold, it's our biggest asset, but some of the others don't agree." The twins had been very vocal about it, counter to what he and Gloria thought should be done, from a strictly financial viewpoint, although they loved the house too.

"You should send Benjie away before he can vote," she said with narrowed eyes, looking at her husband coldly.

"We're not sending him anywhere. If we sell the house, he'll live with one of us." He and Gloria had discussed that too. The most likely option seemed to be the twins, but Gloria had said that she would be willing to take Benjie too. The twins and Gloria could even take turns having him stay with them, if it wasn't too disruptive for him. Stability and structure were important for Benjie, so he didn't get anxious or upset. He needed a stable home.

"You need to stop being delusional about him," Amanda said harshly. "Your parents should have sent him away somewhere years ago. No one has the time to deal with him."

"That's not how we feel about it. He does very well, with some guidance and supervision. My mom used to organize him beautifully. He's totally responsible. He's had the same job for five years," he reminded her.

"So what you're telling me is that you're not going to put him in some kind of group home, and he might even wind up here?"

"I never said he'd wind up here." Lyle knew that Amanda wouldn't be good to him, and he didn't want Benjie treated badly or diminished by anyone. Amanda had made her feelings clear, which ruled them out in offering Benjie a home, if the house was sold.

"You've waited all your life for what your parents were going to leave you, and now you're going to keep the house?" She looked stunned.

"I haven't waited all my life for my inheritance. I have a good job, and we live well on what I earn. I know what you want. You want a fancier apartment. That's not going to influence my decision about selling my parents' house. It's still a valuable asset, whether we sell it or not. And we're all part of that decision. You don't get to vote on this, Amanda, no matter how much you pressure me. We don't need a fancier apartment, or even a bigger one. Ten years from now, our kids will be in college. That time will pass very quickly."

"Not fast enough," she said through clenched teeth. "Don't you want more than we have now?"

"Not really. What don't we have now that we need so desperately?" he asked her.

"I can think of lots of things. A weekend house in the country, a summer home, a better apartment in the city. We could live more luxuriously than we do now, even on your salary," she said, warming to the subject. Visions of his inheritance, and what it could buy them, had been dancing in her head for days, particularly if the siblings sold their parents' home. She knew it could be worth as much as fifty or a hundred million dollars from the right buyer, at currently inflated New York prices. A sixth of that, even after capital gains taxes, sounded very good to her. It was obvious to Lyle that the money he had inherited from his parents, without the sale of their house, was not going to be enough for Amanda. She wanted a showier lifestyle. That didn't appeal to Lyle, whether they sold the house or not. For a girl who had grown up dirt poor, she had very grand ideas. His mother had been right when she had called Amanda ambitious. It had always worried her. None of the Whittiers were greedy or extravagant. Amanda was. She had been talking to her friends and bragging about Lyle's inheritance. He would have been appalled if he'd known. He was always discreet. No one in his circle of friends or in his business life had any idea of what he stood to inherit. He intended to invest the money, just as his parents had, in order to preserve it for his children.

"I don't expect anything in our life to change because my parents died," he told her carefully, and she looked at him with a vicious gleam in her eye.

"What if I told you I wouldn't stay with you unless you spend some of it to improve how we live?" she said. He stared at her and got up from the table.

"I'd say you were making a big mistake. Don't threaten me, Amanda, or try to blackmail me into doing what you want. The decision about the house will be made in due course, for the right reasons, by the people it belongs to now. You're not one of them. Try to keep that in mind." There was something hard and cold about his eyes when he spoke to her, and she hadn't missed his tone. It didn't scare her.

"I mean what I said," she told him, and reminded him of a snake, slithering past him. "I want a bigger life. You can afford it. Why should we live less well than you can afford to? We've both been waiting for this time for ten years. Now it's here. Let's enjoy it." What she was suggesting sounded like dancing on his parents' grave to him, and he had no intention of doing that, or letting her do it. He wasn't going to squander his parents' money on things they didn't need. That was exactly what she wanted to do with his inheritance, and the money his parents had saved for all of them. He knew how his parents had felt about her. His mother had been right.

"Think about it," she said, as he picked up his unread paper and got ready to leave the kitchen. "If things don't get a lot more luxurious around here, then I'm done."

"And then what?" He wanted to see how far

she'd go. What she was saying to him was outrageous and it was hard to believe she meant it. It sounded like greedy, empty threats to him.

"If you don't use some of what you inherited for a fancier life for us, and pressure your brothers and sisters to sell the house, then I want a divorce. I'm not going to stick around for another ten years of what we have now. We've been there, done that, there's a lot more out there than we've had access to until now. Your parents dying is a game changer for both of us."

"You can't sue me for inherited wealth, Amanda. I'm sorry, but that's not how it works."

"Do I need to remind you that we don't have a prenup?" His parents had wanted him to get one before they married, and he had lied and said he had. He had trusted her completely and didn't want to poison their mutual trust by protecting himself from her legally. Now he wished he had. He had no one to blame for not doing it but himself. He had never expected her to turn into this. She sounded entirely willing to divorce him if he didn't use his inheritance to live lavishly, which was of no interest to him. They already lived comfortably now, in a beautiful apartment. All it would mean was more shopping for her, and more showing off to her friends. He made no further comment, and left for his office a few minutes later. He called Gloria from the cab, and told her everything Amanda had said.

"Mom was right," she said in a taut, angry voice, furious on her brother's behalf.

"She wasn't like this in the beginning," he defended her.

"Yes, she was. Mom and Dad saw it. You didn't want to. She's been a gold digger right from the beginning. Look how far she's come from where she started, and that's still not good enough for her. She sees an opportunity now. She wants you to make up for everything she didn't have growing up. How is that fair? You'd better call a lawyer when you get to the office. One way or another, she wants to get her hands on your share of what Mom and Dad left us. Is that really what you want to do with it? Wouldn't you rather hang on to it, invest it, and give it to your kids one day?" The answer to her question was obvious, and then he decided to make a full confession.

"We don't have a prenup, Glo. I told Dad I did, but I never got one. I trusted her, and she cried and said that wanting a prenup was insulting, and like calling her a thief. So I canceled the appointment, and never pursued it after that."

"You're in deep shit," Gloria said, and didn't call him an idiot, but she wanted to. He had been so naïve when he married Amanda. Even he saw that now. He had believed everything she said, and hadn't seen or understood how jealous, bitter, and greedy she was, and how damaged by her youth. "I always thought she got pregnant on purpose," Gloria said angrily.

"We had already broken up when she figured it out. So I went back. But at least I got two great kids out of the marriage."

"And a very expensive, conniving wife. I hope you call a lawyer now. One way or another, she's going to go after you for what Mom and Dad left, either by making you spend it on her, or in a divorce." He was stunned by how little Amanda cared about him and their marriage. Either way would have suited her. He realized his sister was right.

He called Jeff Sampson, an old friend from Yale, when he got to the office. He was a lawyer with a big New York firm. Lyle told him what was going on, and that he had no prenup to protect him from Amanda.

"Do you think she means it? What she said to you sounds pretty harsh," his friend Jeff said to him.

"Unfortunately, I think she does. We haven't been happy for a long time." He wondered now if they ever had been. It had all worked as long as Amanda got what she wanted. And she had apparently been biding her time. She had raised the stakes now, particularly if Lyle and his siblings sold the house. It was clear that she would go after his share. It was a high price to pay for marrying a woman he had never really loved even when he married her. He had done the honorable thing, and he loved their children, but he knew for certain now that he didn't love her. He couldn't stay married to her after what she'd said, and her attitude about Benjie made it that much worse. She was heartless. Whatever had happened to her in her early life had destroyed an essential part of her. She was out for herself and incapable of compassion. It had never been as clear to him before.

He sent Amanda a text at the end of the day, saying that he needed to stay at his parents' house that night to meet with the others. He gave her no hint that he had called a lawyer or how upset he was by what she'd said. He just kept the message short and matter-of-fact. He wanted a night to cool off and think about what to do next. Their mother had kept all their rooms intact at the house, and he knew he had a place to stay. The twins were staying there with Benjie and Annabelle, so there would be five of them sleeping at the house. He was only going to stay overnight, but he couldn't go back to his apartment, and spend the night in bed with Amanda, as though nothing had happened or been said. He needed some time to himself to think of what to do next. He hadn't expected their marriage to implode over his parents' deaths.

Lyle worked late at the office, and showed up at his parents' house without warning at nine o'clock that night. Caroline and Charlie were sitting in the living room, drinking wine, and were startled when they saw him. Benjie had gone to bed early. He'd been tired since the funeral, and Annabelle was out, with the usual vague answer to her brother and sister, "to see friends."

"What are you doing here?" Caroline asked him.

"I needed a night to myself," he said, and she didn't ask him why.

"It feels like old times with everyone staying here." The only one missing was Gloria, who was comfortably in her own apartment on the West Side. Caroline went to get another glass and poured him some wine from the bottle they were sharing.

Lyle sat down in a comfortable chair with them, and started to relax after a long, stressful day, thinking about what Amanda had said over breakfast and his conversation with Jeff Sampson. In a matter of hours, divorce had begun to seem inevitable. He wasn't even sure how he felt about it. Everything was happening so quickly ever since his parents' deaths, and he felt responsible for all of his siblings now.

"What's happening with you two?" he asked them.

"We were talking about work," Caroline answered. "Charlie is trying to talk me into looking for an investor. With what Mom and Dad left us, we can put more into the business, and it will hold us for a while." Fashion was a lucrative business, but an expensive one, and the risks were high.

"We need bigger money than that if we want to get really big now. We've taken it as far as we can on our own. We need real money to take it to the next level," Charlie explained. It was all new to Lyle. All he knew about the fashion industry was what he had learned from them in the past eleven years. Charlie looked serious as he spoke of it. Keeping their ship afloat, meeting production demands and paying for them, was a constant struggle and concern.

They sat together and talked for an hour. It was a relief for Lyle to have something to talk about other than whether or not to sell the house, paying the estate taxes on time, and where Benjie would live if they sold. If he and Amanda separated, he wondered if he could take on having Benjie live with him. He had his own kids to think about too. A divorce would be a huge change for them, and he and Amanda would have to figure out some form of joint custody, with alternate days or weeks or months. He hated to put the kids through it, but all he could see in the future was serious trouble ahead if he and Amanda stayed married. For the first time in ten years, he was seriously thinking of cutting his losses before it got any worse. His brother and sister could see that he was deeply troubled, and Caroline gave him a hug when they left each other on the landing outside their bedrooms.

"It's going to be okay, Lyle, whatever it is," she

said gently, and he smiled at the sympathetic look in her eyes.

"I used to think so too. Now I don't," was all he said, and they each closed their doors to their old bedrooms, remembering how simple life had been when they had all lived there. Their parents had made everything so easy for them, and were so warm and loving. Those days seemed a lifetime away now, and they each wondered if life would ever be the same without Preston and Connie. It still seemed impossible to believe that they were never coming back. They had been due back any day from their trip, which ended in tragedy.

When Lyle woke up the next morning, he showered and dressed for work, and made his way to the kitchen to make a cup of coffee. He found Caro making eggs and bacon for Charlie and Benjie, and she looked up and smiled when she saw her older brother. She put some eggs in the pan for him as well, and he sat down at the table with his brothers with a slow smile.

"Just like old times," he said to both of them, except that when they were young, it was their mother at the stove making breakfast and now it was Caro. She set a plate down in front of each of them a few minutes later, and sat down with them. They had fried eggs, bacon, and toast, and Charlie made coffee for all four of them. And Benjie had made the toast while Caro cooked.

"It's nice staying here," Charlie said as he poured the coffee.

"Yeah, it is," Lyle agreed. Benjie was happy to see him. "I might come back tonight, depending on what happens today," he warned them. Charlie nodded. It was easy to guess there was trouble in his marriage, which didn't surprise anyone. Charlie had smelled a battle brewing after the funeral, although he didn't know what it was about.

"You don't need our permission to stay here," Caro said, smiling at him. "It's your house now too. It's a good thing Mom never took apart our rooms and turned them into closets or storerooms."

"I think she always secretly hoped that we'd come home. And now here we are," Lyle said with a sigh. It wasn't a sign of victory or success in his case.

"I'll call Gloria and see if she wants to come to dinner tonight," Caro suggested. "Then we'll all be together, if we can keep Annabelle here long enough to share a meal with us before she goes out."

"She didn't sleep here last night," Benjie announced. "I looked in her room before I came downstairs." The other three grinned at Benjie's honest report.

"She must have some major romance happening to be out every night," Charlie commented. And a moment after he said it, she appeared in the kitchen, looked at the foursome at the table, and was surprised to see Lyle. She was wearing the same clothes she had worn the night before.

"What are you doing here?" she asked him. He couldn't think of a plausible excuse other than the truth so he shrugged and didn't answer at all. She grabbed a piece of toast and floated out of the room again.

Lyle looked at Caro. "You might want to keep an eye on that."

"I am, but I can't stop her. As she points out to me whenever I ask her about it, she's twenty-one and I'm not her mother."

"Do you think she'll go back to school?" Lyle looked concerned. None of them had dropped out of college, and it didn't seem like a good sign to him.

"Not for now. She's having too much fun," Caro answered. A few minutes later, Lyle stood up to leave for work.

"Thanks for breakfast. See you at dinner tonight," he said, and they all smiled.

There was a touching déjà vu about it from their youth.

Charlie went upstairs to get his coat to take Benjie to work, and Caro put the dishes in the sink to leave them for Frieda when she came to the kitchen to start her day. Charlie came to say goodbye and told his twin he'd see her at the office, and he and

Benjie left a minute later. It was almost like the old days when they all left for school. It was funny being back now as adults, and Caro loved that they were all staying at the house, even if it was only for a short time, until they figured things out. Benjie looked happy too and loved having them around.

Caro was about to leave for work when she decided to stop in to see Annabelle for a minute, and see if she could find out what was going on with her. Annabelle was lying on her bed, looking up at the ceiling when Caro walked in. She looked instantly suspicious.

"What do you want?" Annabelle asked her, sitting up.

"Nothing. I just wanted to make sure you're okay."

"I'm fine," she said, but she didn't look it. She lay down again, looking either hung over or sick. Caro wasn't sure which.

"What's going on, with staying out every night? You must have a pretty serious guy."

"Not really," Annabelle answered, and looked away. "I was seeing someone for a while, but he went back to Brazil two days ago."

"Is he coming back?" Caro asked cautiously, and Annabelle shook her head, and her eyes filled with tears. Caroline sat down on her bed. "It must have been a big deal," she said.

"Not really, and he was kind of freaked out by what happened with Mom and Dad." She lay silent for a few minutes, while Caro waited to see if she'd open up some more, and after a little while, she stood up. Annabelle didn't want to talk. She bent down to kiss her, saw tears slide out of the corners of her eyes, and sat down on the bed again to give her a hug. She thought Annabelle was crying for either their parents or the Brazilian boy, or both. Annabelle clung to her like a child as she cried. She seemed so lost at the moment. They all were, although each of them dealt with it differently.

Annabelle was running from it by partying every night, which didn't seem to be working for her despite the bravado and hostility. "What can I do to help?" Caroline asked her gently, and Annabelle only shook her head.

"Nothing . . . everything is such a mess."

"We all feel that way right now. It's going to take time to get used to Mom and Dad not being around, but we have each other."

"That's not going to help anything," Annabelle said miserably. "I've been partying hard, ever since I left school. It was fun at first, and then it got out of hand. I was seeing someone at school before I dropped out. We broke up before Christmas, and then I met the Brazilian guy when Mom and Dad were away, and that got a little too crazy. I've been seeing the boy from school again, but it's over and he's leaving for Italy. And now everything is just a huge mess."

"What kind of mess?" Caroline asked her. "Most

messes can be fixed, or get sorted out in time. It's never as bad as we think it is when we're in the thick of it."

"This mess is," Annabelle said, looking up at her sister as she lay on her bed. She wanted to tell her, but didn't know how. Caroline was twelve years older and acted like a mother sometimes more than a sister, but she had no one else to tell. "I went to a doctor yesterday," she said, hiccupping on a sob. "I'm four months pregnant, and I never even suspected it. I just thought I was late, or stressed out or something, and then I figured out how long it had been. I did a home test, and thought it was the Brazilian. But then the doctor said it's about four months. So it's the guy at school. He's doing a semester abroad in Florence. I told him yesterday and he doesn't want any part of it. He's kind of a jerk anyway. He cheated on me. I was so upset I dropped out of school and started partying. We saw each other a few times and we broke up again over the Brazilian. Someone told him about him. What am I supposed to do now?" Caroline tried not to look as shocked as she felt, and had the sensation that she had been instantly catapulted into her mother's shoes, and had no idea how to react. She was trying to figure out what her mother would have done in the circumstances.

"Do you love him, the boy from school?" It seemed like a good place to start.

"I thought I did. I don't know what I feel now,

except scared. I don't love him now and he doesn't love me. I don't want a baby, and it's too late to do anything about it. I'm going to have to have it, whether I want it or not. I've been drinking a lot until now, especially since Mom and Dad, and I played around with drugs a few times with the Brazilian guy. What if it comes out all messed up? No one will want to adopt it, and I'll be stuck with it forever. I've been reading about it on the internet."

"Did you tell the doctor?" Annabelle nodded.

"He said I can have sonograms that will show any defects before it's born. I'm having one next week. But Caro, what am I going to do now?"

"It sounds like you're going to have a baby. Do you know when it's due?" Caro wondered how the others would react to the news. She couldn't begin to imagine it.

"Sometime in July. They can give me the date when I get the sonogram. I had a blood test yesterday that will tell me if it has Down syndrome, and the sex if I want to know. I can't believe this is happening. And the jerk from school doesn't want anything to do with it. He said to get rid of it, or put it up for adoption if I can't have an abortion. And I don't want a baby either." She was sure of that.

"This is a big deal to go through without him," Caroline said, "but you have all of us. He really does sound like a jerk. What's his name, by the way?"

"Adam. And he is a jerk, and the others will

probably hate me and think I'm a slut. Benjie keeps telling everyone every time I spend the night out. I was with the Brazilian and drinking a lot. I stopped as soon as I did the test and found out I was pregnant. But maybe it's already damaged."

"You should take it easy now for a while, and get serious about your health. No booze, no drugs." Annabelle nodded. She had already made that decision herself. "I'll go to the sonogram appointment with you if you want."

"Yes, I do. I keep trying to think what Mom would have said. She'd have been nice about it. Dad would have killed me."

"He'd have been upset," Caro agreed. "Do you want to press Adam about getting married?"

"No, and he wouldn't anyway. We used to fight a lot, and he cheated on me twice. I don't want to get back together, and he wouldn't want to either. He's too immature to get married, and so am I." She smiled at her sister, and then looked serious. "I want to give the baby up. I'm not ready to be a mom. I don't even know if I want kids later. But I know I don't want one now."

"That's a big decision. You need to really think about it before you make up your mind," Caroline said seriously.

"Will you help me find an adoption agency that would handle it for me? Probably no one will want it because I drank a lot and did cocaine a few times."

"Someone will want it if you really want to give it up."

"I was so stupid not to be more careful. I stopped taking the pill because it made me gain weight, and I hated feeling fat." She grinned sheepishly at Caro again. "I'm going to get a lot fatter now." Caro smiled and looked at her watch then.

"I have to get to work. We're working on the look book today. They're all waiting for me with a photographer. We'll talk about this more tonight. I'm glad you told me. We're all having dinner here tonight. Stay home for dinner." Annabelle nodded and stood up and put her arms around her sister and hugged her.

"Thank you for being nice about it. I'm sorry, Caro." Annabelle seemed genuinely contrite, and Caro could see she was scared.

"You don't owe me an apology." But Annabelle was going to go through a lot, if she was going to have a baby, and even more so if she put it up for adoption. Caro knew there were women who never recovered from the grief and remorse from the loss. "Just don't make any fast decisions. You have time to think about it. You have five months before you have to decide." Caro smiled at her again from the doorway. "See you tonight. I love you." She rushed out then, and took the subway downtown so she'd get there faster. All she could think about on the train was that Annabelle was having a baby. She couldn't imagine it herself. No matter how foolish her sister had been, Caro felt sorry for her. Annabelle sent her a text while she was on the subway, thanking her again for being so nice about it. The next five months were going to be interesting, and hard for Annabelle.

Charlie gave her a quizzical look when she got to the office. "What took you so long?"

"I stopped to talk to Annabelle. It took longer than I thought it would." But she was glad she had.

"Is there any hope of straightening her out?"

She hesitated before she answered. "Yeah, I think so. She has a lot to think about right now."

"Do you think she'll go back to school?"

"Maybe. In the fall." After she has a baby and gives it up for adoption, Caro thought, wondering how he'd react. But Charlie had secrets of his own. She knew them all. And now she was the keeper of Annabelle's secrets too. It was hard to keep her mind on work for the rest of the day. She had too much to think about. She wondered what it would be like to see the baby on the sonogram when she went with Annabelle. She really hoped Annabelle hadn't damaged it with alcohol and drugs. Caro felt like she had just been thrown into motherhood herself, with a pregnant twenty-one-year-old daughter. More than ever, she missed her mother. She would have known what to do and what to say, and how to help Annabelle. Caro was just going to have to learn as she groped her way along. It was going to be a very long five months for her too. She had lost her parents and her twenty-one-year-old sister was pregnant. It was a lot to adjust to, and their siblings would react too. Caro felt dizzy trying to figure it all out. It was Annabelle's problem, and a heavy price to pay for her foolishness and mistakes.

Chapter 5

As part of his job, Benjie performed small tasks for the animals at the shelter. He was particularly good with the dogs. The shelter occasionally got other animals that had been abandoned or abused as well. All were small domestic animals that people thought were cute as babies, and couldn't deal with when they grew up. Rabbits, hamsters, guinea pigs, birds at times. Reptiles were sent to the live animal section of the science museums. Once they had a miniature horse that had been kept in an apartment. They'd had a number of "miniature" Vietnamese pigs, which the vendors said would be the size of a small dog, and grew to be several hundred pounds. Once the larger animals were healthy, they went to farms or petting zoos. A very young bear cub and a cheetah went to a zoo, and a baby llama to a nature preserve. The only animals Benjie had no affinity for were ordinary house cats. He was uncomfortable around them, and they seemed equally so around him, so he was never assigned to the section for cats to adopt. He had been bitten by a monkey someone had abandoned at the shelter. It had razor-sharp teeth and was aggressive, and Benjie had to have a tetanus shot, so he was afraid of monkeys now. The one who bit him had gone to a zoo in New Jersey that had a female mate for him. Benjie had learned a lot about the animals he cared for, was quite knowledgeable about their needs and habits, and had read a lot about them.

His favorites were the dogs he helped nurse back to health. He had a real gift with them, and all the vets and technicians he worked with loved him and considered him a valuable member of their team in a very special way. He genuinely loved the animals he cared for.

The morning that Caro spent talking to Annabelle in her room, Charlie dropped Benjie off at the shelter on his way to work. Benjie was chatting with one of the techs at the front desk about bandages they needed for one of the injured animals, when a driver for Animal Care came in with two new dogs for them. One was a very skittish Great Dane who was missing an ear. He had been severely abused, and Animal Care had rescued him. He had scars along his back where he'd been bitten in the past by other dogs. He had no recent wounds but had clearly been mistreated and was too thin for his size. Benjie bent down and reached out a hand to him, and the huge black dog went straight to him, jumped up and licked his face, sat down next to him, and held out a paw. He had shied away from everyone else. It was as though he knew that Benjie was safe.

"He's wearing a tag that says his name is Duke," the driver said, as they all watched the instant bond between Benjie and the Great Dane. "Oh, and we have another customer for you." The driver smiled, and put a small cage on the desk. A pointy little face with ears that stuck straight up peered out at them. She was some kind of long-haired breed, which they saw was an unusually tiny Chihuahua when the driver took her out of the crate and handed her to the tech at the desk. She was white with black spots all over her that looked like polka dots. "We found her in a garbage can last night. She's about a year old, no tags, no license, no chip. Someone will adopt her in about five minutes once she has a bath. She's a cutie." She looked adorable, and Benjie picked her up and held her and stroked her gently.

"I'll give her a bath," he volunteered. She had a fluffy tail that she wagged excitedly while Benjie held her. Duke glanced in her direction, and had no interest in her. "I'll take them upstairs." They both had to be examined by the vet on duty as part of their intake. The tech at the desk signed off on them, and the Animal Care driver left, as the tech started paperwork for both of the new dogs. They could hear Benjie talking to them, as he headed up the stairs to the adoption center.

He spent most of the day with both dogs. They both checked out as healthy, and he alternated caring for them. The Dane was ravenous and devoured the food Benjie gave him, and cried for more. Benjie very carefully followed all the rules for new dogs at the shelter, until the staff knew them better. But the Dane wasn't ominous, and was obviously as starved for affection as he was for food. He climbed onto Benjie's lap and sat there, looking like a colt and acting like a lapdog, and the little spotted Chihuahua followed Benjie everywhere. Both dogs eventually fell asleep, looking very handsome after their baths. Benjie filled out a report on each of them, and handed them in at the desk. "I named the Chihuahua Dottie, like Polka Dottie," he explained.

He was with them when the vet examined them. Benjie looked at the vet seriously when he declared them healthy. "Can I take them home?" He had never asked that before.

"You mean like for the night?" The vet was startled. The staff had never had a single problem with Benjie in five years. He followed rules and instructions to the letter. He was one of their most reliable employees. They knew how much he loved dogs and how kind he was to them. It was an unusual request, but they also knew his living situation, and had met his mother several times. He had strong family support. The dogs wouldn't be at risk with him, and his home was huge.

"I mean forever," Benjie explained. "My mom was allergic to dogs and cats, so I could never have one. She's dead now, and my brother moved in with me and my sister. He's not allergic to dogs, so I can have one. We have a big house, they could sleep in my room."

"I was sorry to hear about your mom, Benjie. She was a lovely woman," the vet said gently.

"She and my dad died in an avalanche in France," Benjie said matter-of-factly. "That's why my brother moved in. He likes dogs too."

"A big dog like Duke needs a lot of exercise. Do you think you could walk him yourself?"

Benjie nodded with a grin.

"I can carry Dottie if she gets tired," he volunteered.

"You want both of them?"

Benjie nodded again. "They're friends now. Duke watched while I gave Dottie her bath. He likes her."

"I'll tell you what. How about we give it a try? You take them home tonight. I know you'll take good care of them. You see how it works out, and whether they settle in and you can manage them. And if it doesn't, you bring them back to the shelter, and we'll list them for adoption. We'll call it a trial adoption, sort of like foster care." The vet wasn't worried, knowing Benjie well, and his home situation. He was sure Benjie's brother would bring them back if there was a problem. He felt comfortable with the arrangement.

"I won't bring them back," Benjie said clearly. "I love them, and they'll be happy."

"That's a great start." The older vet smiled at him. He had a grandson with issues similar to Benjie's. "We'll give you enough food and supplies for the first few days, and you can give me a report tomorrow."

"Do you want a written report?" Benjie asked.

"You don't have to do that. Just tell me when you come to work. Do you want to call your brother and ask him?"

"No. He's nice. He won't be mad at me. He never gets mad at me. Neither did my mom. He has a twin sister. They make dresses. And my baby sister won't care. She goes out at night and comes home for breakfast, now that my mom's not there." The vet repressed a smile at the report, and didn't comment. He had been very sorry to hear that Benjie had recently lost his parents. It sounded very traumatic, and the dogs would be a comfort to him. And the vet knew he was responsible and would treat them well.

Benjie took a cab home from work, with the money he always carried. Duke sat on the seat next to him, and Dottie was in the carrier she had arrived in. He paid the driver, and rang the doorbell when he got home. He lost keys so he didn't carry

them. Frieda opened the door and was shocked
when she saw him. Benjie walked Duke past her,
and held Dottie's carrier.

"What is that? A horse?" Frieda asked, staring at
the huge black dog, who was all bones for the moment.

"This is Duke," he said, and held up the carrier
with the fluffy white dog in it. She was barely bigger than a guinea pig. "And this is Dottie. They're
going to sleep with me. I have to walk Duke a lot."

"We've never had a dog," she said, frowning.

"I know. Mom was allergic. She's not here now."
Frieda nodded, stunned, as Benjie walked the two
dogs around the house to show them their new
home, and then took them up to his bedroom. Duke
made himself at home on Benjie's bed with his head
on the pillow, and Dottie curled up next to him
when Benjie put her on the bed. They seemed perfectly at ease, and Duke raised his head from time
to time to make sure Benjie was still there, and then
went back to sleep when he saw him. Benjie took
them downstairs to feed them before anyone got
home, and walked Duke up and down the block.
Luckily, both dogs appeared to be housebroken.
They were an incongruous sight, Benjie with a massive black dog and a tiny white one. Then he went
back to his bedroom, to wait for the others to come
home. He liked knowing that Charlie and Caro were
staying with him now, and Lyle had said he would
spend another night that night too. They were all

going to have dinner together. Benjie loved having everyone at home. He missed his parents, but his siblings were good company.

Caro arrived first with groceries and prepared food she had bought at a deli.

Charlie had said he would make pasta. By seven-thirty everyone was home, and Gloria arrived. At eight, they called Benjie down to dinner. Annabelle was there too. The whole family was in the kitchen talking when Benjie walked in with Duke and Dottie behind him. They stopped talking and stared, as they took in the scene of Benjie with a huge dog and a tiny one.

"What is that?" Charlie asked him, although it was obvious.

"That's Duke and Dottie. I adopted them." Benjie beamed, and Charlie started to laugh. Suddenly they all were laughing.

"You adopted *two* dogs?" Charlie asked him.

"Yeah. They came in together, kind of like twins, like you and Caro," he said, and Charlie shook his head in amazement. It was a bold gesture on Benjie's part, but a sign that he was in good spirits and coping with their parents' deaths, and it certainly added life to the scene. Both dogs were well behaved. Annabelle picked the Chihuahua up and cuddled her, while Lyle stroked the huge, skinny black dog, and Charlie cooked the pasta.

"I always wanted a dog growing up," Gloria said, stroking Duke too. "We couldn't have one because of Mom's allergy. I don't think I've ever seen a dog this big." Duke stood up and put his paws on Lyle's shoulders and looked him in the eye, and when he got down, he shook hands with Gloria. She noticed the missing ear and Benjie explained it, and she felt sorry for the dog. By the time they sat down to dinner, everyone had made friends with Duke and Dottie. Duke sat looking longingly at their meal, hoping for scraps from the table, but wasn't aggressive about it, and Dottie slept on Annabelle's lap.

Everyone was in good spirits, happy to be having dinner together, despite whatever problems plagued them, like Lyle and his agonies with Amanda. For an hour or two, they could forget their problems and just relax as a family.

At the end of the meal, Lyle admitted to all of them that he thought he would be getting a divorce. He and Amanda hadn't told the children yet, and he had to find an apartment. He was going to ask Amanda for alternating weeks in joint custody, and he needed a place big enough for them. After ten years of marriage, he was starting over again, with two children in tow. He was worried about Tommy and Devon's reaction when they told them. He and Amanda hadn't finalized anything yet, or discussed any of the details. He had just made the decision after her threats the day before.

"I think it'll be a dogfight over the money. And

we don't have a prenup," he said, and Gloria groaned.

"That's all she ever wanted from you anyway," she said bluntly. "I'll be happy for you when you're out of that."

"I got two terrific kids out of it, I'm not sorry," he told them all. "It hasn't worked for years. If we sell the house now, she'll want at least half my share of the money," he warned them.

"Another good reason not to sell it," Charlie chimed in. Annabelle interrupted him as soon as he did.

"I have something to tell you all too," she said in a soft voice with a glance at Caro, who dreaded what their reaction would be. It was impossible to predict, with their diverse personalities, ideas, and points of view. Lyle and Gloria were more traditional, and she and Charlie more liberal. "I'm pregnant," she said, and it dropped on them like a bomb. There was total silence at the table.

"Are you having an abortion?" Gloria asked her, with a stern expression of disapproval. Annabelle shook her head.

"I'm four months pregnant. I'm having it."

"Are you getting married?" Gloria shot at her, and Annabelle shook her head.

"The father doesn't want to, and neither do I," she said.

"Whatever you do, don't get married because you're pregnant," Lyle said. "I'm living proof that

that doesn't work. Get married one day because
you love someone you're crazy about and are compatible with. In today's world, you don't have to be
married to have a baby. That was the biggest mistake I ever made," he confessed.

"Annabelle can't be having a baby, she's not married," Benjie said practically.

"Yes, she can," Caroline said gently to him, and
he seemed surprised.

"That's just perfect," Gloria said angrily. "You
stay out every night like a slut, and then you come
home pregnant. It would have killed Mom and
Dad. That's disgusting. Are you keeping it?" Annabelle shook her head, crushed by what Gloria said.
She was being designated as the family disgrace
now, and felt like it.

"I'm putting it up for adoption," she said softly.

"I'll adopt it," Benjie offered, and she smiled
gratefully at him.

"It's okay, Benj. We'll find good parents for it." At
least she hoped so. She still had to look into it with
Caro, who was being far more compassionate than
their older sister, who acted like the vice committee
and didn't mince words. Charlie was the only one
they hadn't heard from about Annabelle's pregnancy and he and Caroline were exchanging meaningful looks, and she whispered something to him.
It was a time for confessions around the table.
Lyle's divorce, Annabelle's unwanted baby.

"It's time," Caro whispered to him while the others were talking. Annabelle was in the spotlight for the moment, on the hot seat. Lyle felt sorry for her. He remembered the chaos it had caused in his life when Amanda had gotten pregnant. His parents had been heartbroken, but had been decent about it. He had done the "right thing" and gotten married, which turned out to be not the right thing at all.

"True confessions," Charlie said with a quaver in his voice. He hadn't intended to share it with them, and never had before, but it seemed to be the night for it, and they were all more open and more vulnerable with their parents' recent deaths. "I've never told any of you, except Caro. We all know how Dad felt about those things. He was old-school and conservative, and Mom thought it would break his heart if he knew. But I told her. I'm gay. There, I've said it. It's out. My darkest secret is right out there."

He felt totally naked, and hoped saying it hadn't been a terrible mistake. He could never have done that if their parents were alive. Their mother had begged him never to tell their father. She said it would break his heart or kill him, so Charlie had kept the secret to himself for the past fifteen years. He had realized at eighteen that he was homosexual. He had told Caro very quickly, and their mother a few years later. She had always been very accepting and loving about it, but she knew her husband wouldn't be, would never accept it, and would have considered it deeply embarrassing, so Charlie had to lead a secret life around his family, and had since he was eighteen.

"Why didn't you tell us?" Gloria asked. When she thought about it, she wasn't surprised, but was disappointed that he hadn't told them.

"I didn't know how any of you would react, and I was afraid you might tell Dad. Mom said it would kill him."

"He was a Neanderthal on that one subject," Gloria said with her usual bluntness. "But he was a decent man and he loved you. Mom always over-protected him. He would have survived it and ac-cepted it," she said in defense of their father.

"Maybe not. I was afraid he might not see me anymore, or let me come home."

"How sad," Lyle said, and reached out and touched his arm. "I'm sorry, bro. I must be as blind as Dad. I don't know what's wrong with me. I never even suspected. You used to talk about girls a lot in college."

"They were just friends. I figured it out senior year in high school."

"Do you have someone in your life, a partner?" Gloria asked him, and he shook his head and smiled.

"Yeah, my twin." He smiled broadly at Caro. "No one else special at the moment. We work too hard to maintain relationships. We work in a crazy business, with crazy hours. The hundred-and-forty-hour workweek. That's why we're both still single."

"He's right." Caro looked resigned when she said it. She glanced around the table to check on Benjie. She didn't see him, and thought he was in the bathroom, or had gone upstairs to get something with the dogs.

"You know, you could do a lot for gay rights," Gloria said to him with an intense expression. He could tell that she was serious and he laughed.

"I'm not running for public office, Gloria, I just want to lead an open life without secrets. That's good enough for me. And Caro was right when she pushed me to tell you. It was time. I don't know when I could have come out if Dad were still alive. Maybe never. So now you know."

"You should have told us sooner, but now I understand why you didn't. It must have been a hard fifteen years for you keeping it secret. I'm sorry," Lyle said. He had the sense that he had failed Charlie as a brother. As he said it, he glanced around to see how Benjie had taken the news, and he didn't see him. "Where's Benjie?"

Charlie glanced around too, and realized he hadn't seen him in a while. They'd been busy with their confessions and hadn't paid attention to him. "Maybe Duke is holding him hostage in his room. I'll go up and check," he said, and left the table for a few minutes. When he came back, he looked worried. "He's not upstairs."

"Did you look in all the rooms?" Caro asked him, and they all headed upstairs to check their rooms, and were back a few minutes later.

"I don't know where he went. He didn't say anything, and I didn't see him leave the table." No one had. They searched the whole house room by room, including the basement, and were back in the kitchen ten minutes later. There was no sign of him anywhere. "Shit, he can't just vanish, like he used to as a child." A few times, strangers had brought him back to the house when he got lost in the neighborhood.

"Maybe he took the dogs for a walk," Lyle suggested. They went outside and looked up and down the street and saw no one. But the dogs were gone too. "Come on," he said to Charlie. "Let's go a few blocks and see if we find him. He probably just took the dogs out."

"He should have told us," Caro said, worried. "We need to make rules for that now. He can't just disappear without telling someone. Mom was always very relaxed about it, and Benjie communicated well with her. He was used to it. He's not used to telling us where he's going."

"No one is going to kidnap him with a dog that size," Lyle reassured her.

They all put their jackets on then and headed outside, spreading out in all directions.

Half an hour later, Caro and Gloria were back at the house with no sign of him, and Annabelle came back a few minutes later. The boys were still out, and Benjie was still MIA, and so were Duke and Dottie.

Lyle and Charlie had met at the entrance to Central Park, and thought it unlikely that Benjie would venture into the park at night. He knew it was dangerous. But his brothers didn't know where else to look, and headed down the path into the park. They walked briskly for ten minutes together, calling out Benjie's name, and listening for sounds, and then they saw him. He had Duke on a leash, and as they approached, they saw the Chihuahua tucked into Benjie's jacket to keep her warm. He waved as he saw them walking toward him, and smiled broadly.

"Dr. Riley, my boss, the vet said Duke needs to walk a lot," he explained. He was completely unafraid in the park at night, especially with Duke to protect him. "I'm sorry I forgot to tell you I was going out. You were all talking and I didn't want to interrupt you."

Charlie and Lyle walked out of the park with Benjie as Charlie explained that he needed to tell someone when he went out, and he needed to stay on their street and not go so far away or into the park at night. He was a dozen blocks from the house when they found him. Benjie said he understood, but he knew he was safe. Charlie and Lyle exchanged a look. It made them both more aware that they needed ground rules now that their mother was gone and they were responsible for Benjie. She had always been fully aware of the range of his abilities and his needs, and he had reported to her. He wasn't used to reporting to them.

"You were talking to Annabelle about the baby, and I didn't want to bother you. I'm sorry if I worried you. I was fine with Dottie and Duke," Benjie said to both his brothers. Their faces were red from the cold when they got home, and Duke bounded up the stairs to Benjie's room. He knew where he lived now.

Their three sisters came out of the kitchen when they heard the front door close, and everyone looked relieved.

"Where was he?" Caro asked Charlie in a low voice.

"Halfway to the West Side in Central Park, with the dogs. He was exercising Duke. He was fine. He just needs to stay closer to home when he walks the dogs, and tell us when he's going out. He was used to telling Mom. He needs to get used to telling us. He didn't want to interrupt us. I told him it's okay to do." Charlie smiled at her. It had been quite a night for all of them. Lyle's sharing his news about planning to get divorced, Annabelle's announcement that she was pregnant, Charlie's long-hidden secret that he was gay, and Benjie going out on his own without telling them and going too far from home.

"We covered a lot of ground tonight." Caro grinned at her twin.

"Never a dull moment at the Whittiers'," Charlie said, and put an arm around her. He missed their parents, but he loved spending time with his siblings. It was the only blessing that had come from losing Connie and Preston, and he was free to live his life now, without lying or hiding from his siblings who he really was. He wished that he had told them sooner, but at least now he could be honest. As usual, Caro was right.

He peeked into Benjie's room when he went upstairs. He was sound asleep in his bed in his pajamas with an arm around Duke, and Dottie on his pillow next to his head. Charlie smiled as he walked to his own room, feeling like an honest man for the first time in fifteen years.

Chapter 6

Lyle had sent Amanda a text message that morning when he got up, asking to meet her at the apartment on his way to work. She had texted back that it wasn't convenient since she had a ballet class, but she would meet him at nine as a favor. She had far more to gain from the meeting than he did. He had a strong sense that all his dealings with Amanda from now on, if he proceeded with a divorce, would cost him money. She was nobody's fool, and he suspected that she already knew what she wanted and had a number in mind. She had a calculator embedded in her brain and talked about money more than he liked, especially in front of their children. He wanted them to have better values than that. Amanda wasn't a romantic, and never had been. He had thought she was at first, but now there was no question about it. She had seemed so vulnerable when she told him she was pregnant, and he had felt sorry for her. Like Gloria, he wondered now if she'd gotten pregnant on purpose in order to hook him. If so, she had done a good job of it.

He had provided her with a very comfortable lifestyle, security, and all the material things she wanted: jewelry, expensive clothes from big-name designers, all the status symbols that impressed her girlfriends. Being married to a successful man had become her job, the only well-paid one she'd ever had. As he looked back now, he had gotten too little in return, neither warmth nor comfort, and she barely took care of their children.

He spent far more time with them than she did, although he had a demanding job. She wasn't interested in the children, or in him, only in the expensive things he paid for, that she shopped for constantly. She was always very fashionably dressed, and a little too sexy for him, like at his parents' funeral with her miniskirt and thigh-high black suede high-heeled boots. It was mostly false advertising since they no longer had sex. He arrived at the apartment on time. She was waiting for him in a red velour Chanel tracksuit and Christian Dior jeweled sneakers. They walked into the kitchen together and sat down. He'd been playing the scene over in his mind for the past twenty-four hours. He wanted to be reasonable with her. She was the mother of his children, and ten years of marriage seemed long to him, and worthy of respect.

He made himself a cup of coffee and looked at her, not sure where to start. "I've been thinking a lot about what you said, about my parents' house, and my brother, and your threat to divorce me if I don't up the ante on our lifestyle. You made it pretty clear about where things stand between us now. It sounds more like a business arrangement than a marriage." It still shocked him to realize that she was willing to leave him if he didn't put enough money on the table to keep her.

"You're going to have more money now," she said simply, looking unemotional about it. "There's no reason why I shouldn't too." She had done nothing to earn it, and they weren't her parents. To Amanda, money was money, whatever the source. There was no sentiment about it, which shocked him even more.

"I think we're done, Amanda, or we should be. There's not much left except the accounting."

"There could be," she said. He realized now that money was the only way to her heart, if she had one, which he doubted. You couldn't think like that and love at the same time.

"You can't buy love, and I'm not going to try. I want a divorce. I'm going to take you up on your offer." She nodded and looked undisturbed by what he'd said. She didn't seem to care one way or another as long as she got what she wanted. "I want joint custody of the kids. I'm thinking alternate weeks. It won't be easy for them at first, but I hope they'll get used to it. And I'm willing to give you half ownership of the apartment," although he had paid for it entirely. "I'll still pay for their schools, and a reasonable amount of child support, and I'll keep paying Molly, so there's no change of lifestyle for you or them." Half the apartment was worth two million dollars, which was a healthy amount to give her, for ten years. She nodded and didn't comment, and didn't counter anything he said, nor thank him, which he noticed too.

"Is that it?" she asked expressionlessly, and voiced no sorrow that it hadn't worked out, or regrets for any way she might have failed him. She didn't discuss the offer with him. She didn't reject it either.

Their meeting was over in half an hour, and he told her that he wanted to see the children in the next day or two, to break the news to them. He offered to do it with her, but she said she was willing to have him explain it. She said she'd already told them she and Lyle might be getting a divorce, so it wouldn't be a surprise. She informed him that Tommy was upset about it, and Devon didn't fully understand, since she was only seven. So she had already broached the subject and upset them, without including him.

Amanda didn't seem worried about them.

Lyle felt dazed as he took a cab to his office. The

meeting had been completely bloodless and un-emotional. He was worried about his children, and annoyed at Amanda for jumping the gun and warning them of what might happen.

He talked to Caro about it that night at dinner, and she asked him what he was going to do about an apartment for him and the children. He admitted that he hadn't thought about it yet. It was all happening so fast, he wasn't prepared.

"I'll have to get an apartment big enough for the three of us on the weeks I have them."

"Why don't you stay here until you find one? Frieda can help take care of them when they come home from school. There's even room for Molly if she comes too. And it will be company for the kids, with Charlie and Benjie here, and I might stay for a while too." She didn't want to go back to the loft in SoHo now that Charlie was living uptown. It was lonely there without him. "There's plenty of room here, and it might be fun for them and distract them, just until you find a place you love." He thought about it for a minute and nodded. It had advantages, if his kids didn't mind not having a place of their own for a while, and bringing Molly to care for them was a good idea. Frieda was getting old, and she had been somewhat overwhelmed by three of them moving back into the house. Annabelle and Benjie were enough work for her, but she was used to them. The siblings were still paying

Frieda from the funds their parents had left, and running the house with it.

"I'll talk to the kids about it. I'm taking them to dinner tomorrow night. If I stay here temporarily, we can start the joint custody arrangement of alternate weeks right away. I won't have to wait till I find an apartment."

He called them that night but Amanda said Tommy was in the shower and couldn't talk to him. When Lyle called back, Tommy was doing homework and couldn't be disturbed. Amanda said he had a paper due for science class. Lyle talked to Devon and she sounded sad, and was excited to see him the next day. She told him she missed him, which made his heart ache. It was painful not living with them suddenly. And they'd had no time to prepare and get used to the idea. The marriage had come to a dead stop with no warning. He wondered if Amanda had planned it that way. Even he realized she wasn't as innocent or spontaneous as she pretended to be. She calculated everything.

The next day at the office, he had ample proof of it. Her counteroffer to his came from an attorney who had obviously had time to plan it. She wanted to own the entire apartment, not half, although she had contributed nothing to it. The custody arrangement seemed fine to her. The child support amount she wanted was outrageous. She was also demanding alimony, half of his current investments, and half of his inheritance. And half of his share of the proceeds from his parents' house if they sold it. Basically, she wanted half of everything he had, and all the contents of the apartment: antiques, art, furniture, appliances. She wanted the apartment and everything in it. And half of every penny he had, either earned or inherited.

He called Jeff Sampson after scanning the document to him. "Your ex-wife isn't shy. She left no stone unturned," he commented dryly.

"What kind of chance do I have of mitigating that?" Lyle asked him.

"We'll negotiate it, and we can offset the value of your share of the apartment against some of it. Where we'll fight her is on what you just inherited, and the house if you sell it. The alimony she wants is excessive. She's young. The judge will give her child support, but a decent judge will tell her to go to work after a year or two. She can't ride the gravy train forever," although she certainly intended to try. "Her attorney knows she won't get all of it, but they're starting high as a negotiating tactic. What are you willing to give her?" Lyle had been thinking about it since he read her demands. There was no question now about what kind of person she was. The gloves were off.

"I'd give her the whole apartment, if you discount that from my investment portfolio. I'm fine with the child support, which she'll benefit from too, with young kids. I don't want to give her half of all my investments, and if I have to pay alimony,

I'd like it to be less. She shouldn't get a penny of anything from my parents. If we'd gotten a prenup, that would have been excluded."

"But you didn't," Jeff reminded him, which Lyle knew too. "Let's see what we can do, and conclude this quickly. I assume you don't want to go to trial."

"I'd rather not, if she's willing to be reasonable. If she holds out for half my inheritance, I'll fight her. That's just not right."

"I don't sense a lot of sentiment here," Jeff said dryly. "She's in it for the money."

"My family thinks she always was," Lyle said in a subdued tone. He was facing harsh reality now, and it was hard to hide from the truth.

"If she has a good head for business, she'll give in on some things and not others. We'll do our best," Jeff said, and for the first time Lyle felt like he hated Amanda. He felt guilty about it, but she had him by the throat and was going for the jugular. She was mean and conniving, and merciless in her approach.

Lyle picked up Tommy and Devon at the apartment that night, and took them to an early dinner at a hamburger restaurant they usually loved. They barely ate, and Tommy looked sullen and smoldering through the entire meal. Devon sat as close to him as she could get, and told him how much she missed him at home. "We'll have every other week together, starting next week. Mom and I have agreed to that." He tried to sound cheerful about it, although living away from them depressed him. He already missed them terribly after only a few days.

"Mom says you hardly want to give us any money to live on and you want to take the apartment away from her, so we'll have to move to a bad apartment," Tommy said angrily as he picked at his food. Lyle was shocked that Amanda was willing to lie to their children in order to manipulate him.

"Tommy, look at me," he said softly. "Have I ever deprived your mom or either of you of anything?"

Tommy hesitated and shook his head. "But you're getting divorced now. That's different. Mom says you hate her and you want to punish her, and you want the divorce and don't care about us." Lyle felt rage rise up in him and fought to control it. The only thing that mattered now was reassuring his children. Amanda was a monster.

"You don't need to know about the money in the divorce, which your mom suggested first. I'm never going to deprive you or her. I offered your mother the whole apartment, all of it, my share and hers. She'll own it, I won't. You won't have to move, unless she decides to sell it to buy another apartment. But she'll own the apartment you live in now. And I offered her a big amount for child support so nothing will change for you. The rest is just business, and you don't need to worry about it. I'm never going to leave your mom short of money, or either of you."

"And where are you going to live, Daddy, if you give Mommy the apartment?" Devon asked him with wide eyes. She was worried about him, which touched him.

"I'm going to find a new apartment for us. In the meantime, I'm staying at Grandma and Grampa's house, with Uncle Charlie and Aunt Caro, Uncle Benjie, and Aunt Annabelle," he explained. "And you can stay at the house with us."

"Are you having fun with them?" she asked him. They liked their aunts and uncles, although they didn't see a lot of them, and they had loved their grandparents and were sad that they were gone.

Lyle smiled at the question. "I am sometimes, except that I miss you a lot. It's nice being with them. And Aunt Gloria came to dinner the other night. And Uncle Benjie got two dogs." Tommy showed some slight interest in that. He didn't admit it, but he had been reassured by his father explaining the financial arrangements for their mother, which wasn't what she had said.

"What kind of dogs?" Tommy asked.

"A Great Dane and a Chihuahua." Lyle smiled when he said it.

"That sounds crazy." Tommy smiled in spite of himself.

"What are their names?" Devon wanted to know, and he told her. "Where are we going to sleep if we stay there with you? In your room?" She looked so concerned it made him want to cry.

"Grandma and Grampa had some extra bedrooms right near mine. You can sleep together in one room, or have your own bedrooms if you want."

"I want my own," Tommy spoke up quickly.

"Molly can share a room with you or you can have your own," Lyle reassured his daughter. "She can stay with us there too." Devon seemed pleased with that. "We start next week, and I'm seeing you for dinner on Sunday," he told them. Amanda had confirmed the schedule through her attorney. But he was angry at her for lying to Tommy about the apartment and the child support. It was an ugly game to play, using the children, and he didn't intend to play it with her. He realized that it shouldn't have surprised him. Nothing would with her anymore, and she was out for every penny she could get. She had her eyes on his inheritance, which in theory, she shouldn't be able to touch, but it had been done by others before. There was legal precedent for what she wanted, which he was sure she knew. Amanda was no fool.

Tommy and Devon's first night at the house they were all living in now started out by being fun. Tommy loved playing with Duke, and walked him with Benjie, and Devon loved Dottie, and Benjie let the little dog sleep with her. Dottie was just the right size for Devon.

The children were nervous on their first night, and Lyle stayed with each of them until they fell asleep. Caro made them pancakes in the morning. She had become the breakfast chef for all of them before she went to work. She felt like a house-mother in a boarding school, and they all had a good time together. Tommy and Devon had brought their clothes for the week. They had brought some toys, too. Tommy had his iPad, and Devon brought her favorite Barbie dolls and the teddy bear she slept with. It was a very full house while they were there. Benjie loved being with them when he came home from work. It was going nicely. And Frieda appreciated Molly's help.

On their last day, Benjie wanted to do something special with them. He was sad that they were leaving for a week, but happy to know they were com-ing back and it would be a regular occurrence. He found a box of cupcake mix left over from when he had made cupcakes with his mother before she left on her last trip. He invited Tommy and Devon to make them with him. He told them he knew how. They found some sprinkles in a cupboard to deco-rate them with, and a tin of chocolate icing.

Devon clapped her hands with excitement, as Tommy mixed the batter and Benjie lit the stove. It came on without a problem, and they filled the cups in the muffin tin with the batter. It all went perfectly and they put them in the oven, and went upstairs to play with the dogs while they waited for the cupcakes to bake. It was the most exciting thing they'd done all week. Benjie said he knew how to do them, and had made them often with his mom. Tommy understood that Benjie was "different," as his dad had explained to him, but Devon didn't. She thought he was a grownup like everyone else. And Lyle had never explained it to her. She was too young.

They had just put a little doll sweater on Dottie when Annabelle came out of her room to check a burning smell. It was much stronger in the hall, and there was smoke in the hall, coming up the stairs from the kitchen. She rushed downstairs and dashed into the kitchen. There was smoke coming out of the oven when Annabelle opened the oven door and saw the charred remains of the cupcakes. She turned off the stove and opened the windows to dispel the smoke that filled the kitchen. Tommy, Devon, and Benjie had come down the stairs to see where the smoke came from. They had forgotten their cupcakes, and ten minutes later, they heard sirens and the firemen arrived. The smoke alarms in the hall had gone off, connected to the fire department. Annabelle explained that a baking session had gone awry, apologized, and they left. Lyle came home a few minutes later, and the threesome looked sheepish as Annabelle scolded them and told them they needed to stay and check what they were baking.

"You can't put something in the oven and walk away and forget it," she explained to them. "You have to stay and watch it."

"I forgot how long you're supposed to leave them in. Mom did that part when we made them," Benjie said apologetically. Devon looked sad about the burned cupcakes when Annabelle took them out of the oven and set them on the stove. They were charred beyond recognition. "We'll do them next week when you come back," Benjie promised them.

"What's going on in here?" Lyle asked. "Good Lord, what is that? Or what was it?" he said when he saw the muffin tin with the charred remains of their cupcakes.

"Cupcakes," Devon told her father. "We were going to put sprinkles on them, but we forgot them in the oven," she said, and Annabelle gave her brother a meaningful look.

"Did you have a grownup with you?" he asked them.

"Yes, Uncle Benjie," Devon answered, and Lyle exchanged another glance with his sister. She got the drift. They needed an adult around for baking projects and Molly had been packing. Keeping track of time was not Benjie's strong suit. He had meant well and gotten distracted by the kids and the dogs, and was embarrassed about it. Annabelle saved the

day with some cookies they decorated instead and
used all the sprinkles, so the kids were happy and
there was no harm done.

It was a reminder to Lyle and all the adults in
the house that they had young children there now
who needed supervision, and at times Benjie
needed assistance, and cooking was one of them.
Devon explained that Molly had been packing their
things to leave the next day to return to their
mother. They were going to leave some things at
their dad's, but there were favorite toys and items
of clothing that they wanted to take back and forth,
so they'd each brought a small suitcase. Their new
life was going to be somewhat nomadic and already was, but they had enjoyed the week with
their father, and having so many people at the table
every night. There were lots of people living in the
house now, and they loved Benjie's dogs. Tommy
and Devon were sad to leave everyone, but coming
back was something to look forward to. For the
most part, their first week of joint custody, bounc-
ing between their mother and father, had been a
success.

The house seemed painfully quiet when Lyle
came home from work the next day and the children were gone. The dogs wandered into their
rooms and were disappointed not to find them
there.

Lyle had had another counter from Amanda that
day in her string of outrageous demands. She was

unrelenting and Lyle wondered how he had ever married her. He had only just begun to understand that the financial settlement of their divorce was going to take a very long time, but he didn't care. Some things were worth fighting for, and fair play was one of them. Amanda had no intention of treating him fairly. She was out for blood. This was her big chance, and she was going to do whatever she had to to get what she wanted, no matter who she hurt in the process, even her kids. Lyle was her target, and the children were collateral damage. She didn't care.

Chapter 7

Gloria called Charlie in his office a month after he had mentioned looking for an investor. She hadn't said anything about it since, and he'd been thinking about pursuing it more vigorously, now that the initial turmoil after their parents' deaths was settling down. Lyle and Gloria still had a lot to do for the estate. But the twins weren't involved in the financial details. As the executor, Lyle was buried in them, and Gloria had time and was helping him to the extent she could. But she hadn't forgotten Charlie's request to help him find an investor for their fashion business. Charlie was startled when she called him, since she rarely did. She was more given to sending him texts from time to time.

"How are things at the house?" she asked him.

"Busy, crazy, nice. It's fun having Lyle's kids there every other week. And Benjie's keeping us all entertained with his dogs. Caro and I are enjoying living there for now, keeping an eye on the younger ones. We haven't been to our apartment in weeks."

"And how is the family slut?" she said, her voice tightening as she said it. He knew who she meant, their pregnant youngest sister.

"She's behaving for now. She's been tired, so she's been going to bed early every night. She hasn't gone out." The daily walk of shame, returning in the morning, had stopped since she found out she was pregnant, and Joao left for Brazil.

"Talk about closing the barn door after the horse got out. I still can't believe she managed to get knocked up. What a mess that's going to be." Charlie told Gloria that Caro had been spending a lot of time with Annabelle.

"I called because there's someone interesting I think you should meet. He's Italian, from Milan. His family owns the biggest textile mills in Italy. He's been investing money in the States for a long time with my help, mostly in high tech, and I mentioned you and Caro. He knows your line and he loves it. He wants to meet you both. Has Caro warmed to the idea of having an investor?"

"We haven't discussed it since . . . the accident. What Mom and Dad left will help us, but not on the scale we need, as I mentioned."

"I'd be happy to arrange a meeting if you want. But Caro had better behave. This guy's a big deal.

He has investments in Asia too. I've been advising him on investments in the U.S. for years."

"What's his name?"

"Giorgio Silvestri."

"Of course. We buy fabrics from him. They have gorgeous things, and they always deliver late. They're worth waiting for, though."

"When do you want to meet him?"

"As soon as he wants. That's a real opportunity. Thank you for arranging it, Glo."

"Anything for my little brother," she said, and Charlie laughed. They talked for a few more minutes and hung up. Ten minutes later, she texted him. They were meeting at the Bemelmans Bar at the Carlyle in two days at six o'clock. It was quiet and a good place to talk, and not far from the house.

He told Caro about it two hours later when they had a meeting in his office. All he said was that they were seeing Gloria with Giorgio Silvestri at the Carlyle.

"The textile guy from Milan? Why?" She was surprised. "What does Gloria have to do with him?"

Charlie took a quick breath and plunged in. "She's been handling his investments in the U.S. for years."

"And?" She waited for the rest.

"He's interested in us."

"As an investment?" He nodded. "Oh, here we go. How did Gloria get mixed up in it?"

"I asked her for advice about an investor. It won't kill you to meet him. Let's see what he has in mind. It's not a marriage, it's not even a date. It's a reconnaissance mission. He's one of the richest men in Italy. He and his brothers are worth billions." They were all in the business together. It was family-run, like many important businesses in Italy related to fashion. "If he likes us, he might give us some decent money and not take too big a piece of the pie."

"I'm not selling any piece of the pie," she said firmly.

"Be sure to tell him when you meet him," Charlie said.

"Don't worry, I will," she said, annoyed at him for setting it up without discussing it with her first. They sat down for their meeting then, to rough out the costs of their next show. It was going to be expensive, the fabrics alone cost a fortune, but they were worth it. Some of them were Silvestri fabrics, which seemed ironic now.

The meeting ran longer than expected, and they got home late. Lyle was having dinner in the kitchen with Annabelle and Benjie. Frieda had roasted two chickens and left them for whoever wanted dinner. They were just finishing eating when Caro and Charlie arrived. The chicken smelled delicious and the twins sat down to join the others. The conversation was easy. They loved meeting up at the end of the day. Annabelle went to bed shortly after, and

Benjie took the dogs for a walk. He stayed on their block now and ran Duke back and forth up the street, or around the block. Having Duke was like having a child in the house. In a few days, Tommy and Devon would be back. And no one was talking about selling the house at the moment. It was serving them all well. Gloria was the only one not living there. All the others were.

The meeting at the Carlyle took place on schedule two days later. Caro grumbled at Charlie all the way uptown in the cab. She kept reminding her brother that she was not going to agree to anything, and was planning to complain to Silvestri that his fabrics always shipped late and made every fashion show they did more complicated as a result.

"I'm sure he can't wait to hear it," Charlie said ironically. "I just want you to know, if you're a bitch to him, I'm going to kill you. I know you don't want an investor, but don't screw this up for us. At least give the guy a chance to talk. He's a big client of Glo's and I promised her you'd be nice. Don't make a liar of me."

"All right, all right. Italians are such bullshitters. But they're charming as hell."

When they walked into the restaurant, Gloria and Giorgio Silvestri were already there, waiting for them. Traffic had been heavy getting uptown. As the twins approached the table, they both noticed that Silvestri was shockingly handsome and impeccably elegant. They had never met him before, only the Silvestri reps. He was somewhere in his late forties, close to fifty, with a mane of silvery white hair. He had a ready smile, and he was straightforward and at ease while talking to Caro. He didn't seem like a "bullshitter" at all to Charlie. He was charming but not unctuous, and very complimentary about Caro's designs. And he seemed sincere and excited about meeting them.

"My brother is actually the final word," Caro said to him. "Nothing gets on the runway without Charlie's approval. He designs as well as I do, he just prefers finance." Caro always gave Charlie credit for what he added to the collection. He had an infallible eye.

"I wanted to design menswear," Charlie chatted with Silvestri, "but I never got there. I got side-tracked by the money side of fashion. It's a high-stakes game these days," Charlie said, and Giorgio nodded.

"I'm very honored that you use our fabrics." He explained that he was one of six brothers who all headed up different divisions of the firm. Like Charlie, he was CFO, but he was interested in the twins' business as a personal investment, or his brothers might want to get involved once they knew more about it. It was a possibility either way. For the moment, he was there for himself, not the family firm, although he handled their investments too. His exploring it as a personal investment gave him greater flexibility on the terms and the amount of his investment.

They talked about their business for an hour, and Giorgio asked intelligent questions, that Caro and Charlie would have asked too in his shoes. He made it seem like a friendly conversation and was very relaxed as he talked to them. His English was flawless.

"May I come to see your center of operations, where you do business, and your workshops?" he asked them, and Charlie told him they'd be happy to have him visit anytime.

"I'd like that. How about tomorrow? I go back to Italy tomorrow night, so I don't have much time." But it was a good first step to show him their business. And it occurred to Charlie that someone in a field related to fashion, like textiles, would make an excellent investor. He'd understand what they were doing and hopefully not get in their hair. They set a meeting time for the next morning, and left the bar an hour and a half after they'd arrived there. A great deal of information had been exchanged. Gloria looked pleased, as did her twin siblings. Giorgio had deferred to Gloria several times, and seemed very comfortable with her. He watched her carefully through the meeting and was very respectful of her.

"I think he likes you, Glo," Charlie commented afterwards.

"He liked the two of you too." She was pleased.

"Not in the same way. He acted as though you walk on water, with a lot of sex appeal thrown in," Charlie commented, and Gloria was quick to deny it.

"That's what Italians do," Gloria commented dismissively. Giorgio had always been warm with her, but she didn't take him seriously on a personal level, only in business. She was delighted to have brought him and the twins together, and hoped something good would come of it for both sides. And Charlie had the definite feeling that Giorgio was interested in Gloria as a woman, not just as the matchmaker for a deal. He kept talking about how brilliant she was and how successful his investments with her had been. And he flirted with her when he said it. Gloria denied it when Charlie said it to her after Giorgio left.

"He likes you, Glo," Charlie insisted. "Is he married?"

"Don't be ridiculous. He's widowed. His wife died in an accident last year. She was in the business with him. He's a good-looking guy," she conceded, but she was sure he was just being charming, not pursuing her. "Stop pimping for me. He's interested in your business, not in me. Besides, I'm perfectly happy as I am." The problem was that it was true. She loved her family and her work, and she made no effort anymore to meet a man. She scared most men away with her straightforward business expertise and sometimes harsh outspoken style. But Giorgio seemed to like that about her, and admired how smart she was.

She went back to the house with Caro and Charlie to have something to eat, stayed for a glass of wine afterwards, wished them luck at the meeting the next day, and then went home.

"What did you think?" Charlie asked Caro after Gloria left.

"I liked him. He seems like a straight shooter, but I don't want a partner or a boss. We're doing fine without him."

"A European investor might be a good thing for us. He'd be in Italy, we'd be here. He may not want to be that involved in the business. He's got plenty to do with his own."

"We'll see," she said. "You'll have to take care of him tomorrow. I'm going to be late. I have to take Annabelle to her sonogram. I promised I'd go with her." Charlie was relieved to hear it. Without Caro breathing down their necks or trying to discourage Giorgio from investing, he might get further, and openly discuss how big a share of the business Giorgio would want in exchange for the investment he would make. It was an important point for the twins. Neither of them wanted to lose control of the business or the brand they had built for the past eleven years. Gloria had told Giorgio that too, and he said he understood. He hadn't been aggressive

with them at the meeting, and seemed very relaxed, collaborative, and respectful. "I'll catch up
when I get to the office," she promised. "I should be
there by ten-thirty. The sonogram's at nine. It
shouldn't take more than half an hour, unless they
find something wrong."

"Do they think they will?" Charlie asked her,
worried.

"She partied hard before she knew she was
pregnant. She's scared." He nodded. He hadn't
thought of that before. It was something else to
worry about. He felt like the parent of a wayward
twenty-one-year-old, and he knew Caro did too.

Annabelle and Caroline arrived at the hospital for
the sonogram at eight-thirty, as they'd been told to
do. They were ushered into a cubicle after a fifteen-
minute wait, and Caro sat down on a chair next to
Annabelle, who was lying down, and very nervous.
She was afraid of what they would see and tell her,
fearing possible bad news of something abnormal
about the baby. The technician arrived a few minutes later, and applied gel to Annabelle's abdomen.
Caro realized then that the baby was starting to
show. Annabelle had been wearing shirts and loose
clothes so she hadn't noticed it before, and Annabelle was tall. But there was a small noticeable
bump. The technician began swirling the wand
over her rounded belly, and they watched the sono-

gram screen. Caro had never seen one before, and didn't know what to expect, and all of a sudden, the baby came into view, in Technicolor. It looked like a baby, and was waving its arms and legs, and they could see its fingers and toes. Its face was already formed, and it sucked its thumb as they watched, then removed its thumb and yawned. The sight of it brought tears to Caro's eyes. It was a whole tiny human, and not even that small. The technician said it was about five inches long and weighed about six ounces.

The tech said it was a healthy size, and the computer told them it was due on July fourth. Annabelle watched the screen intently and then looked away. She wasn't sure how she felt about the image, except she was shocked to see that it looked like a baby, not a blob. It suddenly made it all so real.

"Is it okay?" she asked the tech. "Is everything normal? No anomalies?"

"Nothing I can see. The radiologist will have another look. It looks like a healthy baby to me." The sonogram technician had measured the head, chest, abdomen, and femur, the fetal heart rate and rhythm. She had looked closely at its face and spine, and its extremities, as well as assessing the amniotic fluid and placenta. "Do you want to know the sex?" Annabelle hesitated and then nodded and held her sister's hand.

"It's a boy," the tech said decisively. "We knew that from your blood test anyway," and then she pointed to the screen where they could see his sex. "We'll give you a printout so you can show his dad." She smiled at Annabelle, who was fighting back tears. The doctor came in then and confirmed what the tech had said. Everything looked normal and healthy. They hadn't seen anything that concerned them. The tears rolled down Annabelle's cheeks as she dressed, and Caroline wasn't sure what to say.

Annabelle had seen the baby she was planning to give away. Caro knew she had spoken to Adam, the baby's father, again. He had just left for the NYU campus in Florence. He had been six months behind Annabelle in school, so it was his next-to-last semester. He was still unhappy about the baby, and definite that he didn't want to be involved, and was glad that she was putting it up for adoption. Neither of them was ready for a child. They were still children themselves, although they were also adults, and could have been parents if they wanted to be. Neither of them did, so Annabelle had made the best decision in the circumstances. But she still had to go through the whole delivery, and the entire process, and then would have to give him away to a couple who really wanted him. Caro had already promised her in one of their late-night talks that she'd be at the delivery with her.

A nurse handed Annabelle two copies of the photograph of the sonogram. You could see the baby clearly. Annabelle put both copies in her purse, with a grim expression, and they left the building, and hailed a cab. Caro dropped Annabelle back at the house, and was headed down to her offices on the Lower East Side, to meet up with Giorgio and her brother. Annabelle hadn't said a word since they left the sonogram. She had turned her head away, and was crying.

"Are you okay?" Caro asked Annabelle in the cab on their way to the house.

"It looks so real," she said softly. It had shaken her.

"It is real," Caro said. "Very much so." She was sorry for Annabelle. And she didn't have a mother to get her through it. All she had was Caro, who knew nothing about pregnancy or babies, but she loved Annabelle. But she wasn't her mom.

"I didn't expect it to be like that. It already looks like a baby. It was sucking its thumb."

"'He,'" Caro corrected her. It was going to be even harder to give the baby up now. They were both thinking that. He had a face and tiny hands, and was a whole person. Caro was relieved that the baby looked normal and seemed healthy. Seeing it had been very moving. She dropped Annabelle off and headed downtown.

When she got there, Giorgio and Charlie were sitting in his office. Charlie had already taken Giorgio around, and he looked excited by what he'd seen and heard from Charlie. Caro stepped easily into their conversation, and added some details to what they were discussing about their volume of production, and how they would use the funds if he invested in them. Everything had checked out well so far, and he left an hour later, and said he'd be in touch in the next few weeks. He wanted to discuss it with his brothers.

The Silvestris were a family operation and he said he had been very impressed by Caroline and Charlie. He and his brothers had discussed ballpark figures for the potential investment. They would be willing to provide a large influx of money if they got involved, and wanted 25 percent participation, which Charlie thought was extremely reasonable, and much less than most American investors would have asked for. The Whittiers would remain in control of their company. It sounded ideal. Even Caroline didn't object. Giorgio hadn't decided yet if he wanted to make it a corporate investment with his brothers or a personal one.

They called Gloria and told her, and she said that Giorgio had just called her too. They had made a great impression, and now all they had to do was wait for Giorgio's decision. He was due back in New York in three weeks, and Gloria didn't tell them that he had invited her to dinner when he got back. She was surprised by the invitation and then decided that it was simply to thank her for finding the opportunity for him. She didn't want to believe that it was more than that. But she felt a flutter in her stomach when she thought about it. She liked him more than she wanted to admit. And he had told her that he had always wanted to get to know her better, and now this was their chance. She had always been strictly business with him, which was her usual style.

After Caro and Gloria hung up, Charlie asked her about the sonogram. "How did it go? Do we have a nephew or a niece?"

"A nephew." She smiled sadly at her brother. "And it went fine, but don't forget she's not keeping him. Don't get too invested in the idea. He's going to be someone else's son or nephew." Caro felt sorry for Annabelle. It seemed like a lot to go through in the coming months, and then to give the baby away. But Caro thought her sister was making the right decision. Annabelle was too young for motherhood, and too immature, and she knew it. Caro thought it was brave of Annabelle to admit it, and she didn't disagree. But it wouldn't be easy, whatever she did.

"Poor kid," Charlie said sympathetically, about his sister, not the baby in her womb.

They got busy at work then, and stayed at the office late, to make up for the time they had spent with Giorgio Silvestri, showing him around.

It was ten o'clock that night when they got home, and they were both too tired to eat.

"I hope they invest in us," Caro said, as they climbed the stairs to their bedrooms.

"I never thought I'd hear you say that." Charlie smiled at her.

"The money's great, and the participation would be right for us," she said, and then they both went to their respective bedrooms. Charlie peeked into Benjie's room. He was sound asleep, surrounded by his dogs. All was well in their world. In her room, Annabelle was staring at the photograph they'd given her of her baby. She slipped it into a drawer in her bedside table and wiped a tear off her cheek. She missed her mother more than ever. She had never realized how much she loved her until that moment, and now she had to go through the hardest experience of her life without her. It was a high price to pay for the mistake she'd made, and she hoped that whoever adopted the baby would love him. She was more certain now than ever that she wasn't equal to the task herself. She just wanted it to be over so she could go back to being a kid, but nothing would ever be the same for her again. Whether she wanted to or not, she was going to grow up hard and fast in the next four months. There was no easy way out. Being careless and irresponsible wasn't an option anymore. She was going to be a mother, whether she kept the baby or not.

Chapter 8

Tommy and Devon's visits to their grandparents' house to stay for a week with their father went relatively smoothly, thanks to him, Molly, Frieda, and their Aunt Caro, who loved having them there. Their Uncle Charlie was nice to them too, and they loved Benjie. He was a fun uncle, and the dogs made their stay even better. Both children had nightmares occasionally, and Tommy went in and out of being angry at his father for moving out. Their mother made nasty comments about Lyle constantly, which upset the children. Lyle refrained from doing the same about her, even after Tommy accidentally let slip that Amanda was dating. They had already met two of the men she was seeing. According to Tommy, one of them had a cool car, a red Ferrari, and had taken them for a ride in it. And the other one had his own plane, which they hadn't seen yet. Devon looked at her father, worried about him, and told him both men were ugly. She didn't want his feelings to be hurt. Lyle didn't let on to the kids but he was livid. Their marriage was barely cold in its grave, and Amanda was already dating, and introducing her dates to their kids. He thought of saying something to her about it, but decided not to. She had a right to date if she wanted, and so did he. Dating was the farthest thing from his mind at the moment. He couldn't even imagine it. All he could think about were his children and how they were adjusting, and wanting to finalize the divorce with Amanda. He was in no frame of mind to meet new women. He said something to Caro about it, after Tommy told him.

"She hasn't even finished cashing in on me yet, and she's already looking for a new one." It didn't surprise his sister.

"Do you still love her?" Caro was curious.

"No, I don't," he answered quickly. "I'm not even sure now if I ever did, or, if I did, when I stopped. But it's been pretty miserable between us for the last five years. We haven't had sex in three."

"Was that okay with you?" She was surprised by what he'd said.

"No, but it was just the way things were. I got used to it. I think we gave up on each other around the same time. No big event happened. Our feelings for each other just seemed to evaporate. And the kids kept me busy and happy enough. It's kind of pathetic what you wind up settling for. You don't plan it that way, it just happens. And by the time you realize what you've done, it's been that way for too long. It's not a great way to live, or what I wanted out of marriage. But we never had much in common. It was a duty call right from the beginning, because of Tommy." In Caro's opinion, Amanda had never been grateful for Lyle, or the sacrifice he'd made when he married her because he was a decent guy with a good heart.

Lyle loved the weeks when the children were with him, and he used the alternate weeks to stay late at work and catch up. On the weekends he worked on papers for the estate. He and Gloria had made good progress. The issue of the house sale still hadn't been decided, but five of them were living there now, and Lyle's children on alternate weeks. The house seemed full and alive again, and was useful for the months of transition after their parents' deaths.

Every week, Amanda made some new demand to add to the divorce settlement. Her greed knew no bounds. He was furious when the kids returned for their week with him and Devon asked him who the Addamses were.

"I don't know." He smiled at his daughter after reading her a bedtime story. Dottie was already asleep on her bed, and loved it when Devon was home. "I don't know them."

"Mommy says that's who we are. The Addams family," she said, as a muscle tightened in his jaw. He instantly got the drift.

"There used to be a TV show about them. It was funny. It was about a weird family living together."

"Are we related to them?" Devon asked him.

"No, they're not real. I think Mommy was being funny."

"She thinks it's crazy that we all live together with Aunt Caro and Uncle Charlie, and Aunt Annabelle and Uncle Benjie." The children and Amanda didn't know about Annabelle's baby yet, but Lyle could easily imagine that she'd have a field day with that too. "Do you think you'll ever come home to live with us again?" Devon asked him wistfully, and he answered her as gently as he could.

"No, I don't. Mommy and I both love you, but we don't want to be married and live together anymore. We're very different."

"I know," she said. "Mommy likes to be fancy. You like to be plain." He smiled at the wisdom of children. It summed them up nicely.

"That's right." He didn't add that she liked being fancy with his money, as much of it as she could lay hands on. He easily assumed that the men she was dating had money too, especially if one had his own plane and the other a Ferrari. It was clear what she was after.

"Mommy says we're going to move. She's going to sell the apartment. I like living here with you, Daddy. I wish we could stay longer when we come here." He did too, and constantly worried about what it would do to them, switching homes and parents every week. It didn't seem right to him. They were constantly disrupted and on the move, but it was how custody was handled these days. Some children alternated nights between their parents, which seemed like a nightmare to him, for the children. Alternating weeks was hard enough.

He tucked Devon in then, and went to check on Tommy. He was listening to music with earphones on, as he and Duke lay sprawled out on his bed. Lyle waved and left the room, thinking about what Devon had said about Amanda being fancy and him being "plain." It was a funny way to express it, but she was right. He told Caro about it later.

"You're not all that plain," Caro reassured him. "You just like a quiet life. You always did. Charlie was a lot wilder than you were in college. He partied all the time. But you were a better student."

"Sounds pretty dull to me. I guess I am," Lyle said.

"You're a good husband, and a great father." Caro smiled at him. "Charlie loves the whole fashion scene." It was fertile ground for gay men, and he had been wild for a while in his twenties and settled down at thirty. He'd been very circumspect for the last three years.

"How's the little mother doing?" Lyle asked about their youngest sister.

"All right. She misses Mom a lot. She's struggling trying to get used to the idea of the baby, she wasn't ready for that."

"Dad would have had a fit," Lyle said, and Caro nodded.

"Mom would have been cool about it. I'm trying to guess what Mom would have said to her. Gloria has been really tough on her and calls her a slut every time she talks to her. I didn't think Gloria would be so old-school about it. She was fine about Charlie being gay. But she thinks that Annabelle being pregnant out of wedlock, as she calls it, is a disgrace for all of us."

"I don't," Lyle said simply. "It happened to me."

"Yeah, but you were thirty-one years old, had a good job, and got married immediately, even if no one liked Amanda. Annabelle is ten years younger and just a baby herself. No job, no husband, not even a boyfriend to share the burden with her. She dropped out of school, and now she's going to have a baby. And whatever she does about it, it will be traumatic for her, whether she puts it up for adoption or keeps it."

"What do you think she should do about it?" he asked, and she hesitated before she answered.

"If she were mature enough, I think she should keep it. Women do now, without getting married. It's not the social disgrace it used to be. But I don't think she could handle it, and she doesn't want to. She's never had any responsibility. Mom and Dad babied her and shielded her from everything. If she keeps him, we'll all end up taking care of him for her. And I'm not ready for a baby either. That's years away for me. I want to build our business into a big success first. That's my priority and will be for the next several years. Maybe I'll have a kid when I'm forty, if I meet the right guy. That's seven years away. And I don't meet straight men in our business anyway."

"What about your Italian investor? Charlie says he's hot. Is he straight?"

She laughed at the question. "Yes, he's a widower. He seems nice, but he has a thing for Gloria. He couldn't keep his eyes off her during our meeting, and he kept telling us how brilliant she is."

"What did Gloria think?" Lyle asked.

"She wasn't too impressed. She just wanted to help us close the deal. Gloria keeps her eye on the ball, where business is concerned. That's all she cares about." They both knew it was true about her.

"Maybe your Italian investor would be right for you, if Gloria's not interested," Lyle suggested. Their older sister was always picky about men, and perfectly content alone, and actually preferred it.

"He's not my type." Caro dismissed the suggestion. "Besides, he wants her. He didn't look at me twice, not like that."

Caro and Charlie hadn't heard back from Giorgio yet about his investing in their brand.

Gloria had guessed it would take a few weeks, and Caro and Charlie were getting anxious and wondering if Giorgio's brothers had advised him against it. It was a close-knit family like theirs. And all Caro and Charlie could do was wait.

Lyle was working from home one afternoon, after a meeting about some land in Oklahoma his group wanted to invest in, when he got an email asking him to call the counselor at Tommy's school. They didn't say why, and he called her immediately.

The counselor was in her office and took Lyle's call. She explained that Tommy had been aggressive lately, particularly in the past month. He had gotten in a fight a few days before, and had punched a boy in the face. There had been no injury but the behavior was inappropriate and the counselor was concerned. She wanted to know if there was anything unusual happening at home. He felt sick when she asked.

"My wife and I are separated," Lyle said in a serious tone.

"I'm sorry to hear that. That could explain things. Do you think it's temporary, or do you even know yet?" she asked.

"We're filing for divorce. We have a temporary custody order in place on a trial basis. We're alternating weeks. I'm staying in a family home, with four of my siblings. It's our late parents' home. Tommy and his sister spend a week with me, and then go back to their mother for a week, and then back to me."

"I know that's the current trend, and a week isn't bad, but it can be hard on some kids. Some of them don't mind going back and forth, others don't like it." From what Lyle could see, Devon was more at ease with it than Tommy, maybe because she was younger and more adaptable, and she was closer to her father and would have followed him to the ends of the earth. Tommy's loyalties were more divided between father and mother, and he felt protective of Amanda, with his strong male instincts.

"There's no question, it's a big change for them," Lyle admitted.

"Are they seeing a therapist?" she asked him. He had thought of it but Amanda didn't think it was needed.

"No, they're not."

"I'm going to recommend it for Tommy, given the aggression he's demonstrating. You might want to consider it for your daughter as well." She knew that Tommy had a sister, from his records, at a different school. They were each at a same-sex school.

"I'll have to discuss it with their mother."

"It's just a suggestion, but therapy might make things easier for Tommy. He seems to be struggling right now. And his grades have slipped a little in the last month. Not dramatically, but enough to cause some concern. It's just a yellow light for now, not a flashing red one yet," she reassured him, but Lyle was upset and worried about his son.

He called Amanda to talk about it, and she brushed off the suggestion of counseling.

"He's fine, he doesn't need it," she said blithely.

"Amanda, he punched a boy in the face. That's a danger sign. If he'd broken the boy's nose, his parents would be suing us. He's obviously upset."

"Boys get into fights. That's what they do."

"We're getting a divorce. That's upsetting for all of us, and he's obviously having trouble coping."

"Maybe the other kid was a jerk to him." She didn't want to hear about it, or deal with it, and Lyle realized that he would have to decide himself. After he hung up, he called their pediatrician and got the name of a child psychiatrist she recommended, a man, whom she thought Tommy would like. She told Lyle she was sorry to hear that he and Amanda were getting divorced. He was less and less so as time went on. Amanda was a nightmare to deal with and he realized again how little she engaged with their kids. All she cared about was herself. Lyle called the therapist and made an appointment for Tommy in two weeks. It was the earliest appointment they had. Lyle was planning to take Tommy there himself. He talked to Tommy about it when he came home from school.

"He called me an asshole, Dad." Tommy was incensed. "And he stole my thermos."

"I don't care what he called you," Lyle said calmly, "you don't punch anyone, especially in the face. You could have really hurt him."

"I wanted to," Tommy said. "He's a seventh grader, he's bigger than me, and he's always bugging me."

"Then we need to report him to the school for bullying."

"So why do I have to go to a shrink?"

"Because you punched a kid in the face, even if he's a bully."

"That's not fair."

"Those are the rules," Lyle said. "When you punched him, you became the bully, not the other kid."

"I'm not going to therapy," Tommy said stubbornly.

"I'll go with you," Lyle said gently.

"That's even worse. People will think I'm a head case."

"No, you're a kid who punched another kid, and whose parents are getting divorced. Maybe you'll like talking to the therapist."

"No, I won't. You can't make me go." He looked sullen and belligerent, more than Lyle had seen so far.

"Yes, I can," Lyle said softly, "because it's good for you and the school counselor recommended it."

"I hate you," Tommy said angrily. "Mom isn't making me go to a therapist. Why are you?"

"It's what the school wants you to do. It's not a big deal, Tommy. Don't make it into one." Tommy stormed out of Lyle's room then, ran into his own and slammed the door. He looked sullen that night at dinner and wouldn't talk during the meal. Later, Tommy spoke to Caroline about it when he was alone in the kitchen with her, helping with the dishes.

"That's not so bad," she said. "I go to a therapist."

He looked surprised. "Why?"

"They're good to talk to sometimes. It helps me figure things out, especially when I'm upset about something."

"Why don't you talk to Charlie?" he asked her.

"Because he has his own ideas, and I like talking to an outside objective person. Why don't you try it? Maybe it'll help, or you can tell your dad if you don't want to go back." He thought about it and nodded, and looked calmer when he went back to his room after dinner. Caroline told Lyle about the exchange, and he thanked her.

"Amanda is no help. She doesn't give a damn if they're upset or need therapy. She's too busy shopping and dating." And spending Lyle's money, Caro thought. "Thank you for talking to him." Sometimes she felt like a housemother to all of them. She was beginning to feel like her mother. But it was actually helping all of them to be together under one roof, to help each other however they could.

The next day, Caroline took Annabelle to the obstetrician. Annabelle hadn't liked the one she'd called randomly, recommended by a friend. Caro suggested going to the practice she went to, and Annabelle was open to it. Caro's own OB/GYN wasn't taking new patients, and Annabelle was seeing one of her partners. His name was Ted Kelly, and Caro had never seen him before. Annabelle wasn't sure how she felt about having a male doctor, but he was the only one in the practice taking new patients.

They spent half an hour in the waiting room, while Annabelle filled out forms. She frowned when she read one of the questions on the clipboard, and pointed it out to Caro.

She was signing in as an obstetrical patient and the question was if she used drugs. "How do I answer that?" she asked her sister, who didn't hesitate.

"Honestly. He needs to know, in case the baby has a problem, or a defect."

Annabelle looked pale as she nodded, and wrote in "Previously. Not now." She listed what she had used, and when, as closely as she remembered. She had stopped once she knew she was pregnant, but had smoked marijuana before that, drunk alcohol, and listed cocaine use twice.

When she handed back the forms, a nurse took them to an exam room, and Annabelle undressed and put on a gown.

"Do you want me to go?" Caro asked her, and Annabelle looked panicked at the thought.

"No! What are they going to do?"

"Probably just examine you. Maybe more blood tests, give you vitamins, all that stuff. And he'll have the results of the sonogram." Annabelle nodded and looked scared. And five minutes later, a tall good-looking man with blond hair and blue eyes, wearing a white coat with a stethoscope in his pocket, strode into the room and smiled at them both. He introduced himself, and Caro explained that she was Annabelle's sister and she was there for moral support. He could see that Annabelle was young, and he was relaxed and friendly as he asked her pertinent questions and made notes on a chart.

"You're not using drugs or drinking alcohol now?"

She shook her head and looked embarrassed.

"I stopped when I found out. I didn't know I was pregnant before. My periods are never regular, so I just thought I missed one or two . . . or three." He nodded and seemed casual, but Caro could tell he was paying close attention. "I'm not keeping the baby," Annabelle added in a soft voice. He looked serious then and nodded.

"Have you been to an agency and started the process?" he asked her, and she shook her head. "I can give you some names of attorneys and agencies we've worked with." He didn't seem judgmental to Caro, and kept his attention focused on the patient. After he examined her he said everything seemed fine. He had seen the sonogram, and the baby was healthy, had no visible anomalies, and was the right size for the due date they had given her.

"Is the dad in the picture?" he asked her, and she shook her head.

"No, he's not. He said he'd sign the papers so we could put him up for adoption. We've been broken up since I got pregnant, and he's in Italy now."

"That's got to be hard," Ted Kelly said sympathetically. Caro guessed him to be in his late thirties, or forty at most. He seemed very professional, despite a kind of informal style, which she thought would work well for Annabelle.

"Yeah, it is," she admitted. "I didn't expect this to happen. I stopped taking the pill, but we tried to be careful. We kind of got drunk, and forgot."

"That happens." He smiled at her. "Any other problems or questions, nausea, vomiting, cramps, spotting?" He went down a list and Annabelle said no to all of them. She was young and healthy, and had had no worrisome symptoms that Caro knew of since she'd learned of the pregnancy. "Are you living alone?" he asked her.

"I live with my sister and brothers," she said.

"We just lost our parents in January, and five of us are staying at their house. It's a big house," Caro explained.

"I'm sorry about your parents," he said to both of them. "It must be nice to be together, though."

"It is," Caroline agreed, and Annabelle nodded.

"Depending on the arrangements you make with the adoptive parents, you'll relinquish the baby at the hospital when you leave. You can have whoever you like at the delivery, family member, friend, the adoptive parents if you want, or not. They can wait outside the delivery room if you prefer. You've got time to make all those decisions after you speak to the agency and meet the parents. You're more than halfway through the pregnancy now, so you don't have too long to wait," he said kindly with a warm smile. "And we can talk about the delivery closer to the time, whether you want natural childbirth or an epidural, if you get to the hospital in time for one."

"I want drugs," Annabelle said immediately. He smiled and Caro laughed.

"An epidural shouldn't be a problem. You won't feel anything with that." He checked her forms again and looked at her. "Your bloodwork is all in order and up to date. So, unless you have any other questions, I'll see you in a month." He handed her a card. "My cell phone is on there, if you need to call me directly. And given your circumstances, I'm happy to be at the delivery even on my day off, if you'd like me to be. Or one of my partners can deliver you if I'm not on call. I'm fine with it either way."

"Thank you, Doctor," Caro spoke up. She realized that he had just done Annabelle a huge favor. Most obstetricians only did deliveries if they were on call. If they weren't, the patient got someone else, whom she might never have met. It might make a difference to Annabelle to have a doctor she knew, since she had no partner, and was giving the baby up. Dr. Kelly wrote down the names of three adoption agencies, and two firms of lawyers who handled adoptions, and gave Annabelle the list.

"Our practice works with all of them." Caro wondered if Annabelle's drinking and drug use early in the pregnancy would affect a potential adoption, but she didn't ask him. The lawyers and adoption agencies would tell them. Maybe some couples would be desperate enough not to mind. "See you in a month, Annabelle," he said warmly, and he smiled at Caro. "And see you too, Miss . . ." He didn't know her name and she hadn't introduced herself.

"Caroline Whittier."

"Nice to meet you. I'm sure I'll be seeing you again." He smiled broadly.

"You will." He left the room then, and Annabelle got off the table and dressed and grinned at her sister.

"He's a hunk," she whispered, and Caroline

laughed. "He's really cute," Annabelle added. "You should ask if he's married."

"Stop matchmaking and get dressed. I have to get to work. I'll call the adoption agencies and lawyers later." Annabelle handed her the list.

"Thanks, Caro," she said. She was dressed and looked as young and beautiful as ever. She was a striking girl. She looked like a model, tall and thin with dark hair and green eyes. Caroline's features and height were similar, but she was blond with blue eyes. "He's nice. I like him."

"So do I," Caroline agreed. She liked his style, he was professional but warm and accessible.

"He doesn't make it seem so scary."

"That was a big deal, that he agreed to deliver you even if he's not on call. Most OB/GYNs don't do that. You get who you get depending on what day it is and who's on duty."

"What's an epidural? I didn't want to ask," Annabelle said as they left the exam room.

"It's a shot in your spine that makes everything numb from the waist down."

"Sounds good to me," Annabelle said, and they left the building together. They took separate cabs, and Charlie was waiting impatiently for Caro, with a thousand things he needed her to deal with.

"Where were you?"

"I had to take Annabelle to the doctor, the OB."

"Something wrong?"

"No. Just routine stuff, monthly exam."

He pulled out a stack of fabric samples then, and sketches. "We have to place orders by tomorrow. I need your selections before I order the wire transfers." He was very intense about it and she smiled at him.

"It's okay, Charlie. We'll get it done. I've already made my choices." She pulled a sheet off her desk and handed it to him, and he smiled.

"Okay, sorry. I panic when you're not here."

"You and everybody else." She called the attorneys and adoption agencies that afternoon, and made appointments with one law firm and two adoption agencies, and she stayed at work until eight o'clock, and then rushed home to make sure everyone had eaten. Charlie had already left the office by the time she did. He had a date that night.

When Caro got home, Annabelle was lying on her bed, talking to a friend on her iPhone. She felt more relaxed now that she had seen the doctor. Lyle had cooked dinner for Benjie, who was watching TV in his room. Lyle didn't have the kids that week and Benjie told Caro he had gone to Gloria's after dinner to do some work. She made a salad for herself, and went to her desk in her small study off her bedroom. She felt as though she had a million things to do now, and wondered how her mother had managed it when they were younger. She had always seemed like a miracle worker to Caro, or Wonder Woman, and now she was even more aware of it. She never had five minutes to herself anymore. She was always helping with something, answering questions, feeding someone, solving a problem, checking on Benjie. Her life had changed completely from her simple single life in her stylish SoHo apartment with her twin. And now, here they were, back in their parents' home again, in their childhood rooms. Caroline thought about their mother as she got to work at her desk, wondering how she would manage to do it all. She had Annabelle's pregnancy to deal with now too. She knew they'd get through it somehow, all of them, together. She could almost feel her parents near them, and her mother telling her what to do. She had never admired her more, as she concentrated on the designs she had to correct by the next day, and she felt like a miracle worker now too, or a magician. It was what they all expected of her. She hoped that Giorgio Silvestri would make up his mind about investing in their business soon. They needed the money. And she needed six more hands and ten more hours in the day. She finished the sketches at three A.M., lay down on her bed for a minute, and fell sound asleep, fully dressed with the lights on. She'd been too tired to get undressed.

There just weren't enough hours in the day.

Chapter 9

Caroline took Annabelle to the two adoption agencies first. They handled private adoptions in accordance with the state laws of New York. It seemed very cut-and-dried. They had strict procedures and standards. Neither of the agencies was particularly warm or welcoming, although they admitted that babies like Annabelle's were rare, from well-educated young mothers from good homes. They called infants like that "designer babies," although they said that her drug use early in her pregnancy would disqualify her for many couples. But they were happy to put Annabelle on their lists and promised to get in touch when they had a couple who was interested.

Then, at the end of the day, Caro and Annabelle saw the lawyer Dr. Kelly had recommended. The attorney, Rachel Adams, was in her fifties. She seemed a little tough to Caro, but she was smart, outspoken, and kind to Annabelle. She didn't like the early drug use either, but she said that some people, desperate enough for a baby, would probably overlook it. And Annabelle's circumstances were clean otherwise. The father was willing to relinquish too, which was sometimes a problem. Everyone involved was educated, healthy, no one was in prison, there were no dark circumstances in Annabelle's history. Adams explained that her firm worked with an agency in L.A. and did many celebrity adoptions. In each case, the circumstances were different, and the adoptive parents imposed their own conditions. She said that in most cases, they would want no further contact with the birth mother after the adoption, although some would be willing to send her a photograph once a year. Others would be more inclusive. But most parents wouldn't want her showing up at birthday parties and holidays. She asked Annabelle if that would be a problem, and Annabelle answered immediately. "Not at all. I don't want any further contact either. I want to give the baby up. I can't take care of him, and I don't want the responsibility. I'm not ready to be a mother. I'm twenty-one. I need to have my own life before I settle down. And I don't want to have a baby without a father."

"You're the birth mother everyone wants." Rachel Adams smiled at her. "No hassles, no ties, no father. Other than two hits of coke, some tequila and wine, you're everyone's dream, as long as you stay straight now. No drugs or alcohol," she said with a severe look, and Annabelle nodded. "They'll want you randomly drug-tested regularly to prove that you're clean. Fail one test, and you're history, so you have to take it seriously."

"I will," Annabelle promised. It also wasn't lost on the attorney that Annabelle was a beautiful girl and would present well to prospective parents if her child would look anything like her one day. She was gorgeous, and her sister was too. Rachel Adams gave Annabelle and Caro a mountain of forms to fill out, which they did in her office, and the lawyer was satisfied with the result. At the end, she said that she currently had two couples who might be interested in meeting her. She would have to discuss her case with them, and see how they felt about the cocaine and tequila. One couple was fairly racy, in the film industry in L.A., and she had the feeling they would overlook it. She wasn't as sure about the couple in New York, who were both lawyers themselves. She promised to be in touch soon, and Caro and Annabelle left her office. Annabelle went home, drained by the meetings all afternoon, and Caro went back to her office and walked in at six o'clock. She'd had five messages from Charlie and hadn't read them yet.

"Where the hell have you been?" he snapped at her.

"At adoption agencies and attorneys with Annabelle," she said, looking exhausted as she took off her coat and threw it on a chair. "Why? Is the building on fire?"

"Did you see my texts?"

"I didn't have time to read them. I thought I'd just see what was up when I got here. I thought Annabelle's adoption was a little more important, and I don't see you taking her to see doctors and attorneys," she said in a strained voice. It was emotionally draining dealing with the crisis their sister was in.

"I can't take her to the doctor." He calmed down immediately. "I'm sorry, Caro. You've been terrific with her."

"I'm trying to pretend I'm Mom. I don't know how she did it all, especially when I think of all the headaches I gave her in high school. I feel guilty as hell about it now. I argued with her every day for four years."

"Me too." Then he smiled broadly at her. "Giorgio Silvestri is going to invest with us. It's a personal investment, but his brothers are interested too. They might want to get in on it if we need more money later. They're all very excited about us. Giorgio is arriving in three days to sign the papers. His attorneys are going to email us the contracts tonight so we can have them looked at and make changes if we need to. We're in, Caro. We're going to have the money we need, and we're preserving three-quarters ownership. It's a miracle." She was smiling too.

"Holy shit, you did it!" she said, threw her arms around his neck and kissed him.

"*We* did it! I know it's not what you wanted, but the terms are terrific." She knew it was true and had made her peace with it. She was willing to have an investor now. And Giorgio seemed like the perfect one for them and his terms were fair. Charlie danced her around the room, and as he did, Gloria called her, and Caro took the call. Gloria sounded panicked.

"What's wrong?" Caro asked her, waiting for the next crisis to land on her.

"Giorgio Silvestri is flying in from Milan in three days, and he invited me to dinner. He says he's investing in CCW, and he wants to thank me. I don't know what to wear. Will you style me, Caro?"

"That's why you called me?" Gloria had sounded like the building was burning.

"Yes, everything I own makes me look like a librarian or a prison guard. I don't own anything I can wear to dinner with someone as fashionable as he is."

"You've met with him before," Caro reminded her.

"For meetings in my office, and lunch once. This is dinner. Will you do it?"

"Of course. Will you wear makeup? I'm not going to lend you anything unless you wear makeup and brush your hair." Gloria usually wore her hair in a ponytail or a knot at the base of her neck, and looked like she had combed it with a fork. She was brilliant in business but paid no attention to how she looked. And suddenly she wanted to look chic and beautiful. "Does this mean you're interested in him?" Caro was curious.

"I don't know. I just don't want to embarrass myself and look awful. You always look chic whatever you wear. So did Mom. I didn't get that gene. I look more like Dad every day."

"He looked pretty good too," Caro reminded her.

"That's because Mom dressed him and bought all his clothes." That was true, but he was a handsome, distinguished-looking man, and Gloria looked very aristocratic. She just needed to add a feminine touch to it.

"I promise we'll get you looking so hot, he'll propose to you by dessert," Caroline told her.

"It's probably not even a date, just a thank-you dinner for introducing you to him."

"It's a date," Caro assured her. "He's not taking us to dinner. Come in tomorrow, and we'll pick something for you to wear, and I'll come to dress you before you have dinner with him."

"You're a saint," Gloria said, and hung up, sounding flustered and grateful. Caro told Charlie and he looked amused.

"Now you really are officially a magician, if you

can dress Gloria for a date and get her to wear makeup."

The contracts came in that night, and the twins looked them over together and sent them to their lawyer, who called them the next day. He suggested a few changes, but essentially they were fine.

"It's one of the best deals of its kind I've seen," he told them. "He's giving you full autonomy to run the business the way you want and already do, as long as your numbers hold up. If your sales drop markedly, he'll step in with a support team."

"Our numbers won't drop," Charlie told him, and reported his comments to Caro.

They emailed the pages back to Giorgio, indicating the minor changes their lawyer had suggested. And Gloria came in after work to pick something to wear.

Caro had already pulled several options from their current collection for her sister's dinner with Giorgio. One was too sexy, another too severe and made her look like a dominatrix. They agreed on a sleek, very chic, simple white wool dress with a high neckline, long sleeves, and a flattering silhouette. It was very stylish, and Gloria had a good figure from her daily rigors at the gym. The moment she put it on, it looked like it had been made for her. Caro had kept one of the sewers in case they needed alterations, but they didn't. She had shoes in Gloria's size to try on. They picked a simple pair of black suede high-heel pumps that looked perfect with the dress.

"I can't wear those, I'll kill myself," Gloria complained about the high heels.

"Yes, you can. Practice. You just have to get from the cab to the table and back again. Pretend you're a runway model." She took a pair of simple diamond studs off her own ears and put them on her sister's.

"I don't wear earrings." Gloria looked skeptical. She wasn't used to being fussed over.

"Now you do. The guy works in fashion. He looks like a movie star. He's sane, available, single, and straight. You can damn well wear a crown of thorns if you have to. No whining." They put the whole outfit together, and Caro did Gloria's hair in a simple French twist and then paraded her past Charlie, who was on the phone with the lawyer again. Giorgio's lawyers had made a few minor changes to what they'd sent, but nothing that altered the deal significantly. He gave an enthusiastic thumbs-up when he saw his older sister, and she beamed at him.

"Fantastic!" he whispered, covering the mouthpiece of the phone. He ended the call a minute later. "He's going to kidnap you and take you to Italy when he sees you," Charlie said, and Caro looked delighted with the end result of Gloria's makeover.

"I'll come over and dress you and do your makeup and hair before the dinner," she promised.

"I look weird in makeup," Gloria said, worried again.

"You look weirder without it. Your days as a librarian are over. From now on, you have to look glamorous when he's here. You want a second date, don't you?" Gloria nodded and felt like a teenager going on her first date to the prom.

"This is stressful," she said, sitting down at Caro's desk. "I need a drink." Caroline poured her a glass of wine, and the three of them sat talking about the deal they were making. Gloria came alive when they did. As long as she was involved in finance and business, she felt supremely competent and sure of herself. As a woman, she felt like a novice and a bumbling idiot. She always failed first dates.

"Just pretend you're making a deal with him. The way you look will do the rest. Once you're dressed, forget about it. The clothes are just there to enhance you. You're not showing off the clothes." Gloria liked the way Caro expressed it, and looked more confident when she stood up. She almost tripped in the shoes, and then caught her balance, and looked sexy and elegant as she walked around Caro's office. The dress rehearsal was a success. She felt like a different person with her new look.

*   *   *

Giorgio Silvestri arrived two days later on schedule, and all the changes had been made to the final contract by then. Everything was set for the signing the next day. He stopped by Caro and Charlie's offices as soon as he came in from the airport, just to say hello. He gave them both a hug, and was to be there the next morning at nine o'clock with their respective attorneys for the signing. He had an attorney with him that he used in New York.

He was taking Gloria to dinner that night, and left to dress for dinner and pick her up.

As soon as he left their offices, Caro ran out the door with the dress and shoes in a garment bag, a stylist's kit of safety pins and thread, and all the little tricks of the trade they used on the runway, like glue and double-sided tape. She took a cab to Gloria's apartment and went to work. She had brought her own makeup, and Gloria still had her earrings. In exactly an hour, Caro had her looking like a model, and Gloria was really beautiful. She was nervous but it didn't show. Caro hugged her and left before Giorgio came to pick her up.

He arrived with a car and driver, and Gloria went downstairs when the doorman called her. Giorgio had made a reservation at La Grenouille, on the East Side, and the headwaiter recognized him immediately and took them to their table. Gloria looked calm and elegant, as Giorgio followed her to their table.

The evening rolled out like a red carpet, and he

told her he loved her dress as they sipped champagne and studied the menu. He told her how excited he was about the investment he was making in CCW. He and his brothers were sure that their collaboration would be a huge success.

"And it's all thanks to you for introducing me to your brother and sister. We're almost related now." He smiled at her. He looked happy and relaxed despite the flight from Italy and the time difference. He said he had slept on the plane, to be ready for their evening together. "I was excited about seeing you, Gloria," he said over the champagne. "I feel like a boy again." But he looked like a very handsome, sophisticated man, and he made her feel like a stylish, fashionable woman, in her borrowed dress from Caro and Charlie's collection. "I hope we will see more of each other now, with this connection. I'm going to spend a week or two in New York every month, to be sure it goes smoothly. We're going to make an announcement to the press next week. It's interesting too that I have five brothers, so there are six of us, and there are six Whittiers. It is the joining of two great families, even though I'm the only one investing, with only two of the Whittiers. I would like to meet the other Whittiers soon," he said after they ordered. "And all my brothers want to come to the next show, just to see it."

"We are a bit of a motley crew," she said, smiling. "We're all very different."

"My brothers and I are too. And our wives even more so. My wife was a textile designer I met at our factory when she was very young."

"Do you have children?" She hadn't thought to ask him before, in all the time she'd known him. Their dealings had never been personal before his wife died. Now, suddenly, they were. He had been widowed for just over a year.

"No, unfortunately not. No children, but I have fourteen nephews and nieces, and more coming soon. Do you have children?" He hadn't asked her either. They had only spoken about business before.

"No. I've never been married, although these days that doesn't seem to be a prerequisite for children."

"I'm shocked that you've never been married. How did that happen?" He smiled as he asked her.

"Too much work, which I love. And the wrong men. And I think it's best to be married to have children."

He nodded. "I agree with you, although two of my nephews and one niece have children and aren't married, and they're very happy. I'm old-fashioned that way too." He smiled.

She didn't tell him about Annabelle. If she was giving the baby up for adoption, it seemed best to keep it secret, and no one would ever know. "My oldest brother has two children. They live with him and the others half of the time right now, in my parents' home. All five of my brothers and sisters are living there, in the home where we grew up. I'm the only one who isn't. My parents died in January, and we're trying to decide whether or not to sell their house."

"Big families are wonderful," he said, "although very noisy at times, and sometimes rather stressful. My brothers and I have many arguments, but we love each other. Italians can be very crazy, and emotional." He laughed when he said it.

"I think all big families can be a little crazy. We are sometimes too," she admitted.

They chatted as they ate the delicious food, and the evening went by too quickly. He looked wide-awake and energized at the end of the meal. He said he wasn't tired at all, despite the time difference. They'd talked about Italy, growing up, their families, their work lives. He was fascinated by her and loved her looks, and she was surprised by how at ease she felt with him. She couldn't remember the last time she had been on a date, and it had never been like this. They hated to leave the restaurant, and he was sorry to take her home and leave her.

"Would you have time to have dinner with me again on Saturday, Gloria?" He couldn't wait to see her again. He had never realized how interesting she was, and she looked beautiful. And he liked how strong she was. And how well educated. "I'd love it," she said, as he kissed her on the cheek and

walked her into the building. He was a perfect gentleman, and she loved his European manners and
Italian charm. She wanted to introduce him to her
family, but she wanted to get to know him better
first. The Whittiers were a lot to deal with when
one first met them, although he said he had a big
noisy family of his own. But she liked having him to
herself too.

She went upstairs to her apartment with a smile
on her face. She sent Caro a text, and assumed she
was asleep.

"Perfect evening. Need to book expert stylist
again for Saturday night. Love, G."

The response from Caro was immediate, she
was still working. "Double rate on holidays and
weekends. We need to go shopping for your dating
wardrobe."

"You're hired at any rate," Gloria answered, and
carefully took off the beautiful white dress and
stepped out of the heels, to return them to Caro.
The evening had been magical, and so was he.

And as Giorgio walked into the Four Seasons,
where he was staying in one of the suites, he was
smiling too. The signing went smoothly the next
day, and Giorgio, Caro, and Charlie had lunch uptown at Majorelle to celebrate. At the end of the
meal, Giorgio mentioned Gloria to Charlie, and
how grateful he was to her for introducing them.
His eyes lit up when he spoke of her, which Charlie
told Caro after lunch.

"I think he really likes Glo. How did it go last night? Did she say?"

"It sounds like a ten-alarm fire. We're going shopping for a new wardrobe on Saturday." Caro smiled and he laughed.

"Good for Glo. She deserves a good guy, and this one was worth waiting for."

"I have a feeling she thinks so too. She sounds giddy in her texts, or drunk." He was happy to hear it. And they were thrilled with their deal, thanks to her.

They got home late from the office, and when they got to the house, Benjie was waiting for them, sitting on the staircase in the main hall, with both dogs. He looked very serious, and Charlie was concerned.

"Is something wrong?"

"I have to talk to you."

"What about?" Caro waited to hear it too.

"I heard Annabelle talking today, on the phone. And I heard her and Caro talking yesterday. Annabelle is going to give her baby up for adoption. I don't think he should leave the family. It's our nephew, yours too. He's going to need a mom and dad. I want to adopt her baby. Will you tell her for me? Then I can be its dad, and she can still be its mom." To Benjie, it was a simple process, like his adopting Duke and Dottie. He looked very serious as he said it, and it brought tears to Caro's eyes. She sat down next to him on the steps.

"Being a mom and dad to a baby is a big responsibility. And Annabelle doesn't feel ready to be a mom," she explained to him.

"Can't she get ready now? The baby's not here yet. She has time to learn how to do it."

"Some people don't feel ready till they're older, or never feel ready to have children, like Gloria."

"I'm ready to be a dad. I could be a dad, and she could be a mom later when she's ready. But we can't give her baby away to strangers. They might be bad to him. I want to adopt him." They could see that he meant it, and it made Caro feel guilty that she didn't feel ready to do the same, but it was so much to take on, and she had the business to run. She couldn't imagine being married or having a child herself for at least the next five years. And she hadn't met the right person. Neither had Annabelle. "Can I adopt him?" Benjie's eyes pleaded with them. "I don't want her to give him away. He belongs to all of us."

"Actually, Benjie, he's Annabelle's," Charlie said to him. "Like Tommy and Devon are Lyle's. It's up to him what he does with them. And Annabelle's baby is up to her. We can't decide for her."

"I want to be his dad. Will you tell her?"

"I promise," Caro said seriously, as Charlie wiped a tear from his brother's cheek. "But we have to respect what she wants to do."

"Why?" It was a lot for Benjie to take in and process. He had been thinking about it all night and day. He tended to obsess about things sometimes if they were important to him.

"Because she's the mom."

"You're like our mom now," Benjie said to her, changing the subject. "You do a good job, like Mom. She would be proud of you," he said, and Caro put her arms around him and hugged him. He was such a sweet boy, and such a good person.

"Mom would be proud of you too."

"She wouldn't be happy about Duke and Dottie. She wouldn't let me have them here," he said seriously, and Caro smiled.

"I'm sure she's okay with it now." He nodded, and they walked up the stairs together. Duke and Dottie were waiting for him at the top of the stairs, as though they knew the conversation had been too serious for them to join in.

"You'll tell Annabelle about the baby, right? You'll ask her?" he said, before he ran off to his room with the dogs.

"I promise," she said solemnly, and turned to look at Charlie, who had followed them up the stairs.

"He makes me feel like a shit," Charlie said when Benjie's door was closed. "Do you suppose we should take the baby? He has a point."

"She really doesn't want it," she said gently. "And it wouldn't be fair. We're not going to have a spare minute for the next five years, if we make the company grow the way we want to."

"Why does it have to be either/or? Other people have kids."

"Yes, but we don't. Our business is crazy. The fashion industry is. I can't see myself with a baby for years. Can you?"

"Maybe," he said, and she was surprised. "If I met the right person," which he hadn't either. None of them had, and Lyle's marriage had been a mistake from start to finish.

"We don't have time to meet anyone the way we work," she reminded him.

"Gloria just did."

"But not at our age. She's six years older than we are. And she doesn't want children, ever. She never did. She wants work."

"Maybe Giorgio will change that," he said optimistically.

"Even if he does, she'd be forty when she had a baby."

"So? Other people do it. I just think we need to stay open to the possibilities. There's more to life than just work. You should go on a date once in a while too."

"Are you kidding?" She laughed at him. "With who? When? At midnight after I put Benjie to bed? There's no time. Mom was a magician, but she wasn't dating. I don't know how she did it all. And she had Dad to help her."

"She wanted to do it all, and she loved it," he reminded her.

"I guess that's the secret. But I'm happy like this. You, the business, the house, the others, Lyle's kids here every other week. That's enough for me."

"What about Annabelle's baby?" he asked her again, and she hesitated.

"I don't know. I think that should be up to her." He nodded, and they each went to their rooms. There was much to think about with a baby coming. It didn't seem real yet, to any of them, least of all to Annabelle. But it did to Benjie. His offer to adopt the baby had touched their hearts. He was so full of love, and had so many special gifts of his own.

Chapter 10

Gloria's second dinner with Giorgio went even better than the first. He took her to a small Italian restaurant he knew, where the food was superb. They stayed until closing time, and she invited him upstairs for a drink when he took her home. He kissed her, and it was gentle and sensual and searing, but he didn't try to go any further, which made it all the more enticing. He was a gentleman until he left. She was dreamy-eyed afterwards, thinking about him. She felt like a teenager, and he said he did too. He said he had been thinking about her for months, and this was the culmination of a dream for him. He thought she was a very special woman. She felt like one when she was with him and admired him too. She felt very lucky to know him.

*   *   *

The fashion press went wild over the announcement of their deal, and Caro and Charlie were called for interviews as soon as the news broke of Giorgio Silvestri of Silvestri Textiles investing in their business. It gave them greater stability and credibility than they'd had before. Every fashion and business publication wanted to interview them. Charlie was impressed when the editor of *The New York Times* business section wanted to do a story on them, and *The Wall Street Journal* was also in hot pursuit. Charlie couldn't resist saying yes to the *Times*. They assigned a writer he'd heard of and never met, whose credentials were excellent. Brady Walker, the journalist, was a Stanford graduate, and had a master's degree from the Columbia School of Journalism, the same university Lyle had attended for his MBA.

Walker arrived for the interview with a photographer, who took a quick shot of Charlie and Caro, and then Caro and the photographer left them. Brady Walker settled down in Charlie's office for the solo interview. Charlie was surprised by how young he was. They were about the same age. Brady was wearing jeans, and a crisp blue shirt open at the neck. Charlie was wearing almost the same thing, with a blazer. Charlie laughed as he looked at him.

"We look like twins," he commented, and Brady laughed too.

"I hadn't noticed. What's it like being a twin?"

Brady asked, curious. He was friendly and open and personable. His questions weren't tricky or snide or jealous.

He was a straightforward, serious interviewer. Charlie told him about what it was like growing up with Caro, and how close they had been and still were. How much he loved working with her and how talented she was.

"You're lucky," Brady said almost enviously. "I'm an only child, so I've never had that sibling relationship, which sounds like a best friend, only better. It also means I'm a spoiled brat and can't share." He laughed at himself and Charlie laughed with him. The interview was more like a conversation between two people who enjoyed talking to each other and were compatible. Brady brought out the best in him, and Charlie could sense it was going to be a great interview.

When it was over, and Brady put his recorder in his briefcase, and put his notepad away, he lingered for a few minutes, and didn't seem to want to leave. He appeared to want to say something more. "I don't usually do this. In fact, I never have. I don't hit on my subjects," he said, looking embarrassed, "that's frowned on, and unprofessional. But do you want to have lunch sometime? I loved talking to you. I really enjoyed it. It's going to be a fantastic piece."

"I really enjoyed it too, and I'd love to do lunch,"

Charlie said. Brady wasn't obvious, but Charlie could sense that he was gay.

"I'll call you," Brady promised, and they exchanged a warm look of mutual appreciation before he left.

He called Charlie the next day. "Is this too soon? Do I seem ridiculous?" Brady asked, and Charlie laughed. "I told you, I've never done this before with a subject. It's really not my style."

"No, it's not ridiculous, and I was hoping you'd call. I would have, if you took too long. Yesterday was too good to let slip away."

"Yeah, it was," Brady said. They made a date to meet the next day at a deli they both knew. The article was due out on Sunday.

Caro happened to see Charlie the next day when he was leaving for lunch, which he hardly ever did. He usually ate at his desk, if he ate at all. He didn't eat much and was fashionably thin.

"You're going out for lunch?" she asked him.

"I . . . yeah . . . uh . . . the guy who did the *Times* interview wants to do some fact-checking. I told him I'd meet him for lunch."

"He couldn't do it over the phone?" She looked surprised.

"We . . . I thought I'd take him to lunch. He was a nice guy." And then suddenly she got it. She was too close to Charlie not to, and she knew him too well. He had never been able to keep a secret from her.

"Oh my God. Why didn't you just say it? I missed that completely. He was a hottie," she teased him, "and so are you."

"He's smart too. Stanford and Columbia."

"Don't be such a snob. He seemed nice. And good for you. It must be contagious after Gloria. Now it's you and this guy. What's his name again?"

"Brady. Watch out, you're next," he teased her back. He was glad she had guessed. He didn't like having secrets from her.

"I am not next! I have a full-time job as house-mother. Romance is not in the cards for me."

"It would be, if you want it to," he said.

"Well, I don't. I have to get Annabelle through her pregnancy, and Lyle through his divorce. And help him with his kids . . . and Benjie . . . and dress Gloria for her next date. I like my role as the spinster sister. I can babysit for your children." Charlie rolled his eyes and left a minute later. He took an Uber to the deli, where Brady was waiting for him in a Stanford sweatshirt, jeans, and running shoes. He looked handsome and young, and Charlie looked equally so in an almost identical outfit yet again.

"We keep dressing the same," Brady noticed.

"That's telepathic," Charlie told him. "Caro and I used to do that. It's actually a phenomenon."

"I really like you," Brady said simply. "You're just a tiny bit crazy, just enough to be fun and interesting, like a dash of salt and pepper." Charlie thought about it and decided he liked the comparison.

They talked nonstop, exchanging information all through lunch, and then Charlie had to get back to the office. Brady's time was his own, except for deadlines. He worked from home.

"See you again?" Charlie asked before they left each other on the sidewalk outside the deli.

"I hope so," Brady said with a look of longing. "This is too good to stop now." Charlie nodded in answer. "Where do you live?" He hadn't asked him, and Charlie laughed.

"With almost my entire family. Four of my brothers and sisters, in my late parents' house. We just moved back in, in January. It's actually working out pretty well."

"It sounds great, but I won't be dropping by," Brady said, slightly intimidated. "I live in the West Village. Do you want to come to dinner sometime?"

"I'd love it." Charlie's eyes danced at the prospect.

"This is fun," Brady said. "It's like teenage romance, except we don't have to hide being gay. You're out, right?"

"Very recently," Charlie said, "after my parents died in January. It was a secret before that."

"Wow. I told my parents when I was sixteen. They were fine with it," Brady said.

"I told my mom at eighteen. My dad would have

killed me, or had a heart attack. My mom was the only one who knew, and my twin, for fifteen years."

"And how is it now?"

"A nonevent. It's fine. It's not an issue."

"That's good. It always shocks me how many people still have parents like that. It must be really hard."

"It was. My father had major denial. My mother always said it would kill him or break his heart if I told him."

"I'll cook dinner for you at my place," Brady offered.

"Sounds perfect." Charlie smiled at him. They hugged, then Charlie grabbed a cab back to the office, and Brady disappeared into the subway. It had been a nice interlude, and Charlie couldn't wait to read the article when it came out late Saturday night in the Sunday early edition. He was having dinner at Brady's apartment that night.

"How was lunch?" Caro asked him when he got back to the office.

"Nice," he said, glowing and trying not to show it. "He's cooking dinner for me on Saturday night at his place."

"Not at ours?" she teased him. "He could cook for an army."

"I'm not ready to bring him home yet. I want to get to know him first. So far, I really like him."

"Good. Enjoy it. You deserve some time off."

"So do you," he said to her.

"That's not my reality at the moment," she said, and rushed back to her office for a meeting, with no time to chat more.

Lyle's kids arrived on Friday for their week with their father, a few days early since their mother was going to Palm Beach for the weekend with the man who had the plane. Tommy gave his father bulletins, although he didn't want them, and Lyle had gotten a notice from his son's science teacher saying that Tommy had flunked a quiz and his science grade was slipping. Lyle was taking him to the shrink on the weeks he had him, but it didn't seem to be changing anything. Tommy had had another incident at school. He had tripped one of his classmates on purpose and the boy had bumped his head. They had given him a day of suspension for it, during the week he was with Amanda.

"What's happening?" Lyle asked him over dinner. Everyone else was out, and Caroline wasn't home yet, so they could talk freely.

"Nothing's happening," Tommy said, staring into his plate. He was beginning to smolder. He did that a lot now. The psychiatrist said he was angry about the divorce, and at Lyle for leaving. Tommy thought Lyle should have stayed. He felt that Lyle had abandoned them and their mother, and Amanda fed that impression by playing victim to the kids.

"You can't go around hurting other kids," his father said. "You'll get kicked out of school, and it's not a nice thing to do."

"I just tripped him. Big deal." Tommy tried to dismiss it.

"It is a big deal, and he hit his head," Lyle completed the picture. He was really upset about it. Tommy didn't appear to be, and he had always been a sweet, docile boy. "He could have gotten seriously injured."

"He called me a name," Tommy tried to justify it.

"That doesn't make it all right."

"Emerald Berman called me a sissy, and I didn't trip her," Devon said primly, which didn't help, and Tommy stormed away from the table, went up to his room, and slammed the door. "He does that at Mommy's too," she said to console her father. "He called Mommy a name this week. He said she was a bitch to you, so you left. She sent him to his room without dinner. But he ate ice cream when she went to bed." Lyle knew it wasn't good to let her tell tales, but it was a relief to know that Tommy was angry at his mother too, and acting out there as well. So he wasn't just angry at his father. He blamed them both for the divorce. They heard the front door open then, and it didn't close, and after ten minutes or so, Lyle went to check what Tommy was doing. He was sitting on the front step of the

house, with the door open behind him, looking
glum.

"Do you want to come finish your dinner, and
behave?" Tommy didn't answer, but he followed his
father back to the kitchen. When he got there, Lyle
asked him if he closed the door.

"I think I forgot," he answered finally.

"Then go close it, and come back." Tommy did
as he was told, and didn't talk to his father or his
sister, but he finished his dinner and put the plate
in the sink. Then he went back upstairs to his room,
calmly this time, and he didn't slam the door.

Lyle had just finished cleaning up the kitchen
when Caro came home, looking tired, with a briefcase jammed full of sketches to complete. Charlie
arrived a minute later, and the three of them were
talking when Benjie arrived from the shelter after a
late shift, went to his room, and came back downstairs seconds later, with a look of panic.

"Duke and Dottie are gone!" he exploded into
the group.

"They're probably asleep on someone's bed,"
Charlie told him. "Check the bedrooms. They have
to be there." He took the stairs two at a time, and
was back minutes later.

"They're gone," Benjie said, and Charlie went
upstairs with him to look, but the dogs were nowhere. They opened the doors to Tommy's and
Devon's rooms too, and they weren't there either.

They were nowhere to be found. Charlie looked mildly concerned.

"A dog the size of Duke can't just disappear," he said to Benjie. Dottie liked hiding under beds, so they checked those too. Everyone spread out to look for them, and came back a few minutes later. The dogs had in fact vanished. Annabelle came home from seeing a friend to find them all in the front hall, trying to decide where to look next, and Benjie burst into tears when he saw her.

"My dogs are lost!" he wailed.

"They can't be lost. They have to be here some-where," she said, and joined the others searching for them.

"Someone stole them." Benjie couldn't stop cry-ing by then, and suddenly, Lyle remembered the incident with Tommy at the front door. He had for-gotten to close it, and Lyle had sent him back to do it. He wondered if the dogs could have escaped during those few minutes. He bounded up the stairs to ask Tommy, who had his headphones on, listen-ing to music. He took them off when his father walked in.

"Have you seen the dogs?" Lyle asked him hur-riedly.

"No. Why?"

"They're gone, and Benjie is upset. Did you see them go out when you were sitting on the front step?" Tommy shook his head. It was the only time that Lyle could think of when they might have escaped. He went back downstairs and reported to the search party that the front door had been left open for a few minutes, and the dogs might have gotten out then. Hearing it, Benjie only cried harder.

"They're going to get killed. We see it at the shelter all the time, dogs that get run over. They'll be hit by a car and Dottie is so little, she'll die." He was sobbing, and Caro was trying to calm him down.

"Benjie, Duke is a big dog, people will see him and avoid him. We're all going to go out and look for him."

"They won't see Dottie," he sobbed. He loved his dogs, they were his best friends, his babies, and he was so responsible with them.

"Do you want to wait here or come with us?" Caro asked him.

"Come with you," he answered with a hiccup. Caro looked at the group, and they all left together and went in separate directions down the nearby streets. Charlie and Lyle headed toward the park, with Caro and Benjie a short distance behind them, to turn left on Madison Avenue. "Duke likes the park," Benjie told them, but they were all aware that crossing Fifth Avenue to get there, with heavy traffic, would have been dangerous for both dogs. Caro was just praying that they didn't come upon one or both severely injured or dead in the street. There had been no sign of them anywhere yet. All four of them eventually walked into the park at a brisk clip and looked around, but didn't see them. Lyle climbed up on a little hill and pushed apart the bushes, and then ran down the other side. Charlie searched behind some trees, and Benjie walked to the places where he walked them, with Caro following. All of a sudden Lyle gave a shout, and then she heard him whistle, and Duke came bounding down a path, his tail wagging and long legs flying, with a tiny ball of white fluff trotting behind him as fast as her short legs could carry her. She had leaves tangled in her long hair. Duke stood up with his paws on Lyle's shoulders to lick his face, and then he spotted Benjie and ran to him. Benjie had stopped crying and was laughing, and ran to hug the dog. He knelt down and put his arms around Duke, who pushed him over and kissed his face, while Dottie barked frantically. Both dogs were unharmed, and Benjie lay on the ground with Duke standing over him, and his siblings looked at each other in relief. All of them had been afraid of the tragedy they might encounter and Benjie would see. He had been beside himself with worry and grief. "Thank God," Lyle said softly, and Charlie nodded and smiled at his twin.

Caroline called Annabelle on her cell and told her to go back to the house and watch the kids, they had found the dogs and they'd be home in a few minutes.

On the way back, Lyle explained that Tommy had briefly left the front door open and they must have gotten out then. He promised to be more careful in future, and Tommy was waiting in the front hall with Annabelle and Devon when they got back. Tommy looked immensely relieved, and apologized to Benjie, who hugged him and forgave him immediately. They all went to the kitchen, and Benjie gave the dogs treats to welcome them home. Both dogs looked very happy with all the attention after their adventure.

"I thought they'd get hit by a car," Benjie said, still shaken by their disappearance and what could have happened. They had all been afraid of finding one or both dogs dead on the street. He took them up to his room then, and the others all had a glass of wine to calm their nerves and relax. Benjie didn't drink alcohol, he didn't like the taste or the effect, except for a rare sip of champagne to celebrate something.

Caro checked on Benjie later, and he was asleep on his bed, with his arms around Duke's neck, and Dottie snoring softly beside him. Caro stood in the doorway, watching them, and Charlie came up behind her and saw them too.

"All's well that ends well," he whispered, and she softly closed the door, grateful that nothing terrible had happened.

*   *   *

Charlie had dinner at Brady Walker's apartment in the West Village on Saturday.

He had a terrace that overlooked the Hudson River, and was an excellent cook. He prepared a delicate Indian meal, and they talked for hours about their work and their families, and what it had been like knowing that they were gay and fitting into their world. They had both grown up in New York and had friends in common, but had never met. They read the interview together in the early edition of the Sunday paper, and Charlie loved it. It was fun and respectful, and relevant, and even flattering, and all of the quotes were accurate.

"I wanted you to love it," Brady confessed.

"I do," Charlie said, smiling at him. They went for a walk afterwards along the river, and kissed in the moonlight. They sat on a bench and talked, and then Charlie went home. He didn't want to get in too deep too soon. He wanted to give their feelings for each other time to grow. He didn't want to jump in right away, and have it be fast and furious and burn itself out. And Brady liked what they were doing. They were courting each other, and learning about each other. They didn't want hot fast sex and then it would be over and be meaningless. They wanted to take their time and wait.

Caro was surprised when he came home that night and asked him about it. "We're taking it slow," he said, and looked happy.

"I want to get to know him," she said with a gentle smile.

"You will," he promised. "I want to get to know him too."

Giorgio and Gloria were trying to take it slow too, but were less successful at it. Their mounting passion was almost uncontrollable by their third dinner together. And after the fourth one, they wound up in bed almost as soon as he walked through the door of her apartment for a drink afterwards. It was what they both wanted. The flame that had ignited between them burned so brightly that they couldn't get enough of each other.

They made love until the sun came up, and then lay in each other's arms, totally spent and sated, and drifted off to sleep, knowing that their world would never be the same again. They had come home. Gloria had never been in love like that before in her entire life.

Chapter 11

Caro went with Annabelle to her next visit with Dr. Kelly. She was six months pregnant and couldn't hide it anymore. The two adoption agencies hadn't called her, but Rachel Adams had called a few times. She had some prospects but nothing definite yet. Annabelle's partying early in the pregnancy had put some people off, but there was still time to meet the right couple and arrange an adoption before the baby was born.

Dr. Kelly questioned her about her decision, and she was still definite about not wanting to keep the baby. She was bored at home, and seldom went out. Since she couldn't drink, it wasn't fun to meet in bars while her friends did. She was home almost every night. And she didn't want everyone to know about the pregnancy since she wasn't keeping the baby.

There were no problems with the pregnancy, and another sonogram showed that the fetus was growing nicely. It was a good size. She only had three months left, but it felt like an eternity to her, with nothing to do except sit around the house.

Ted Kelly spoke to Caro in the hall while Annabelle was getting dressed. "Something tells me you have your hands full at home," he said, and she laughed.

"That's a pretty accurate description, more than you know. Seven of us are sharing my parents' house. Two children, five adults, and two dogs. It's never boring," she said with a smile, as Annabelle joined them.

"Are you in fashion?" he asked, curious about her, and she nodded. "I thought so." She had a simple, crisp, very neat, stylish look about her. He had lingered with them longer than usual. He liked talking to Caro, even though she wasn't a patient, and he admired her for her staunch support of her younger sister, who was having a baby she clearly didn't want and said so. Annabelle seemed to have no maternal instincts at all, and he thought she was doing the right thing, given her attitude and her age. But he also knew it was probably going to be harder to give up the baby than she expected. In three more months, she would get more attached to it than she thought she would. He had seen it happen before, and he wanted to warn Caroline at some point, if not Annabelle. Giving up the baby was liable to be much more traumatic than Annabelle imagined. It wouldn't be easy to just hand over a baby she'd just given birth to. Her hormones would be running rampant, and giving the baby away went against nature.

The sisters left, and he walked into the nearest exam room to see his next patient.

Annabelle grinned at her sister in the elevator on the way to the lobby of the medical building.

"He likes you," she said smugly.

"He likes you too. He's a nice guy," Caro said, thinking with awe that Annabelle was only three months from having her baby. The concept was still hard to absorb. Her baby sister was having a baby and giving it up. Caro always wondered what their mother would have said about it.

"That's not what I meant," Annabelle corrected her. "I mean he *likes* you, like a guy. You're not his patient, so it's okay."

"He does not 'like' me, 'like a guy,' Annabelle, don't be ridiculous. He just talks to me because I'm the only other adult in the room. He's just being friendly."

"You're blind. He thinks you're hot."

"I'm not 'hot,' I'm your sister. I'm standing in for Mom."

"Well, you're not Mom. She was sixty-five years old. You're thirty-two years younger, and gorgeous."

"Thank you. Let's just get through this baby, so you can get past it. We don't need to pick up your

OB in the process," Caro said matter-of-factly. She thought Ted Kelly was very good-looking and seemed very nice, but she wasn't open to doing anything about it. Thinking of him reminded her that she wanted to call Rachel Adams and push her. Time was passing, and they needed to find adoptive parents for Annabelle's baby pretty soon. Caro wanted everything organized and in place by the time Annabelle had the baby, so the handover would be swift and smooth, to minimize the trauma for her. She could only guess how hard that would be.

She talked to Lyle about it that night. Tommy seemed happier, but Lyle said he was still having problems at school, and outbursts of anger that got him in trouble.

Amanda paid no attention to it whatsoever, and had just made a new batch of demands. She wanted a new car every year at Lyle's expense, a global amount to pay for her shopping, tutors for the kids if they needed them, and a summer vacation he would pay an astronomical amount for. Amanda liked to travel in style to expensive places, and she wanted Lyle to pay for that too.

Tommy was going to camp in Maine that summer for six weeks, which Lyle thought was a long time, and Devon was going to a fancy day camp for July and August. It was run by her school. She didn't want to go and was trying to find a way to get out of it. Caro was trying to organize some kind of vacation in August. She couldn't go anywhere in July with the baby coming. She wanted to be there for Annabelle before, during, and after. It was going to be challenging for her. Lyle was staying in town in July too, to work on a new commercial real estate deal. And Charlie was talking about taking a trip with Brady, but he didn't know where yet. Maybe Turkey or Greece, or somewhere closer. Giorgio wanted Gloria to come to Italy. So their summer plans were starting to take shape. And after the baby was born, Annabelle wanted to take a trip with friends, to celebrate her liberation. The pregnancy hadn't been hard for her so far, but the last few months could be. Just the idea of getting the baby out seemed terrifying to Annabelle. She would have preferred to be asleep, or even have a Caesarean, but Ted Kelly had told her there was no medical reason for it so they wouldn't do it. The best they had to offer was an epidural, but Annabelle was afraid it wouldn't be enough to counter the pain. There was no reward at the end of this for her, so she wanted it to be as easy and painless as possible. She had no motivation to be brave in order to have a baby she wouldn't keep.

Gloria announced the day after Annabelle's doctor visit that she wanted Giorgio to meet all of them, and was suggesting a family dinner on Sunday night. The others liked the idea and were curious about him. There had been some hints that Charlie was seeing someone too, but he wasn't ready to introduce him to them. He was being very low-key and somewhat secretive about it. He had told Caro that he didn't want to jump the gun, introduce Brady too soon, and scare him off. It made sense to her. And Giorgio could hold his own in any crowd. Caro didn't know if Brady could, although as a journalist, he should be able to talk to anyone.

On Sunday night, Giorgio showed up at the front door at the appointed hour. Caro and Annabelle were frantically cooking. Benjie, Tommy, and Devon had set the table. Lyle was doing whatever he could to help, and opened the wine. Charlie had been out with Brady all day and came home just in time for dinner, and was happy to see Giorgio. Giorgio was looking mildly flustered as he tried to remember the cast of characters, who belonged to whom, and all their names. Benjie chatted easily with Giorgio and introduced him to the dogs. And Giorgio said he loved dogs, and had two cocker spaniels in Italy.

There was always a celebratory feeling when they all got together, like a birthday party, and tonight was especially so with Giorgio in their midst. He was a good sport spending the evening with them, with so many new people at once. He kept glancing at Gloria and smiling, as though to reassure her that he was fine. She relaxed as she watched him, and he leaned toward her at one point and whispered.

"Wait until you see my family dinners. They are much crazier than this!!" She laughed and he patted her leg under the table and couldn't wait to get her home to bed. He was glad that she wasn't living with her family. He was enjoying being with her on their own, but he had a good time with them all at dinner that night. He laughed and drank wine, enjoyed the food, and flirted with Gloria. He loved meeting them all and told her so on the way back to her apartment, where they fell into each other's arms like starving people as soon as they walked in and closed the front door behind them. They never even made it to her bedroom and made love on one of the living room couches.

"So what do you think?" Caro asked Lyle after they left.

He smiled in response. "I think our sister has never looked happier. He's a great guy. I hope it works out for them."

"Do you think they'll get married?" Annabelle asked them.

"Who knows? I'm not sure it matters," Caro responded, and Charlie agreed.

"Mom always said Gloria wouldn't get married until her forties. As usual, she was right."

"They look so happy," Annabelle said. It was beginning to weigh on her that she was having a baby by a man she didn't love, who didn't love her, a baby she couldn't even keep, and didn't want to. She could feel the baby moving constantly now. It kept her up at night. She was worried about the delivery and how bad it might be. And what if no adoptive parents turned up? Then what would she do? When she saw Gloria, it suddenly put into sharp focus for her what love should look like, between two people who genuinely cared about each other.

It had touched them all, seeing them together. Gloria was absolutely glowing, and Giorgio seemed like a genuinely good person. It was all very new, but it looked very promising to all of them.

They were still talking about it at breakfast the next day. And Caro and Charlie were in a good mood when they left for work. Lyle was too. He had meetings all morning, and no time to check his emails until noon. When he did, he read one that nearly stopped his heart. He couldn't believe that Amanda would do that to him, but she had. He called his lawyer immediately. His voice was shaking when Jeff came on the line.

"What's up? My secretary said it was urgent." He had come out of a meeting to talk to him.

"I just got a notification from the Administration for Children's Services that I am under investigation for subjecting my children to the unsuitable environment I live in. That we live in chaos and disorder with unsafe members of the family in our midst. It says that I am suspected of exposing my children to neglect and dangerous elements, and my son has behavioral problems in school as a result." Lyle was on the verge of tears as he read it to him.

"Is any of that true?" Jeff asked him. He thought it highly unlikely that Lyle could be guilty of any of it. His ex-wife was just jerking him around to get more money out of him. Any trick or form of harassment would do.

"It's true about my son. He's having problems in school. He's been meeting Amanda's boyfriends and he's upset about the divorce. He's been seeing a shrink when he's with me."

"Then you have nothing to worry about."

"I hope you're right. You can make anything look bad if you try hard enough. I'm living at my parents' house until we decide whether to sell it or not. It's a twenty-five-thousand-square-foot house, so several of us are living there, at a great address off Fifth Avenue. It's a beautiful home. Four of my siblings are there with me, all respectable people, but ACS may not think so. My younger brother is at the high end of the autism spectrum, with slight signs of Asperger's. He's terrific and has a job, is living there with his two dogs. My youngest sister is twenty-one, single, and pregnant. She's giving the baby up for adoption. My twin brother and sister are also living there. He's gay, which they may consider unsuitable."

"This isn't the dark ages," Jeff reminded him. "Are any of them drug addicts or falling-down drunks?"

"No."

"Been in prison, or jail recently, or alcoholic?"

"No."

"Have partners living there, or have sex in plain view of the kids?"

"No to both."

"Is there physical or verbal abuse in the home?"

"Of course not."

"Are the dogs you mentioned vicious? Have they attacked the children?"

"No, but one of them is a Great Dane."

"If it's not a pit bull, we're fine. What's the other one?"

"A Chihuahua. And they said we had a fire recently, which was my brother trying to make cupcakes with my kids. They forgot them in the oven and burned them but they never caught fire. The smoke alarms went off, that's all." She was determined to make trouble and make him look bad.

"You're going to be fine, Lyle. It's not illegal to be gay or have Asperger's or get pregnant out of wedlock, or even to burn cupcakes. It sounds like any normal family. Believe me, they see a lot worse every day, and not in a twenty-five-thousand-square-foot house just off Fifth Avenue. Do you have supervision for the kids, and does your brother need a helper?"

"A housekeeper and nanny for my kids. And my brother and sisters and myself are there for the kids and my brother. He has a job in a pet shelter and goes to work every day just like the rest of us. My pregnant sister doesn't work and is home most of the time right now."

"Amanda is just messing with you. The ACS people are going to walk out of your house laughing."

"I hope so." But Lyle was terrified he could lose his kids.

"ACS has to follow up on these reports. Some are bogus and some are real. They'll recognize this for what it is immediately. I'm sorry to say it but that woman you were married to is a witch. And I'm not worried at all. They'll assign someone to the case, who will contact you in twenty-four hours, and they have sixty days to conduct an investigation and reach a conclusion."

"What do they do? Do they just show up?"

"Usually. They don't like to give people warning. Just don't give any wild parties with naked women, or start dealing drugs out of your house for the next few weeks," he said lightly. "Other than that, you'll be fine."

"I'll warn my siblings not to." He tried to be lighthearted too. It was the nastiest thing Amanda had done to him so far, and he knew he'd never forgive her for it. What would he tell his kids? He just hoped that the people who came to investigate were reasonable and could see that they were a loving family living a decent family life.

He warned the others of it that night and they were shocked and sympathetic. "She really is a piece of work," Charlie said, sorry for his brother.

"It'll be fine," Caro reassured him.

"Do you want me to move out?" Annabelle offered. "I could stay with a friend if it looks bad for you to have me here, unmarried and pregnant." Everyone wanted to help him as best they could.

"I can go back to the loft," Charlie said quietly.

"No one is moving out," Lyle said. "We're a respectable family. As my lawyer said, we're not dealing drugs here, shooting up, or beating each other up. We're all decent people, and Tommy and Devon are lucky to be here with me. I can move out too, if you want me to, since I'm the cause of the problem," he said, feeling guilty and ashamed.

"No one is going anywhere," Caroline said in a firm voice. "They can investigate whatever they want. We're a family. We're real people. And we stick together and take care of each other. We're proud of each other, just as Mom and Dad were proud of us. We're what family is supposed to be about. And we'll deal with it when they come. No one is moving out." She looked around the table and they all nodded. She was becoming more and more like their mother. Strong and caring for everyone.

Lyle lay in bed that night, thinking about

Amanda, and hating her even more than before. He had wanted to be fair with her, and generous. Now he wished he had never met her, except for the children she had given him. He was dreading the investigation and what they might think, but he knew Caro was right. They were a family, with all the weaknesses and foibles and strengths of any family, and better than most. Whatever lies Amanda told them wouldn't change that. Whenever the investigators turned up, the Whittiers would be ready and waiting to show them what a real family looked like, no matter what Amanda said.

Chapter 12

It took ACS less than two days to call in response to the complaint Amanda's attorney had filed against Lyle Whittier. They were overloaded and understaffed, and handled complaints on a triage basis, usually within twenty-four hours, as required. Given the fact that Amanda's complaint did not report physical harm, but alluded to unsuitable, irresponsible surroundings, and no one had gotten hurt so far, the complaint sat at the bottom of the pile. The caseworker it had been assigned to assessed that no one was at physical risk, which made it lower priority than most of the cases she had.

The mother's report said that the Whittiers "lived like gypsies," that the family was dysfunctional, that a "disabled" member of the family posed a potential threat and had caused a fire that involved her children. She referred to them as a real-life Addams Family, with unsavory family members the children were exposed to. The report was full of innuendo and bitter descriptions of Lyle's family members, and reeked of vengeance against her ex-spouse, so the supervising investigator did not give it a great deal of credence. He had seen too many reports like it before as part of aggressively hostile divorces, usually among high-end people with money, which was often at the root of the complaint. But they had to check it out anyway, once a complaint was made.

Sometimes reports like this one were all lies, occasionally there was some truth, but not much, or an ex-wife was angry about a new girlfriend and accused her of being a prostitute. There was no allusion to sexual misconduct or incest being committed by the father. Those reports went to the top of the pile and were acted on immediately, although sometimes too late. But in this case, the mother's claim of wild dogs roaming loose in the house, and a family resembling a comedy TV show and living like vagabonds didn't impress him. The family's home address, where the children were living half the time, didn't arouse his concerns either, although child abuse and incest could happen in the wealthiest homes. Supervisor Ike Fellowes read the report again and sighed. He hated it when people used their already limited staff and time just to piss each other off. He had seen it all before, and this report had that smell to it to him.

He assigned it to a more recent member of his staff, Daphne Dawson. She was getting her Master of Social Work degree from Columbia, and completing the 1,200 hours of supervised fieldwork she needed to get her license. She was thirty-two years old, a responsible, serious young woman from Chicago who handled every case with the utmost diligence and left no stone unturned to verify the claims made by either police or private citizens. Ike had found her at times a little too zealous, but better that than casual and negligent. No one would have accused her of that. Before going to graduate school, she had earned a degree in sociology at Northwestern, and had graduated at the top of her class. He called her in to see him and handed her the initial report.

"Take a look at this," he said with a dour expression. The description of the number of people living there made it sound like a tenement. And the tenants like the inmates of an insane asylum.

"That doesn't sound like a healthy environment for children. It implies that the disabled member of the family is an arsonist, and dangerous," she said, as she handed the report back to him.

"This investigation may prove to be part of your education as a social worker, Daphne. It could be real, but smells of a nasty divorce to me, possibly to blackmail more money out of the husband. I may be wrong, but you see reports like these from time to time. They're usually bogus, but we can't ignore them. The fancy address may hide a multitude of sins, or they may all be harmless. I've checked out a lot of these in my day, now it's your turn. More than likely, you'll be wasting your time." Daphne had already been exposed to how cynical Ike was, and he could see that she didn't entirely believe him. She was conscientious to a fault, somewhat naïve, and determined not to leave any child in danger. In the six months she'd been there, she had removed at least a dozen children from truly dangerous circumstances and placed them in foster homes, which wasn't always better. Daphne Dawson was a good person, and would be an excellent social worker one day, and he could sense that she was from an upper-middle-class home. Both her parents and an older brother were doctors, and she had chosen social work as her path instead.

"Should I do a home visit right away unannounced?" she asked him. She wasn't sure if the ground rules were different at a fancy address. All home visits were unannounced to capture the real atmosphere of the home.

"Would you normally?" he asked her, leaning back in his chair. She had a girl-next-door look to her, wholesome and innocent. He was close to retirement and she was a breath of fresh air compared to all the tired, angry, jaded, disillusioned people he worked with. They had seen too many real tragedies to remain unaffected, children who had had bleach thrown at them or had been beaten senseless and were brain-damaged forever, pregnant eleven-year-olds who had been brutally raped by their fathers. The heartbreaks were endless. He didn't expect the Whittier report to be one, but you never knew. There were always bad surprises anywhere in the city.

"Normally, I don't make an appointment, I just show up," she answered his question, "as we're supposed to."

"Then do that," he advised her. "Always trust your instincts. In some cases, don't just believe what you see. There's always more to the story, and most people are hiding something." She nodded agreement. "It may be something perfectly benign, or not."

"I have time to go by there today, for an initial assessment. It may be a little late."

"That's fine, you'll see more then. They won't be expecting you. Good luck." He smiled at her as she left his office, looking very serious. She treated each case like the most important one she would ever handle. He hoped that this one would turn out to be as lightweight as he thought it would be. The reference to the Addams Family made him somewhat optimistic.

Daphne had a busy day after that. She needed to visit a brain-damaged child she had placed in a group home to see how she was doing, and to make a home report on two foster families. There had been a suspicious report about one of them. She was going to visit a nine-year-old girl the police had rescued who had been used as a sex slave in a sex-trafficking operation. She had a grandmother on her list who was on welfare and taking care of seven grandchildren for her daughter who was in prison. Social services wanted to split up the children and put them in foster homes and the grandmother was begging them not to, but she was selling marijuana to supplement her income. A neighbor had turned her in. Almost every case on Daphne's list was a tragedy waiting to happen, or that had already happened, many of them irreversible, with children who would turn into severely damaged adults, some of them even dangerous, trying to get even for what had been done to them. Too many of them ended up back in the system, in prison.

It was five-thirty when Daphne finished the last of her visits. She hadn't had time for lunch. She rarely did, or she ate a sandwich on the subway between clients she visited. She looked at her watch and wondered if it was too late. She knew she couldn't get to the Whittiers' until six o'clock. She didn't mind working late and often did, and she often saw more at those hours, when the element of surprise played in her favor, as it might in this case. She decided not to put it off, and stayed on the subway to the right stop. She lived in Brooklyn and had two roommates, and the neighborhood she ventured into, heading west toward Central Park, was unfamiliar to her. Her parents in Chicago lived on the lake, and she had grown up in an affluent environment, thanks to her parents' hard work as professionals. She had a strong work ethic as a result, and so did her brother, who was five years older than she was and a plastic surgeon in Chicago. Their father was a renowned cardiologist, and their mother was an obstetrician.

The apartment buildings she saw along her path were nothing like the ones where she made home visits in the worst neighborhoods in the city. These were elegant buildings with uniformed doormen waiting to let people in. In the last two blocks there were several handsome old turn-of-the-century mansions, with grandiose façades and impeccably trimmed hedges in front of them. She checked the address she was looking for and arrived at the largest of the old houses. It was an enormous double-width house that must have belonged to someone very important when it was built. It had a spectacular, ornate stone façade. She looked up with admiration, climbed the front steps to the heavy wooden door with the brass knocker, and rang the bell. It looked like a butler should open it to her, and she smiled as she stood there. No one answered and she rang again and waited.

Then finally, the door swung slowly open, and no one was there as she looked straight ahead at her own eye level. Her gaze drifted down, and she found herself looking at a little girl in pink ballet slippers, a pink leotard, and a tutu with sparkling hearts on it.

"Hi, I'm Devon. My aunt is cooking. I'm not supposed to open the door, but everyone else is busy. I'm having my ballet recital tomorrow."

Daphne's normally very serious face broke into a slow smile, like ice melting in spring. "Your tutu is very pretty," she said. They stood there eyeing each other. She couldn't push past the child and was waiting for an adult to show up. No one did. She could hear loud music coming from upstairs, the kind that teenagers listened to, and she could hear voices from the rooms beyond. "Could you go and get a grownup to talk to me?"

"Okay," Devon agreed, but she was afraid that someone would scold her for opening the door to a stranger, so she didn't tell anyone that Daphne was there. The door yawned open as Daphne stood in the balmy spring evening, outside what had once been a magnificent home, noticing that the antiques in the front hall looked a little worn, but there was an aura of old-money elegance to the interior. She was peeking inside when a tall, gangly young man walked by and was surprised to see her. What looked like a small horse was loping behind him, then suddenly dashed forward, stood up, put a paw on each of her shoulders, and nearly knocked her down, as Duke licked Daphne's face and the young man stared at her.

"You're not supposed to leave the door open," he scolded her. "My dogs will run away." Daphne was trying to push the giant dog off her, despite his affectionate exuberance, as a pretty woman walked into the hall and saw the scene. She was visibly pregnant, and called Duke to order and addressed the dog's owner.

"Benjie, take Duke upstairs." The young man pulled the dog by his collar and removed him from Daphne, as Annabelle approached her. "I'm so sorry. Are you okay?" Daphne was trying to straighten her jacket and wipe her face, while still trying to look official and dignified. "Can I help you?" Annabelle had no idea who the woman was. Maybe a friend of Caro and Charlie's, although she didn't look chic, just a little frumpy. She was carrying an overstuffed, battered briefcase, and she was pretty and young.

"I'm Daphne Dawson, from the Administration for Children's Services," the young woman said officially. Annabelle looked blank for a moment and then remembered what Amanda had done. She had almost forgotten about it, but Lyle had warned them an investigator might show up.

"Oh, of course. I'm sorry. My brother isn't home from work yet. Would you like to come in?" Daphne nodded and followed her into the once-elegant hallway with the still-grand staircase. Caro came out of the kitchen and addressed her sister, ignoring the woman with her.

"I burned the pizza. Should I order another one?" It was Caro's turn to cook. They had designed a rotation of kitchen duty, and she had come home to do it. She was still wearing a chic dress from the office and Louboutin high heels. She looked gorgeous and Daphne stared at her, impressed.

Annabelle looked at her intently. "This is Ms. Dawson, from Children's Services, ACS. The front door was open and Duke was trying to love her to death."

Caro looked instantly concerned. "I'm so sorry. He's big but he's harmless. He loves everyone. Would you like to wait for my brother? He's not home yet."

"I'll wait," Daphne said with determination, although her introduction to the house had been somewhat unnerving. "Are the children here? I already saw one of them. She let me in, she was wearing a tutu."

Caro frowned. "She's not supposed to answer the door. I didn't hear the bell. And yes, of course, the children are here." She didn't like the idea of letting Daphne meet them without Lyle present, but she didn't want to refuse the investigator either. She turned to Annabelle and asked her to get Tommy and Devon, then led Daphne into the large, elegant living room and offered her a glass of water, which she refused. Daphne sat primly on an enormous an-

tique chair with slightly threadbare velvet uphol-
stery, and Caro excused herself for a minute. She
sent Lyle a frantic text, telling him the ACS investigator was there and to get home immediately. He
texted back that he would be home in fifteen minutes, and Caro went back to sit with the visitor. A
minute later, Tommy and Devon joined them. Their
father had warned them that this would happen, but
Caro wasn't sure if they remembered. Daphne smiled
at the children, and Annabelle disappeared and
went to sit in the kitchen.

Benjie was feeding Duke and Dottie. "Who is
that woman?" he asked Annabelle.

"She's here to see Lyle." She didn't want to explain it to him.

"He's not here," he told her.

"I know. Don't let the dogs out. Keep them in
here."

"Duke liked her."

"He might scare her," Annabelle said, wondering
what would happen. She knew how worried Lyle was
about it. Reporting him to ACS had been a rotten
thing for Amanda to do, and Annabelle was sorry for
him.

In the living room, Caro and the children were
sitting politely while Daphne chatted with them.
She asked them if they also lived in another house,
which she knew they did.

"Yes, with our mom," Tommy answered, and
Devon nodded.

"She has an apartment," Devon added. "She's going to sell it. She wants a fancier one."

"Do you like living here?" Daphne asked them, as Caro listened.

Devon answered first. "Yes, and our aunts and uncles live here too, except Aunt Gloria. But all the others live here with us." She pointed at Caro, who smiled at the investigator, and tried to look relaxed and welcoming in her high heels and chic black dress.

"My brother and I live in SoHo, but our parents died a few months ago, and we all wound up living here while we settle the estate and figure out if we want to sell the house. So we're using it for now."

"It's a beautiful house. How many bedrooms are there?"

"Fourteen. It's a huge house. We all grew up here, and we hate to sell it. But it doesn't make much sense to keep it. We're kind of staying here for old times' sake right now, and it gave my brother, the children's father, time to look for an apartment. The children are with us on alternate weeks."

"How many of you are staying here?" Daphne inquired.

"Five siblings. You just met my sister, and my brother who owns the dog. All three brothers are staying here. Their father, my twin, and my youngest brother, who lived here with my parents. So did the sister you just met. We all still have bedrooms here, and more to spare."

Daphne spoke to the children directly again then. "Do you have your own rooms?" It was a standard question, which seemed foolish here. They nodded enthusiastically.

"And Dottie sleeps with me," Devon volunteered.

"Who's Dottie?" Daphne asked, confused again. There were so many people to keep track of.

"She's my uncle's dog. She's a Chihuahua. Duke sleeps with Uncle Benjie."

"Yes, I think I met Duke." Daphne smiled.

And as she did, Lyle walked in like a strong breeze, looking rushed and flustered. He hastened toward Daphne and held out a hand to shake hers. He was surprised by how young she was. She didn't look like an investigator or a social worker. She seemed kind of meek to him, and embarrassed as she looked up at him, as though she felt she was intruding. "I'm sorry. I was on my way home from work. Rush-hour traffic," he explained.

"It's my fault for coming so late, I just thought it might be a good time to catch you at home." She blushed then. "I didn't mean 'catch,' I meant find you." She felt overwhelmed by the number of people and the grand house and felt foolish being there, and Lyle was so handsome it startled her, and he seemed genuinely nice. Now she understood what Ike had meant. She had a feeling that there was a motive behind the report, other than protecting the children. The family didn't look like vagabonds to her. They looked like nice people.

The sister who had been sitting with her was very chic and sleek-looking and seemed totally responsible. The pregnant one looked young but seemed wholesome and respectable. Lyle was wearing a business suit and had come home to his children at a decent hour. There were plenty of adults in the house, and Devon said they had a babysitter. The dog was a bit much but obviously friendly. There were a lot of them living there but with fourteen bedrooms in a huge mansion, why not? And their reasons for living there temporarily before they sold their childhood home made sense to her, and even touched her.

"We've been expecting you," Lyle said calmly and sat down.

"We've been swamped at ACS," she said.

"Do you still need the children to sit with us?" he asked her.

"I can talk to them again later." She intended to speak to Tommy's school about the reports of his disruptive, aggressive behavior. Lyle told the children they could go upstairs. Caro left the room with them, and Lyle turned to Daphne. "My ex-wife made this report to ACS only to harass and upset me. You're welcome to access everything about my life, and the kids', but this was all about money, not them. I know you can't take my word for it, but that's what this is about." She was beginning to suspect that was the truth. There was a warm family feeling to the mild chaos she saw around them, which wasn't unusual in a big house with a lot of people in it.

"Your children look very happy." They looked clean, well fed, and relaxed. They didn't seem stressed or uneasy, even with a stranger. She knew the signs of dysfunctional homes and this wasn't one. They weren't being abused. They looked loved in a stable environment, even if a busy one.

"They are, though my son has been showing signs of distress over the divorce. We've been seeing a psychiatrist. My ex won't take him, so he goes once a week when he's with me. I think it's helping. He's angry about the divorce. Devon has adjusted better, maybe because she's younger."

"A lot of kids lash out over divorce, particularly boys."

"His mom is dating a lot, and I think it worries him." He threw Amanda under the bus knowingly and figured she deserved it. The point was not lost on Daphne.

"Are you dating?" she asked him, looking embarrassed again. She felt more than ever like a nosy intruder. He was an intelligent, respectable man and she was asking him if he was dating, but it was part of her job.

"No, I'm not. Honestly, I don't have time with the kids here, and I don't want to. I'm trying to settle my parents' estate, which is a full-time job, along with my day job."

"What is your job?" She couldn't remember.

"I'm in land development and commercial real estate. Some days, I can manage to take meetings at home on the phone, but most of the time I'm at my office. I try to be home by six or seven every night when my kids are here, and we eat dinner together," he informed her, and she nodded. She had the feeling that what he did was very lucrative, and his ex-wife probably wanted money. "Is there anything I can tell you or show you to assure you that my children are being well cared for? Would you like to meet my brothers and sisters?"

"I think I've met the two sisters who live here," she said hesitantly. And as she said it, Charlie walked in and waved from the doorway to the living room. Lyle beckoned to him and he approached. Charlie looked handsome and stylishly dressed, in a blazer with jeans, as he smiled at Daphne.

"This is my brother Charlie. He lives here too for now." Charlie looked puzzled as to who she was, and wondered if Lyle had a date. She looked a little uptight to him, and not too entertaining. "This is Daphne Dawson, from ACS," Lyle explained, and a light came on in Charlie's eyes. He got it immediately and smiled at her again.

"Sorry, I didn't mean to intrude." As they were talking, Benjie wandered in to talk to Charlie.

"Can I go to the gym with you?" he asked him.

"I can't go tonight," Charlie told him. "Tomorrow, I promise." Benjie left the room then, and Lyle took the bull by the horns.

"Benjie is high on the autism spectrum, bordering on Asperger's in his social skills sometimes. He's had a job for five years at a pet shelter, and he does very well. Sometimes he's socially awkward and sometimes he's fine. Who isn't? They love him at his job, and he's a loving, kind, responsible person, and he loves my kids."

"I met his dog when I came in," she said with a rueful smile. "He's taller than I am, and he almost knocked me down kissing me." All three of them laughed at that, and then Charlie hurried off. He was meeting Brady for dinner. Daphne stood up then.

"I'm keeping you from dinner with the kids. I'd like to meet with them one more time, just to ask them some more basic questions. And I want to go to Tommy's school about his recent issues."

"And what happens after that?" Lyle asked her, still worried.

"Nothing," she said. "If I'm satisfied that everything is in order and the children are happy and in good shape, we put the file on hold for a year. If we get another complaint, we take it seriously. If not, the file is archived."

"So my ex-wife can do this again and again?"

"Technically, yes, but not really. If we find that her claims have been unfounded, or even irresponsible and frivolous, we're going to pay a lot less attention the next time she calls us. We don't have time for false claims or people using us to punish someone else. We save children's lives every day. We need all the manpower we have to do that. To be honest, your children look fine to me, and this isn't the 'gypsy camp' your ex-wife described. It's a warm, wonderful family, and you're all lucky to have each other." She smiled at him. "I'll make an appointment to see the children again, and then I'll write my report. I'll call you, Mr. Whittier," she said, as he walked her to the door and shook her hand gratefully, and then thought of something. "Would you like to see their rooms?" he asked her.

She hesitated, and then nodded, more curious than professional. He ran her upstairs quickly, as she admired the handsome halls and family pictures, and passed several bedrooms. Molly was tidying Devon's, hanging up a dozen tutus, and smiled warmly. And Tommy's looked like a real boy's room, with posters of his favorite athletes tacked to the walls. She smiled at both rooms. They were lucky kids and she could sense they were much loved. He took Daphne back downstairs.

"Thank you. I'm sorry I wasn't here when you arrived, and that my brother's dog almost knocked you down."

"I'm not much of a dog lover usually," she said, smiling, and he thought she looked prettier when she did. She had looked very stern to him when he met her. "But he was very friendly." Everyone in the house was. She hadn't met a single person who made her uneasy. She liked them all, and Lyle particularly. "I'll get in touch in the next few days for an appointment with Tommy and Devon. I'm pretty jammed, but I'll try to make it soon, so you can put this behind you." Unless they told her something shocking at Tommy's school, which she doubted. As far as she was concerned, this was over, and exactly what Ike had described, a bogus claim by a bitter or greedy ex-wife. There wasn't the faintest sign of neglect or child abuse here, or child endangerment. And if they were "gypsies," they were the nicest ones she could imagine. Mr. Whittier's ex-wife was obviously just trying to make trouble for him. Even Daphne could sense that. The atmosphere in their home made you want to meet them all, and stay. They exuded love and kindness, a welcome she never got on her unannounced visits.

When Lyle walked into the kitchen, Caro looked at him with worried eyes and whispered, "Is she gone?"

"Yes. It went fine. She realized that Amanda was just trying to make trouble. I don't think they take too kindly to that. They have better things to do, and children in real danger. She wants to see the kids one more time, and talk to Tommy's school, and then she'll make a report, and it's over. I don't think they'll even pay attention if Amanda does it again. She blew it." He looked immensely relieved. Caro served them all pancakes for dinner, since she had burned the pizza, and they all talked animatedly. Lyle felt as though someone had lifted a thousand-pound weight off his shoulders.

Daphne Dawson called Lyle in the office a week later and apologized for not calling sooner. She said she was jammed. As promised, she made an appointment to see the children, and offered to come on a Saturday, which was easier for him. When she did, she talked to each of the children alone, and was satisfied with their responses. And the school had seen a marked improvement in Tommy's behavior since he'd been seeing the psychiatrist. Her official visit was over at noon, and Lyle invited her to join them for lunch. He was making pasta for everyone, and all of them were home.

She hesitated for a minute and then accepted, and unbent once she was sitting with them at the table. They joked and played and talked over each other. Gloria showed up with Giorgio halfway through lunch and he tested Lyle's pesto pasta and said it was excellent and cooked just right, al dente, the way he liked it. He had a plate of pasta with them, while Gloria talked to her sisters.

Daphne looked uneasy when Duke walked into the room and sat down next to her. She was afraid he would try to lick her face again, and instead he shook hands with her, as though to apologize for his previous exuberance. She had a good conversation with Benjie about his work at the shelter, and told Lyle afterwards how impressed she was with him. He hadn't felt awkward with her at all. He liked her.

She seemed to fit in perfectly despite her original reason for meeting them. Gloria was outspoken about calling Amanda a gold digger and a greedy bitch when the children left the room, which confirmed Daphne's suspicions.

"I'm not here for ACS now," she pointed out to them. "I'm on my own time, so you can say anything you want. I'm off duty. Just don't beat the children," she said, and they laughed. They liked talking to her. She fit in quietly, and Lyle seemed to like her. Charlie noticed and said something to Caro about it later.

"Is that a romance brewing or was he just buttering up the ACS officer?"

"Maybe a little of both. She's smart, and very easy to talk to. Maybe he should go out with her." She said as much to Lyle later. Charlie had gone out to meet Brady. He was hanging around the house a lot less lately, and Caro missed him. He was seeing a lot of Brady, and spending time at his apartment in the West Village. Caro had the feeling that it had the potential to become serious. Ultimately, she wanted that for her twin, to find a loving partner, but it was going to leave a terrible void in her own life when he did.

"I'm not going to invite an ACS officer out on a date," Lyle said to Caro. "Are you crazy? What if I say the wrong thing? She'll arrest me." He was teasing, but dating Daphne seemed far-fetched to him, although he liked her. She was very calm and well balanced, and had a quiet beauty. She was totally different from Amanda. There was nothing showy about her, and she was nice to his kids, and kind to Benjie, and recognized his intelligence and skills.

He thought about what Caro had said and decided to call Daphne a week later. She told him she had finished her report and filed it. It was over.

"I wasn't actually calling about that," he said, feeling awkward. "I'm sure this isn't how these things are supposed to work, but would you consider having dinner with me?" She was smiling when he asked her over the phone. She had been sad, knowing that she no longer had any reason to see him, and would never hear from him again, and now she had.

"I'd love it," she said, sounding lively and young, and not as shy as she had when she met him. After meeting his family, she felt at ease with him, and she thought his family was terrific.

They picked a night the following week when they were both free, and Lyle was smiling when he hung up. She had asked him if he was dating as part of her investigation, and he said he wasn't, but now he was.

He teased her about it when they had dinner. "You made a liar out of me, Daphne," he told her.

"No, I didn't." She smiled shyly at him. "I was really happy when you said you weren't, which was very unprofessional of me."

"Is that why you asked me?"

"Of course not," she said, blushing again.

"I'll bet it was." They laughed their way all through dinner, and all Daphne could think of when he took her home was that she hoped he would ask her out again.

Lyle already knew he would. He had had a wonderful evening with her and wanted to see more of her. And most ironic of all was that, without meaning to, Amanda had brought them together by filing the ACS report on him. He'd have to remember to thank her for it someday.

Chapter 13

At the next big Sunday family lunch, Gloria and Giorgio were there. They were spending almost every night together, and it was turning into a serious relationship. He loved big families and thoroughly enjoyed being with hers. He was exactly what she had always needed and never found. "It's never too late," Lyle whispered to Caro at the table, and she smiled. She was sitting next to Brady on her other side. Charlie had convinced him to come to lunch, although he was hesitant to engage with Charlie's family. There were so many of them. He found the idea of it overwhelming, although in reality they were warm and welcoming. He liked having Charlie to himself. He loved their time alone, but he also knew how important the family was to Charlie. Caro made every effort at lunch to make Brady feel at home. She knew how close he and Charlie had become. She could see it in their eyes whenever they looked at each other. They were deeply in love.

"Don't be jealous of him, Sis," Charlie whispered to her later in the kitchen, while Brady was at the table talking to the others. "You know I'll always love you most. But he's important to me now too."

"There's room for both of us," she said, and hugged her twin. When they went back to the table, Gloria was harassing Annabelle about going back to school. She still fiercely disapproved of Annabelle's pregnancy and said so whenever she got the chance. She reminded Annabelle how ashamed their parents would have been, and what a disgrace she was. Annabelle cringed every time she saw her. Giorgio had tried to talk to Gloria about it, since he had unmarried nieces and a nephew who had babies, but nothing he said had mitigated how vehemently Gloria felt about it. "If you're not going back to school, you could at least get a job," she said to Annabelle.

"Who's going to hire me like this?" she responded to her older sister. "I'm having a baby in five weeks, and I can hardly move."

"You move fine when you want to," Gloria growled at her, "and you must have had no trouble moving when you got pregnant."

"I'll hire you," Caro said to Annabelle, mainly to keep Gloria from attacking her. She never failed to rub salt in Annabelle's wounds about being pregnant. "We're swamped. I could use a girl Friday, even for five weeks. And you can come back to work after you have the baby," since she wouldn't have a baby to take care of. Annabelle's face lit up when she suggested it. She liked the idea. She was deadly bored at home. Her friends were either finishing school or had jobs now. And those who weren't working would be leaving for the summer.

"Do you mean it?" she asked Caro.

"You can start tomorrow. After we see Dr. Kelly, you can ride downtown with me." Annabelle had to see the doctor every week now. She was getting close. And no adoptive couple had turned up yet. Annabelle was worried about it, and so was Caro.

The next day, Annabelle had her regular weekly OB appointment, and Caro went with her, as she always did. Ted Kelly was at ease with both of them now. He was attentive to Annabelle and addressed all her concerns, and he was always pleasant to Caro and chatted with her for a few minutes at the end of the appointment. Annabelle was increasingly worried about the delivery, and how painful it would be. He reassured her that they'd make it as easy as possible for her. She was young and healthy and he didn't foresee any complications. Caro hoped he was right, and she intended to be there.

*   *   *

After the office visit, Annabelle went downtown with Caro, who put her to work filing fabric samples and sketches. Annabelle answered emails for Caro, and was surprisingly efficient. It turned out to be a very good idea. She did some projects for Charlie too.

Annabelle was tired at the end of the day, but she felt as though she had accomplished something, instead of lounging around at home, watching movies on her computer. And unlike most pregnant women, she had nothing to prepare for the baby, since it wouldn't be coming home. When Charlie came home that night, he took Benjie to the gym with him, which Benjie always loved. He particularly loved the stationary bikes and the treadmill. He roamed around talking to people and making friends.

Charlie was having a boxing lesson, and left Benjie at the treadmills. He couldn't get into mischief at the gym or get hurt. As soon as Charlie walked away to his lesson, Benjie started talking to a girl on the next treadmill. She was beautiful and seemed very young and naïve. She had the same sweet innocence about her that Benjie did. Her name was Rose. As they walked along on neighboring treadmills, Benjie told her about his dogs. She said she'd like to see Dottie, and he promised to show Dottie to her sometime.

When Charlie came back an hour later, they

were still talking and walking. They were fast friends by then, and Benjie blew her a kiss goodbye when they left, and she blew it back to him, and then waved and jumped up and down. She was at the gym with her mother.

"You made a friend at the gym," Charlie said, smiling. She had a voluptuous, womanly figure, but she acted like a young girl. Her interactions reminded him of Benjie, and he wondered if she had issues similar to his. He wasn't sure.

"She's beautiful," Benjie said, looking awestruck. "She wants to meet Dottie. I said she could."

"Maybe we can have her over sometime," Charlie said vaguely as they went home. He had a thousand things on his mind from work.

"I'd like that. She lives four blocks from us," Benjie said. They had figured that out while on the treadmill. She said she could come over sometime to meet his dogs when he got home from work. Benjie loved the idea.

After that, Benjie badgered Charlie to take him to the gym every night, but Charlie only went three nights a week. At Benjie's insistence, Caro took him once, and Lyle another time. They thought it was sweet that he'd made a friend. The only people he had a chance to see normally were the people he worked with at the shelter. It was rare for him to make new friends. He talked about Rose constantly once he'd met her, and begged his brothers and sisters to take him to the gym every night when he came home.

The night Caro went, she chatted with Rose's mother. From what she said, Caro sensed that Rose was very much like Benjie. And she was warm and affectionate like Benjie. Her mother smiled at Caro.

"Rose is crazy about him. She gets so enthusiastic and excited. Benjie seems a bit like that too." They seemed very similar in some ways. She'd noticed it too.

"He's my brother," Caro answered her proudly. "How old is Rose?" Benjie was twenty-eight.

"Rose is twenty-six. She's our only child." Caro nodded, while Rose and Benjie continued to ride the exercise bikes and were laughing hilariously.

Something had struck them funny, and the two women watching were happy to see them enjoying each other. Neither of them volunteered confidential information about them but it was obvious that Benjie and Rose had something in common and were attracted to each other. Caro was happy to see it. Benjie deserved to have company and a new friend.

"I was an attorney," Rose's mother said, "but I gave up my practice when Rose was two. I spend a lot of time with her. She lives with me."

"My other two brothers and a sister and I are living with Benjie right now. We just lost our parents. Our mom took care of him. He really misses her. But having all of us there with him right now is a good distraction for him."

Rose and Benjie had just gotten off the bikes and were heading toward them, holding hands. She gave him a little shove when they got to Caro and Rose's mother, and they both laughed. They were having fun and teasing each other, and then they laughed uproariously again. The four of them left the gym together, and walked in the warm early summer night, until Rose and her mother headed toward Park Avenue, and Benjie bounded up the front steps of their house.

"I LOVE ROSE!" he shouted to anyone who could hear him, with an exuberant expression. "She's my girlfriend," he turned and said to Caro. "She told me so. And I'm her boyfriend." He'd never had a girlfriend before. He told Lyle all about it when he saw him in the hall.

"Well, that's exciting news," Lyle said, looking at his sister, and she nodded. "What does she look like?"

"Devon's Barbie doll," Benjie answered proudly. "She's beautiful."

Lyle raised an eyebrow in Caro's direction, and she told him in a soft voice as they headed toward the kitchen for a snack, "She's like him."

"That's interesting. That should be fun for him." He was happy for Benjie.

"They have a ball together, riding the exercise bikes and walking on the treadmill."

"Good for him," Lyle said. They all worried about Benjie being lonely, and at least he had someone to hang out with now.

"Her mom takes care of her. She was an attorney and retired from her practice for her. Sort of the way Mom took care of him."

"It takes a village," he said, and put some ice cream in bowls for Tommy and Devon and took it upstairs to them. Caro liked being able to see her brothers any time she wanted, living under one roof. She loved sharing the house with them and was glad they hadn't sold it.

Almost as though the Fates were tempting them, Lyle got an email the next day, from an attorney he knew, saying that a client of his was interested in the house, and was wondering if they were going to sell it.

Lyle emailed back that it wasn't on the market, the subject was under discussion among his siblings, and they hadn't come to a conclusion yet. The lawyer responded as soon as he got the email and asked Lyle to call him as soon as possible. He called a few minutes later, and the lawyer told him that his clients were crazy about the house.

"We're crazy about it too," Lyle said simply. "Five of us are living here, and the others seem to have no desire to sell at the moment. We haven't talked about it for a month or two."

"Would you mind asking them now?" The attorney sounded hopeful. "There's no house like it in the city. And my clients are afraid you might sell it to someone else."

"Do you know what kind of price they have in mind? That might make a difference," Lyle said, but he knew that for his siblings, it wasn't about money, it was about sentiment, although money was always nice too. But they had what they needed for the moment, from their recent inheritance. A house sale would be a windfall for them that they could do a number of things with. Lyle didn't want to propose it to them. Things were so peaceful now. He didn't want to get into a big argument with his siblings about selling the house, or start a war between opposing factions. But as executor and trustee, he was obligated to inform them of the offer. He called a family meeting at the house at the end of the day, and asked Gloria to come without Giorgio.

She was curious when she walked into the house late in the day and saw her older brother.

"Why couldn't Giorgio be here? I have no secrets from him."

"It's a family meeting, Glo. He's not family, yet," he teased, and he waited until everyone was there and seated in the living room. "We've had some interest in the house. Apparently there's a couple who would like to make an offer, and they want to know if we're interested before they start negotiating. They don't want to waste our time or theirs. I need to know how you're all feeling about it now. What do we want to do with Mom and Dad's house? We're making good use of it for the moment with five of us living here, and my kids part-time. I don't know if you want to continue that, or if we should try to sell while we have an opportunity. Or at least see what their opening bid is." That made sense to him.

"Do I have to move?" Benjie was the first to ask. They had included him in the meeting too.

"Not yet," Lyle said gently. "And maybe you don't." He looked at the others then. "I don't think it would be practical for us to live here together forever. Sooner or later our lives will change, and we'll want our own places. But right now, it's working for us. And we'll figure out Benjie's living situation with one or two of us." He looked reassuringly at him. "It's all a question of when."

"Why don't we find out how much these people have in mind?" Charlie said sensibly. Gloria agreed. She and Lyle and Charlie were all businesspeople, and they were curious about what the market would be for a house as large and unusual as theirs. The size of it played for and against them. There would be a very small market for it. Few people would want a house that large, except to make it into a club or a small hotel.

"I'll ask them," Lyle said, "and let you know."

He called the lawyer back after the meeting, who promised to discuss it with his clients and get back to him.

The attorney called back two days later. "My clients are thinking in the vicinity of fifty million," he said in an even tone.

"That's lower than we thought," Lyle said bluntly. "We've consulted some real estate brokers in the past six months, and they think we could get close to a hundred."

"If you're willing to wait for it and you're not in a hurry," the lawyer said. "That would be a very, very special buyer. Probably someone offshore."

"We're not in a rush," Lyle said coolly. Even if they were, he wouldn't have admitted it.

"I'll get back to you," the lawyer promised, and did a day later. The person interested in the house was willing to come up to sixty, but no higher, and Lyle knew turning it down was a bold move, but he wanted to. The house was serving them well now, and he seriously believed that when they wanted to sell, they could get more for it than the attorney was offering them from his client.

He called each of his siblings from his office and asked for their vote. Gloria wanted to sell, but no one else did.

"What about you?" Gloria asked him, and he hesitated.

"It may be self-serving, but I'd like to stay here

for a while longer, maybe until I get the divorce. It's great for me and the kids to be here. The divorce will be final in September. Eventually, I want to get my own place, but for now it's perfect. So I guess my vote is to wait, and pass on this round. I hope we don't regret it."

"So do I," Gloria said. But she wasn't living there, and the other five weren't ready to cut the cord to the mother ship yet. Selling the house would be like losing another piece of their parents, and none of them needed money right now. They didn't live extravagantly, and they loved being together. No one wanted to give that up. It wasn't the right reason to make the decision, but it was the one they agreed on in the end. The house enveloped and comforted each of them like a warm blanket, even Annabelle. She had been in a hurry to move out when her parents died, but now she wanted to retreat into her shell here, especially after she gave up the baby, which would be a hard time for her.

She had begun to feel a bond with the baby as he grew bigger within her, and she kept reminding herself that she couldn't think like that. She couldn't keep the baby. She just wanted to know that the adopting parents would be kind and loving and responsible, like her own parents. Living there was like still being with them. She could close her eyes and pretend they would come home. It still felt that way.

The day the family turned the offer down, ev-

eryone came to dinner, even Gloria. It was a giant
step for them, and it felt like a celebration as they
ate dinner and drank wine. Gloria grudgingly accepted their decision. She would have sold the
house if her siblings hadn't overruled her. Giorgio
was there that night too. When the subject of family business came up, he'd leave the table to send a
text or answer an email. As visible as he was, and
noticeably sophisticated, he was also quiet and discreet, and his own family was similar. He was
deeply in love with Gloria, and wanted to share
every aspect of her life. He was going to Sardinia
that summer and wanted Gloria to come with him.
He had a house there, and a sailboat. He had to be
back in New York at the end of August to prepare
for Fashion Week. Caro was already working on it,
three months ahead of time.

"Can I stay?" was all Benjie said.

"We're all staying for now," Lyle said. Benjie let
out a sigh of relief as he looked at Lyle.

"I thought I'd have to move this time."

"We'll give you plenty of warning," Lyle promised. "But we're not selling now."

Benjie let out a whoop of joy.

The attorney gave it one more try. The mystery
investors offered seventy. It was their final offer, or
so they said.

"No, we're not selling, crazy as that sounds,"
Lyle said to the persistent attorney.

"I hope you have no regrets later," the lawyer said tartly, and Lyle smiled.

"Yeah, me too." But their love for their parents' house was greater than their desire for money. Most people wouldn't have understood it, but they all did.

Chapter 14

Rachel Adams, the adoption attorney, finally sprang into action four weeks before Annabelle's baby was due. Annabelle was panicked by then. The agencies hadn't called her and she was afraid that no one would adopt the baby. Caro had called to remind them, and they had told her that everyone had shied away from Annabelle's drug and alcohol use early in the pregnancy. No one wanted to take the chance. But Rachel finally had two couples for her. One lived in Connecticut, the other in Boston. Rachel had clients from all over the country.

The ones in Connecticut were older, in their midforties. They had been trying to get pregnant, and stay pregnant, for fifteen years. She'd had seven late miscarriages before they finally gave up. They were excited about adoption now, and wanted just the right baby. They had already rejected at least ten birth mothers, but they liked Annabelle's background. They had consulted a doctor who had said that the baby could escape severe damage from her brief drug use, if they were lucky, and they decided to take a chance, and wanted to meet her. They also did not want continuing contact, which Annabelle liked too. Caro made an appointment to take her to the meeting.

The second couple, from Boston, was younger, and he was in tech. The wife was a commercial artist, and taught drawing in the fine arts department of Harvard, and classes on French and Italian Renaissance art. Caro was busy the only day they could come to New York, so Charlie agreed to take Annabelle. Both meetings were scheduled in Rachel's office. Annabelle was terrified of meeting the two couples, and that they might confront her about her two incidents of drug use. She was desperately afraid that if they rejected her, she would have no one to adopt the baby and she'd have to keep it. The closer her due date was, the more certain she was that she didn't want the baby. And she was enjoying her job with Caroline and Charlie. She was sorry she hadn't thought of it sooner. She had spent useless months doing nothing, and she found that she enjoyed working in fashion, and thought about going to design school as they had. She wanted to come back to work as soon as possible after the baby, and the twins were impressed

by how hard she worked. She was an adept problem solver. And she was excited about working on
their fashion show in early September. She hoped
that the baby would be a distant memory by then.

Annabelle went to the meeting with the couple
from Connecticut first. They were friendly and
pleasant. They had a long list of questions for Annabelle, all of which she was able to answer posi-
tively and honestly. She had the feeling that it had
gone well, and they would want to proceed with
her, but a week after the meeting, Rachel called to
tell her they had dropped out. A lower-risk birth
mother had come on the scene, and they opted to
adopt her baby instead. It was a bitter disappointment for Annabelle, and made the second meeting,
with the couple from Boston, even more important.
They were her only option now. They were bright
and interesting, and Annabelle liked them and had
a good feeling about them. She was just beginning
to warm to them and relax when the husband be-
rated her for her foolishness to have used drugs
when she was pregnant, and told her how irresponsible she had been. She was well aware of it herself
and told them again that she had been unaware
that she was pregnant at the time. Scolding her for
it didn't change it, and at least she had been honest
with them. She could have lied and hadn't.

Charlie pointed that out to them, and he and the

husband got into an argument with voices raised. Annabelle watched miserably while her brother defended her, and finally stood up and told Annabelle they were leaving. She didn't want to give up her only chance for an adoption, but the couple told her then that they didn't want her baby anyway. They were too afraid that she might have used drugs since and could be lying about it. Annabelle left Rachel's office in tears, with no further prospects for an adoption.

Charlie had been outraged by how badly the couple had treated his sister, to the point of abuse. They had humiliated her. Rachel had called Annabelle the next day to apologize, and said she had tried to calm the couple's fears, but they had decided against adoption and were considering surrogacy instead. They had spoken to a surrogate in New Jersey and liked her.

Annabelle's due date was only a week away when Rachel asked her to come in to meet a couple from California. They were both cosmetic dentists and had a lucrative practice in L.A., with many celebrity clients. They were kind and compassionate to Annabelle, and they all liked each other immediately. Annabelle found all their questions and conditions reasonable. The couple met with her twice, and Rachel called to tell her that they wanted to go forward with her. They were going to stay in New York until she gave birth, so as not to miss it. They wanted to be at the hospital when the baby was born, but were willing to wait in the next room and not be present for the exact moment of the birth. It all sounded perfect, and Annabelle had the adoptive parents she needed. It had all worked out at the eleventh hour.

She had a quiet dinner at the house with Caroline after the second meeting, and couldn't wait for it all to be over now. She was uncomfortable all the time and couldn't sleep at night. The Fourth of July was that weekend, and she hoped she had the baby on her due date, or before. She just wanted it to be over. She asked Dr. Kelly about inducing her and he told her there was no medical justification for it, so he refused to do it. He was sympathetic with her wanting to get the delivery behind her, but he said it was better for both her and the baby to let nature take its course. She was thinking of going to the gym to do some exercise to see if she could get things started. Dr. Kelly had said walking might do it.

Lyle's kids were at the house, Tommy was leaving for camp soon and would be gone for six weeks, when Lyle walked into the kitchen to talk to Caro, with a worried expression. "Rose's mother just called. She wants to meet with us tomorrow. She wouldn't say what it was about, but she was upset, and her husband is coming with her. They're coming at ten o'clock tomorrow morning."

"Did she give you any idea what's up?"

"None." Lyle couldn't guess what they wanted.

Charlie was there too when the Fullers arrived in the morning. Rose wasn't with them. They were very direct with the three Whittiers when they told them that Rose and Benjie had been caught kissing and making out, and the Fullers were afraid it would go further if they continued to see each other, but they were crazy about each other and the Fullers didn't know what to do. Rose had threatened to run away if they stopped her from seeing Benjie. They were very upset.

Caro was touched and Charlie didn't think it was fair to stop them from seeing each other, and Lyle agreed. And Charlie confirmed Benjie was a virgin. He had never even spoken of sex to his brothers. He just said he loved Rose. And she loved him.

"We've put her on the pill in case something happens," her mother said nervously. They didn't want her to get pregnant, understandably. And they were adults. "I think we're going to have a hard time keeping them apart. She's very determined when she wants something, and she says she loves Benjie and wants to do things with him like they do now."

All five of them had a dilemma. They didn't want Benjie and Rose to get into a situation they couldn't handle, but they loved each other, and they had a right to love too.

"Neither of them is mature enough to engage in

a sexual relationship," Rose's mother said, distressed, and her father agreed.

"I'm sorry to ask," Charlie interrupted seriously, "but does it matter? If she's on the pill now, she won't get pregnant. And maybe they have a right to this. They are adults. They're twenty-six and twenty-eight years old. Do we have a right to deprive them?"

Rose's parents looked shocked. "We always hoped she would find someone like her, but I guess I didn't think it would happen and she might want to have sex. Benjie is a sweet boy and they love each other. But it doesn't seem right to just let them do whatever they want and have a real physical relationship. They're so innocent, and they're not responsible."

"Do they even want to have sex?" Lyle asked. "Maybe they don't."

"Maybe they're not as innocent as we think, or as we think they should be," Charlie said with a smile he couldn't suppress. "I think we should just let them have a relationship like any other people, without stopping them. They can't have sex openly in public, but if they're discreet about what they do, and they love each other, why not?"

Rose's parents didn't look enthused at the prospect. "They can't handle that kind of mature relationship," Jane said.

"Maybe they can," Lyle commented. "They're both very intelligent."

After an hour of discussion, Rose's mother and father agreed to think about it. They had come to ask them to keep Benjie away from Rose, and for both families to cooperate to stop them from seeing each other to avoid their relationship going any further. Lyle and Charlie had argued to let it continue with their full support, as long as Rose and Benjie were treating each other well and respectful of each other, which seemed to be the case. They knew Benjie would be heartbroken if he could no longer see Rose.

The Whittiers agreed to supervise them more closely, and monitor the relationship, but not to stop them, and Rose's father seemed inclined to agree. They had coffee together, and then the Fullers left, with a whole new point of view. They all realized that it was a very progressive outlook, but maybe a good one. And it showed faith in Benjie and Rose.

"Wow," Caro said to Charlie after they left. "My baby brother is in love, and I haven't had a date in months. I'm definitely missing all the fun." She grinned, and he laughed at her.

"That's because you work too hard," he reminded her.

"Apparently." She smiled at the irony of the meeting and the end result. Lyle had promised to buy Benjie condoms and teach him how to use them, just in case they went that far, and the Fullers promised to be diligent about giving Rose the pill, so she was covered against pregnancy. That was the one thing none of them wanted to have happen. Neither Rose nor Benjie could have coped with it, the risk of their problems being passed on genetically was too worrisome, and the last thing any of them wanted was a baby to take care of and assume responsibility for. They had decided that sex might be okay, but babies weren't.

And they weren't even out of the woods yet with Annabelle's. The worst part of her experience was yet to come, giving up the baby and never seeing it again. Charlie had had second thoughts about it, after discussing it with Brady.

He spoke to Caro about it a few days later. "Do you think it's right that she gives it up?" he asked her. It felt wrong to him now.

"It's what she wants," Caro said quietly. "It was a hard decision for her. We owe it to her to support it."

"What if it's the wrong decision?"

"Who's to say that? She believes it's the right one for her."

"What if she regrets it later? She can't get the baby back. That's what I'm worried about. And the baby will never know her."

"She knows all that, and it's what she wants. We can't interfere." Caro realized something then. She knew her twin too well. "Do you want her baby?"

"Brady and I have talked about it," he admitted to her. "At least he would be in the family. But Brady really doesn't want to. He wants our own, if we stay together. And right now, it looks that way." He smiled shyly at his sister. "Do you want the baby?" he asked her, and she shook her head.

"Look how hard we work. I'm never home. I don't think I have a right to take on a baby I can't spend time with. There are so many people in the world desperate to have children and they can't, and here's Annabelle, desperate to give one away. It's the way of the world, sadly. Five years from now, maybe, for me, or even three, but not now. I just can't."

"By the time you're ready, we won't even know where the kid went." Caro didn't disagree. But there was no room in anyone's life for this baby Annabelle had so carelessly conceived, except the people who were willing to adopt him. It would be a blessing for them. "I wish it were the right time for one of us," Charlie said. Caroline agreed, but none of Annabelle's siblings had time for a baby. Caro wondered what their mother would have done, if she would have kept the baby. Caro suspected she might have. She wondered if their father would have let her. It was hard to guess.

Caro saw Annabelle when she returned from the gym. She looked like the portrait of womanhood in all her glowing beauty. She had exercised more vigorously than she had in a while, but nothing had started. The baby was choosing his own time.

*   *   *

Annabelle went for long walks after that, every day.
Her due date came and went, despite all the walking. She was utterly miserable by then, and the
baby seemed huge.

She continued to work for Charlie and Caro,
and made a real effort to be helpful to them. She
could hardly waddle around now. And Caro went
to her next visit to Dr. Kelly with her. He did an internal exam this time, which he hadn't recently
until now, and it was uncomfortable for Annabelle.

"I think the baby will come very, very soon," he
said after he examined her. "In the next day or
two." She was a week late by then. "I want you to
have a test to check the amniotic fluid tomorrow.
We won't let you go much longer. If you haven't
gone into labor in a few days, we'll induce," he said
with a smile.

"I feel like an elephant," she complained, as he
helped her off the table. "I've been working, and I
walk miles every day."

"It'll be very soon," he assured her, and glanced
at Caro, as he always did. She had been staunch to
the end, and had been to every office visit with her
sister. "One way or the other, it won't be more than
a few days." The wait seemed interminable to Annabelle, and it even seemed long to Caro now. Annabelle was ready to get the ordeal over with.

They walked for a few blocks after they left his

office. But Annabelle was tired and couldn't go far. They took a cab the rest of the way home, and Annabelle could hardly make it up the front steps without Caro's help.

Caro had just taken her keys out and was opening the front door when there was a splash of water on the ground between Annabelle's feet. She looked down in surprise.

"Oh," she said, and looked at her sister, and Caro looked at her. "I think my water just broke." It was a pool at her feet, as Caro went to get a towel to wrap around her and led her inside. She left a trail across the black-and-white marble floor in the front hall.

"I'll call Dr. Kelly," Caro said, and Annabelle started up the staircase to her room, and turned to look at her.

"I'm scared," she whispered.

"It's going to be fine, and it'll all be over soon. It may not start for a while." Annabelle wasn't having contractions yet, other than the practice ones she'd had for weeks.

Annabelle went upstairs to lie down, and Caro called Dr. Kelly on the cell phone number he'd given them. "Labor should start in the next few hours," he reminded her. "Call me when it does. The baby's big and we may need to do a C-section. I didn't want to worry her. We'll try not to."

"Can I stay with her if you do?"

"Yes, we set up a drape so you can't see anything. And she won't feel anything except some pulling and pressure." It sounded unpleasant to Caro.

She went upstairs to check on Annabelle after that. "Nothing happening?" Annabelle shook her head.

"This baby doesn't want to come out." She lay on her bed, looking frustrated, and got up to take a shower, and then the first pain hit her, like a wrecking ball. It was stronger than she had expected. It knocked the wind out of her, and she couldn't talk while she had it. Caroline looked at her watch so she could time the next one, and sat down in a chair. The next one was seven minutes later. The baby was in no hurry. But things had finally started. Sometime that day or night, the baby would be born. Annabelle was looking at her with wide eyes, and her face was pale. "I'm never doing this again," she said to her sister. But Caro knew she would, hopefully with the right man next time.

Annabelle went to take a shower then, and Caro called Charlie to tell him she wasn't coming to the office. He was excited to hear it. And Caro had a feeling they had a long day and night ahead.

Chapter 15

The contractions stayed six minutes apart for two hours, and then stopped for a while. Then they went to five. Dr. Kelly said to come in at four minutes, and reminded them that first babies could take a long time. The others were all coming home from work when Caro and Annabelle left for the hospital. They waved and wished Annabelle luck when she and Caro got in a cab. The hospital wasn't far, at the East River.

Caro called the Hills, the adoptive parents, before she and Annabelle went to the hospital. They said they were going to leave right away, so they didn't miss it, but Caro assured them they had time.

Annabelle had preregistered, so they went straight to the labor and delivery floor, where they admitted her and took her to a labor room. They handed Caro a blue cap and gown to put on, and paper slippers to wear over her shoes. Annabelle grinned when she saw her.

"You look silly," Annabelle said, in a gown by then too. A nurse came in to examine her, and she cried out and said it hurt when she did.

"You're at three centimeters," she told Annabelle. "It's still early." She had to get to ten. It was still early labor, although the contractions were painful and she'd been in labor all day. By nine o'clock that night, she was at five centimeters. The baby was in no hurry. She was at seven at midnight, and things started to get rough. She was in real labor then, the contractions were fierce and she was throwing up. Caro was giving her ice chips, and Annabelle was in terrible pain with each contraction. Dr. Kelly appeared then. After a few more contractions, he said she was ready for an epidural, and she wouldn't feel anything after that. Annabelle was crying and clutching Caro's hand. The anesthesiologist came a few minutes later and Caro had to leave the room.

She didn't see the Hills outside the room, but she knew they were there somewhere. It had been a long night for them too, but not as long as for Annabelle. She looked peaceful when they let Caro back in the room. She could see on the monitor that the contractions had gotten longer and harder, but she wasn't feeling them now. At two in the morning, the nurse said she was finally at ten centimeters and could start pushing. She had been in the hospital for eight hours by then. It felt like a lifetime to Caro and Annabelle. Dr. Kelly came back in the room then. He had come in and out since he'd first arrived. They put her feet in stirrups and removed the lower half of the bed. The contractions had slowed down slightly from the epidural, so they reduced its strength and Annabelle could feel the contractions again.

"This is so awful," she said to Caro, and looked miserable, while Caroline worried about her. It seemed like such a brutal process, especially for a baby she would never see again afterwards and would never know.

Dr. Kelly checked her again then, and he and two nurses were telling Annabelle to push. She was, and nothing happened. The baby was big, and after two hours of pushing she was exhausted. They put an oxygen mask on her, and she squeezed Caro's hand. The contractions looked like the Grand Tetons on the monitor. There was an additional monitor for the fetal heartbeat, which Dr. Kelly said was fine. The baby wasn't in distress. Annabelle looked like she was. She and Caro were both wishing that their mother was there but they didn't say it. And Caro never left her for a minute. She took an occasional sip of water, and never left her sister's side.

After another hour of pushing, one of the nurses was applying pressure to move the baby downward, and then things started moving at a brisk

pace. A Lucite bassinet was brought into the room
by a pediatric nurse, and a pediatrician was in the
room to check the baby. It seemed like a hopeful
sign that the baby would be there soon. Caro
glanced up at a clock in the room and saw that it
was five-thirty in the morning. She wasn't even
tired, from the adrenaline of wanting to help Annabelle, but there was nothing she could do, except
hold her hand and encourage her.

Annabelle pushed two or three more times but
nothing happened, and Dr. Kelly spoke to her quietly, after glancing at Caro. "Annabelle, I want you
to give us two or three more pushes, great big ones,
and if the baby doesn't move down, we're going to
help you and give you a C-section." She was getting
too tired to push, and the fetal monitor gave an occasional little irregular beep. The baby was getting
tired too.

"I don't want a C-section." She was crying.

"Let's see how it goes." She gave two huge
pushes and there was a slight shift. Another push
and she was crying all the time and looked nearly
unconscious between pushes. Caro could see that
the doctor was doing something, an episiotomy
and applying forceps, and then suddenly everything happened quickly. Annabelle gave a horren-
dous scream, and another push, and suddenly there
was a wail in the room. The baby was out, and the
nurse handed him to the pediatrician to check him.
Annabelle lay limp and looked up at Caro as though

she'd been crucified. And she had been. It was six in the morning and she had done a hard night's work. Caro was still holding her hand, and Annabelle looked half dead.

"Is he okay?" She lifted her head to ask, and the nurse said he was fine, while the doctor delivered the placenta and sewed up the episiotomy. Dr. Kelly said something to one of the nurses. "Can I see him?" Annabelle asked. She had originally said she didn't want to, but it had been so grueling she wanted to now, to make sure he was all right.

"Nine pounds, six ounces," the nurse who had weighed him said, and they brought him over wrapped tightly in a blue blanket. He had a face like a cherub, round cheeks, and he was glancing around, as though he was looking for his mother.

"Can I hold him?"

Dr. Kelly exchanged a look with Caro, and the nurse put the baby on the bed next to Annabelle where she could see him, with the crib sides up so he was safe. He gazed up at Annabelle, and stared at her, and she was smiling and crying as she held him. Dr. Kelly spoke to her gently. "Would you like us to take him to the adoptive parents now? They're outside waiting." He didn't want to push her, just remind her.

Annabelle looked from him to Caro, and she was crying when she spoke to her sister in a whisper. "I want to keep him. I'll do whatever I have to . . . I can't give him away, Caro . . . I love him."

"You don't have to give him away," Caro said, and bent down to kiss her sister. "You're such a brave girl." Caro felt sorry for the couple who wanted him, but if Annabelle wanted to keep him, it was better this way, and the family would help her. They'd all manage somehow. Annabelle was holding the baby, and a nurse lifted him gently and put him to her breast, as Caro looked at Dr. Kelly.

"Should I go and talk to the Hills?" she asked him.

"We'll handle it. I'll go talk to them. These things happen. Better now than in a few weeks when they've grown attached to him." Annabelle had been through so much that Caro couldn't imagine her giving the baby up now on top of it. She'd been through her trial by fire to have him.

Ted Kelly left the room, and came back a little while later. Annabelle had been given a shot and was dozing, and the baby was in the bassinet with a nurse checking him.

"How were they?" Caro asked him in a whisper.

"They were very nice about it. They're kind people. They understand. It happens this way sometimes. You must be exhausted," he said. Between the emotions, and the whole night on her feet, she had been through a lot too, worried about her sister.

"I'm okay. I'm glad she's keeping him. It would

have been awful for her, giving him up. She's young, and we're here to help her figure it out."

"She's lucky," he said, and left to do some paperwork and fill out forms. They took Annabelle to a room then, and rolled a cot in for Caro, and she went out to the hall to call Charlie. The Hills had left by then. The sky was streaked with pink and orange and the day was dawning. Charlie answered immediately in a deep sleepy voice.

"You have a nephew. Nine pounds, six ounces." She sounded exhausted.

"How is she?"

"She was very brave. I'm never having kids," Caro said, and he laughed.

"Are the people there? The parents?"

"She's keeping him," she said, and he was quiet for a minute.

"I'm glad. It's the right thing. We'll manage."

"So will she. She grew up tonight." She had been for months. It had been a rite of passage into adulthood.

"I'll come to see her later. We all will," Charlie said.

"She's going to feel pretty rocky, so you shouldn't stay long."

"We won't. Get some sleep."

Annabelle was sound asleep when Caro got back to the room, and the baby was in the nursery. Caro lay on the cot with a pillow and a blanket, and she fell asleep too. Dr. Kelly came back to check on them. He left a few minutes later and gently closed the door behind him.

Annabelle was awake when Caro woke up, rolled over, and looked at her. She was smiling. She looked tired, but happy.

"How do you feel?" Caro asked her.

"Like a mother. He's so beautiful. I feel sorry for the Hills."

"They'll get another baby. You should have yours."

Annabelle nodded. "Thank you for being there. I'm going to call him Preston after Dad. He'd love that."

A nurse brought the baby in a little while later and showed Annabelle how to nurse him.

Caro left then to go home, shower, and change.

The others were all at breakfast when she got there. They cheered when they saw her, and wanted to know how Annabelle was, and the baby. She didn't tell them how it had really been, just the good news that he was healthy and Annabelle was fine, and that she was naming him after their dad.

Lyle had called Gloria, so she knew. And they were all planning to visit Annabelle that afternoon.

"Keep it short," Caro reminded everyone.

*   *   *

They all went to see her later that day, with flowers and balloons, crowding into the room, Lyle and Charlie and Benjie, and Gloria with Giorgio. They were inseparable. He'd brought a pale blue cashmere Hermès blanket for the baby. Gloria had on her stern face of disapproval, and had come empty-handed. They'd been told that Annabelle was keeping the baby, and Gloria approached the bassinet with caution, and stared down at him. She was frowning, ready to be critical of his very existence. Then she bent down to see him more closely as the others chatted with Annabelle and congratulated her.

Caro saw Gloria touch his face with a finger, and Gloria smiled at him, and she was still smiling when she stood up after her initial inspection.

"He looks just like Dad." Caro didn't think so, but Gloria did.

"I think he smiled. He's huge." Suddenly, Annabelle had produced a miracle. Annabelle asked Gloria if she'd like to hold him and she nodded and sat down so Caro could put the baby in her arms. Benjie stared at him, fascinated. Giorgio took photographs of Gloria holding the baby and told her how beautiful she looked with a baby in her arms, like a madonna. And for the first time, Caro could imagine Gloria with a child of her own. Baby Preston had brought his own magic with him, which touched them all. Benjie said he had a gift for him, that he'd give him when he got home.

They left as they had arrived, like a summer storm, loving but exhausting, and Caro stayed to help Annabelle for a little while and then went home. She was still tired.

Annabelle was a lot younger and on a euphoric high from the baby she'd given birth to. There was no sign of the agony of the night before. It really was a miracle, like magic. And Gloria was showing everyone the pictures Giorgio had taken of her holding him. No baby had ever been more welcome, despite the circumstances of his birth.

Charlie and Caro went to pick up Annabelle and the baby at the hospital the next day. They had had to rush around buying all the things she didn't have since she hadn't planned to bring him home with her. She needed a bassinet for him to sleep in, clothes, diapers, a car seat so he could leave the hospital. Gloria bought the fanciest stroller she could find, and said she was going to take him on walks in the park on weekends. While a nurse taught Annabelle how to change and dress him, Caro waited in the hall with Charlie. He went to get the car just as Ted Kelly arrived to discharge Annabelle. He stopped to talk to Caro for a minute.

"I hope you got some rest. You've been amazing with her for all these months. It's rare to see that kind of support these days." He admired her a lot and had been biding his time.

"That's what big sisters are for." She smiled.

"I've been wanting to ask you something for months. I didn't think it was appropriate till after the baby came." She had no idea what it was. "Would you have dinner with me sometime?" She was stunned.

"Really?" He laughed at her reaction.

"Yes, really. You truly are an incredible person, and I'd like to get to know you."

"Thank you, yes . . . sure." She was embarrassed but touched. She liked him, and had since they met. He had a warm, easy, straightforward, intelligent style.

"I'd like to meet the rest of your family too. They must be quite something."

"They are," she said proudly. "A little wacky, slightly crazy, and really terrific. I'll invite you to dinner with them sometime."

"I'll call you. Dinner, the two of us first." He sounded very definite and looked pleased. They went into Annabelle's room together then. She was dressed and the baby was asleep in a little blue outfit and matching blanket Caro had brought. He was a beautiful baby.

Ted Kelly walked them downstairs, a nurse's aide wheeled Annabelle in a wheelchair holding the baby, and Charlie was waiting for them in the car, with the car seat strapped in. The nurse helped them get the baby into it, and Caro introduced the doctor to her twin. Charlie looked slightly flustered by the mechanics of the car seat, and Annabelle sat in the backseat next to the baby, who was sound asleep. She was totally unprepared for whatever came next, and she would have to learn it all now.

Caro got into the car and before they pulled away, Ted said, "See you soon," to Caro, and she waved as they left.

"See you soon?" Charlie looked at her. "What does that mean? Are you having a baby?" He could guess what it meant from the look on the doctor's face and his sister's.

"He invited me to dinner." She grinned at him.

"Oh my God, you're shameless. Your sister has a baby and you hit on the doctor." Annabelle was laughing in the backseat.

"I told you he liked you," she said smugly.

"Yeah, maybe he does. I like him too. He said he waited till you had the baby to ask me out."

"Very proper." Charlie approved. He was a stickler for rules and manners. The others were waiting for them when they got home, with blue balloons, and all the clothes and equipment they had bought that Annabelle didn't have for him. Brady was there too, waiting for Charlie, and Devon and Tommy wanted to see the baby, and thought he was adorable. Gloria was coming over with the stroller that afternoon. And Benjie presented him with a live white bunny from the shelter. It was a miniature and just a baby.

"I'll take care of it for him till he's older," Benjie

explained. Annabelle thanked him and hugged him, and said the baby was going to love it.

It took Annabelle several hours to settle in and get organized. All the baby's things were in piles and gift boxes around her room. She needed a new chest to put them in. Her milk hadn't come in yet, but she was nursing him for the nutrients he was getting, and so they'd get used to each other. Caro poked her head in from time to time to see how she was. Annabelle looked tired and happy and a little dazed.

"Your family is amazing," Brady said to Charlie. "Whatever happens, they're there for each other and roll with the punches and just turn it around and make it great."

"Not always, but we try." Charlie smiled.

"It must be fantastic to have a family like that."

"It's pretty good," Charlie acknowledged. "It works, most of the time."

Daphne Dawson came over that afternoon too, to see Lyle and the children, and the new baby. She stayed for dinner, as she often did now. The children liked her and she had a gentle way with them. The four of them had fun together. She was always full of good ideas for things to do with the children. Lyle's divorce would be final in September, and the financial details were almost worked out and finalized. Amanda had done well for herself, and Lyle had made his peace with it. She didn't get any of his inheritance, but a big chunk of everything else. And when she found out about Daphne, she tried to poison the children against her, but it hadn't worked so far. She was busy with her new boyfriend with the plane. She was about to put their apartment on the market, and upgrade. And best of all, Tommy and Devon loved staying at the house with their father.

Annabelle brought the baby down to dinner in a Moses basket that night. She put it on a chair next to her so she could keep an eye on him, and Devon handed her the tiny diapers when she changed him. It was like dressing a doll. Gloria and Giorgio stayed for dinner, and Gloria stared at the baby in wonder. No one would have guessed that she had been opposed to his arrival in every way before that. But Annabelle was a kind person and forgave her for it. The baby had brought with him forgiveness and love, and hope for the future. He was the personification of love. Annabelle had written a letter to the Hills to apologize to them, and hoped they'd find another baby to adopt soon.

Dinner was as chaotic as always, maybe even a little more so. Caro wondered how Ted Kelly would take to it. Giorgio and Daphne and Brady had gotten used to the family and were good additions to the mix. The Whittiers were an overwhelming group at times, with good hearts and sharp minds, and now Baby Preston was one of them. The newest member of the family had arrived and was home with all the others. He had turned out to be a gift and a blessing, warmly welcomed despite a bumpy start. Annabelle glowed every time she looked at him. She had crossed the bridge from childhood to adulthood in a single night. She was a mother now, with the example of her own mother to follow, as her role model. The legacy Connie had left them would last forever in their memories, and their hearts.

Chapter 16

Ted Kelly waited two weeks before he called Caro. He wanted to give her time for the baby to settle in, so she would feel free to go out with him. He called her on the number she'd given him when she was the contact person for her sister. He had an office number for her too, but didn't want to disturb her at work. He invited her to dinner on Friday night, since he said he'd be on call for the rest of the weekend, and didn't want to get called away in the middle of dinner, and most likely would be. She accepted with pleasure. She was staying close to home to help Annabelle, who was coping surprisingly well, and so far the baby had been easy. Annabelle was still tired after his arrival, but Ted had told her that was normal at her postpartum visit. She was young and would bounce back quickly. And there were lots of hands to help her at home. Frieda babysat for her when she wanted to get out between feedings. Nursing was turning out to be a full-time job, and little Preston had a healthy appetite. Everything was new to her since she had taken no prenatal classes. She was planning to go back to work for Caroline and Charlie at the end of August, before Fashion Week in September. Frieda had a niece who was going to come in and help. Caro had arranged it all.

When Ted came to pick her up for dinner, there was chaos in the house, more than usual. Tommy was leaving for camp the next day, and his trunk and duffle bags were in the front hall. Devon was wearing little pink shorts she had worn to day camp and was running after Duke, yelling at him. He had taken one of her Barbie dolls, which he loved to do. He didn't hurt them, he just piled them up in his bed, where she reclaimed them.

Rose was due any minute for dinner with Benjie, and he was dressed and waiting for her at the front door. They were going to watch a movie afterwards. Daphne was sitting on the floor next to Tommy's duffle bags, sewing in the last of his name tapes to help Lyle. Amanda had already left for a month in Europe, leaving all the camp preparations to Lyle. She was in the process of buying a shockingly expensive apartment in Tribeca in a building with a gym, a swimming pool, and a doorman. Tommy and Devon said it was nice, but they liked being at the house with their dad better, and they didn't like Amanda's boyfriend. They said he was stuck-up and never talked to them, just their mom.

Charlie and Brady were in the kitchen cooking dinner for everyone, before they left for Brady's timeshare in the Hamptons later that night. Giorgio was cooking pasta carbonara as part of the menu and showing them how to do it, perfectly al dente, and Gloria was holding Preston, asleep in her arms, while Annabelle took a shower. She said she never had time to get out of her nightgown between feedings.

Caro was just coming down the stairs in a white pique summer dress with gold sandals and big hoop earrings when the doorbell rang. Benjie answered it since he was closest, waiting for Rose to arrive. He looked surprised when he saw someone he didn't know. Ted got a glimpse of the chaos inside and smiled at him and held out a hand.

"Hi, I'm Ted. I'm here for Caroline," he said properly. It reminded him of picking girls up at their dorm when he was in college.

"I'm Benjie. I thought you were Rose. Her mom is going to drop her off. She's my girlfriend." Ted nodded, followed him inside, and saw Lyle and Daphne on the floor with Tommy's camp bags, as Duke ran past them with the stolen doll. "That's my dog," Benjie explained. "His name is Duke, he's a Great Dane. He lost an ear in a dogfight. I adopted him. My other dog is Dottie." Ted spotted Caroline coming down the stairs then, and smiled at her. She

introduced him to Lyle and Daphne, who apologized for the mess they were making with Tommy's
camp gear. Lyle stood up and shook hands with
him, and Daphne apologized for not doing so. Gloria watched the scene as she held the baby, and
waved hello.

"Let's get out of here," Caro said, grinning, "before someone asks us to babysit or feed the dogs."
The doorbell rang and Rose arrived while they
were talking. She was wearing a pink cotton summer dress and looked very pretty. Benjie kissed her
and introduced her to Ted proudly.

"This is Rose, my girlfriend. We met at the gym,"
he explained. Ted looked amused by the scene
around him, and not in the least put off by it. Annabelle appeared then, looking beautiful in skin-
tight jeans and a white men's shirt. Two weeks after
delivery, she was as thin as ever.

"Hi, Dr. Kelly. Did you come for dinner?" She
was happy to see him, and Caro guided him toward
the door.

"No, we're going *out* to dinner," Caro said. "We're
trying to escape."

"You're welcome to stay," Gloria said, as she
handed Preston to Annabelle. "My boyfriend is
making pasta carbonara. He's Italian and a fabulous chef. I'm Gloria, Caroline's older sister, by the
way," she said, shaking hands with him. The couple
had almost made it to the front door but not quite,
as Benjie and Rose disappeared to the kitchen, with

the dogs after them, and Lyle handed Daphne a stack of towels he'd just discovered that still needed labels.

Caro and Ted made a rapid escape out the front door, and Caro closed it firmly behind them. "Run before they come out and grab us," she said to him, as they walked down the front steps, and he hailed a passing cab. He was taking her to his favorite little French restaurant, near where he lived, close to the hospital. "I'm sorry. It's like visiting an asylum. There's no way to look cool and sophisticated with all that going on. My family is crazy, but I love them."

"They look like they're good crazy," he said after giving the driver the address they were going to. "They all seem like such nice people." She nodded agreement, and then looked at him slightly more seriously.

"Thank you for being nice to Benjie. He's very excited about his girlfriend, his first, and his dogs. Duke is a little exuberant. At least he didn't knock you down."

"I have a sister like Rose and Benjie," he said simply. "She lives with my mom in San Francisco. She leads a pretty quiet life. I think Benjie is having a lot more fun than she is. It's hard for them to find friends and have a social life. It looks like Benjie's is built-in. He's lucky he met Rose. Do you like her?"

"Very much. She's a sweet girl, and her parents are very nice. It's a little dicey keeping an eye on them. They're like kids, and then suddenly they're adults and can get into situations a little over their heads," she said discreetly. "They met pretty recently."

"How old is Benjie?"

"He's twenty-eight, he'll be twenty-nine soon. My mom was great with him, it's been a big adjustment for him since she's gone. I try to step in, but I can't fill her shoes."

"You seem to be doing fine. My sister Francine is thirty-five. She has a job at a gift shop. She loves it, but it's kind of a lonely life for her, with my mom."

"Benjie works at a pet shelter, that's how we got Duke and Dottie. He's terrific with the animals. He would have made a great vet." She liked that Ted wasn't put off or surprised by Benjie. He could be very direct at times, with no filter to what he said, but the behavior was familiar to Ted. He had recognized it immediately, and he could see that Benjie was happy and having a good life. He always wished he could do more for his sister. But he lived far away and only saw her now a few times a year. Sometimes he felt guilty for living in New York, but he loved it, and the practice that he worked for. He had leapt at the job when they offered it to him. "You're from San Francisco?" Caro asked him on the way to the restaurant.

"Yes. I went to medical school at NYU, and never left. There's so much more to do in New York. San

Francisco is a sleepy little town. You're lucky you have your family here."

"Sometimes," she said, and they both laughed. "We haven't all lived together like this in years, but it's turned out to be really nice, better than I expected. Charlie, my twin, moved in for Benjie. Then I moved back to keep an eye on Annabelle. Lyle split with his wife, so he moved in temporarily and brought his kids. Total chaos, but nice."

"I wasn't sure if Daphne is his wife. She seems very pleasant." They chatted on the way to the restaurant.

"She's a social worker who came to investigate us when his ex-wife filed a report with the ACS that we were, in her words, 'living like gypsies.' She did it to make trouble for him. Daphne is a vast improvement. Lyle is going to get his own place in the fall. And we can't hang on to the house forever," she said with a sigh. "It works for now. Eventually we'll all have places of our own again."

"It looks like it's working extremely well. Annabelle is lucky she has all of you to help her with the baby."

"We want her to go back to school. She probably won't now." They got to the restaurant then. It was small and charming, run by a young French couple, with real French food. It was delicious and it was quiet so they could talk. He had chosen well.

He asked her how she had gotten into fashion. "It was always my dream, and Charlie's. He loves the business side of it. We just took in a partner, from Milan. They run the best textile mills in Italy. It's going to make a big difference in our business now. We can really grow the business."

"What do you do for fun?" he asked her.

"Work." She laughed. "It's all I do. It's kind of a passion for me. And take care of my family, especially for the past six months. My parents took care of that before. Or my mom did. Annabelle and Benjie still need some help. Everyone else is grown up. And Lyle needed a hand with the kids with the divorce."

"I work a lot too," he confessed. "Medicine is my passion, and I love OB. It's exciting every time a baby is born. There's always a story, something special about every mom and every baby. It never gets boring, and it can be incredibly challenging. I'm glad Annabelle kept the baby."

"So are we. My sister Gloria was awful to her about it, but now she's fallen in love with the baby and she acts like it was her idea. It's funny. I've never been dying for a baby. I love my work too much and it would interfere. I'd probably be a bad mother, always at work."

"You're already a great mom from what I've seen with your sister. And it's a lot harder mothering an adult, especially in her circumstances."

"I tried to do what I thought my mother would have, although I wasn't too happy about Annabelle's situation either."

"I see a lot of women like you, who've focused on their careers, don't think they want a baby, and when it happens, they fall in love with it. There's something magical about motherhood and babies." It was obvious that he loved his work too. It made him a happy person who was nice to be with. He had no axe to grind.

"I'll take your word for it," Caro said. "I'm not ready for that kind of magic in my life yet." He laughed and then looked at her seriously.

"And what about relationship magic? Do you have time for that?" he wondered. She had a very full life, and a lot of responsibilities. She hesitated before she answered.

"I don't know. I've never really tried, or had a long-term relationship. It's hard when you're committed to your career. Whenever I've dated, someone was always mad at me for what I wasn't around for or couldn't do. Work is a priority for me, and I don't like disappointing people or getting yelled at, or being the bad girl or girlfriend or wife."

"I'll keep that in mind. No yelling when you have to work."

She smiled, but it was true. "Our industry is crazy all the time, deadlines, new collections, crises every day with production failures, lost fabrics, bad reviews. And twice a year it gets even crazier with Fashion Week, which is really fashion month, with weeks to prepare a show, and then sales afterwards. I start sketching the next collection the day after a show." She was warning him, if he really wanted to go out with her, she wanted him to know what he was in for. "It's a mad business but I love it." Her eyes lit up when she said it. He could see that she did.

"Sometimes I deliver three babies a night, or even four, or don't come home for two days. It works well in a practice like ours, with lots of backup, but things happen you can't predict, and sometimes it's serious when things go wrong. That's the dark side of OB. Most of the time it's a happy event when you hear that first cry. At other times, it's a tragedy. I don't leave then." He was warning her too. "And for me, it's all year round, not seasonal, although there are busier times. The end of September is always nuts for us. If you count backwards, it's everyone who went to a party or celebrated the holidays, had a lot to drink and a good time, and in January I have a whole new flock of OB patients. The holidays are good for business nine months later," he said, and she laughed.

"I never thought of that. I'll be careful over the holidays from now on." They had covered a lot of ground by the time they left the restaurant, and walked for a while on a warm night.

"I love the way you dress," he said randomly, "you always look so chic."

"Thank you. You should see me when I'm doing a fashion show. I look like I was shipwrecked. We work twenty-four hours straight sometimes. Kind of like you, but for a less noble cause. I loved that you didn't leave while Annabelle was in labor. You hear a lot of different stories about deliveries, some not so good. Not all doctors care as much as you do."

"I like my patients. That helps. It's not just a job." He loved the fact that they were both passionate about their work. It seemed like a fair exchange. "So do we do this again?" he asked her as they wandered slowly west.

"I'd like that," she said in a soft voice.

"So would I." He smiled at her, and they walked all the way back to her house, which was about a mile. When they got there, she didn't invite him in. It was eleven o'clock and the house had usually settled down by then, but it might not have and she liked the peaceful feeling the evening was ending on. He was even nicer than she'd thought, and they had many interests in common, travel, theater, books, art, although they had little time to pursue them. But at least the interest was there. He loved sailing, and the ocean, and she did too. He had gone to sailing camp in Washington State as a boy, she had gone to Maine every summer with her parents and siblings. Her father was a great sailor, although her mother got seasick and never left the shore. Once in a while she went out on a boat with them, was green the entire time, and swore she'd never do it again.

The family had loved to tease her about it. Caro

and all of her siblings still loved to sail, and so did Ted. He'd had a small boat he took out on the San Francisco Bay when he was in college. He said it was always freezing.

"I had a terrific evening," he said, as they stood outside her house. He could just imagine the various scenes inside. They were like a TV show, with half a dozen episodes happening at once.

"So did I," she said warmly, and took out her key.

"I'll call you next week. I'm working a couple of long shifts over the weekend, but I'm free next Sunday night."

"Maybe you'd want to come to dinner. We usually cook together on Sunday night for whoever is around."

"It sounds like fun." He realized maybe more than she did that her warm, highly populated family life was probably what fueled her for the hard work in her career, and why she hadn't missed having a relationship. Her life was filled to the brim with people who loved her. It shone in her eyes, and she had unlimited love to give as a result. "I'll call you," he promised. He didn't try to kiss her, he didn't want to spoil the evening or scare her off. There was no rush. He had waited five months to ask her out, and neither of them was going anywhere, except to work.

*   *   *

Charlie asked her about her date on Monday when she saw him at the office. He had stayed at Brady's apartment on Sunday night when they got back from the Hamptons. Caro was trying to adjust to seeing less of him. She wanted him to be happy, and Brady was a good person. They were a good match, but Charlie had less time for her now, which was inevitable in adult lives, even if they were twins. He had spoiled her with his full attention for a long time.

"How was your date?" he asked, and she smiled.

"He's really nice."

"How really nice? Wow, fantastic really nice, you can't wait to see him again? Or really nice, let's be friends, see you next year?"

"More like the first one. He's busy too. Neither of us has a lot of time to see each other," she said.

"That's bullshit. Brady and I are busy too. You make time if you want to."

"I think he said something like that too."

"How old is he?"

"Thirty-nine. He told me at dinner."

"He has a lot of busy years of work ahead of him, and so do you. I think forty is when people wake up, and realize they don't have a life and they'd better make one. Like Gloria, with Giorgio. Speaking of whom, two of his brothers are coming in next week and want to meet us. We should take them to dinner." She nodded. "And I think they're all coming to our show in September. We're a big deal to them now."

"They're a big deal to us," Caro said gratefully.

"I'm going to spend two weeks in the Hamptons with Brady in August, but I can come in whenever you want me to." They had given up the idea of Turkey or Greece.

"I won't get crazy with the show till about the third week in August. Everything is pretty well on track. And maybe now we'll have an in to get our fabrics from Italy on time."

"I thought of that too. Gloria is spending the whole month with Giorgio in Sardinia, and a few days in Milan on the way back." Her whole life had changed in a few months. Caro loved the way life did that sometimes. A spin of the dial, a new person, new job, new city, new life, and suddenly all your dreams came true. It didn't happen often, but when it did, it was terrific. Gloria had blossomed from a tough, fairly rigid, hard, judgmental businesswoman into a warmer person, and a woman who was deeply in love with her man. The twins both loved to see it. Caro loved who Gloria had become, thanks to Giorgio. And she loved seeing Lyle having fun with Daphne. She was easy and uncomplicated and nice to him, not like Amanda, who had made him miserable for years, and had married him to use him.

*   *   *

The house was noticeably quieter once Tommy left for camp. Devon was going to day camp six days a week and loved it. Annabelle was managing well with the baby.

Gloria was at the house constantly now, helping with her nephew. Rose was on a trip to Wyoming with her parents, so Benjie was bored. They talked on the phone several times a day.

Brady and Charlie invited Caro to the Hamptons for a weekend. She went and had fun. They played a lot of tennis, swam, went surfing. Brady introduced Charlie to his friends, and they broadened and enriched each other's lives. She could see why Charlie loved him. Brady was a man of principles and good values, like Charlie.

Ted came to Sunday night dinner for his second date with Caro, and he managed the barrage of questions, people, Giorgio's delicious pesto pasta, and Benjie's dogs, and wound up holding Annabelle's baby while she and Caro served the meal the boys had cooked. They were all good cooks. Lyle told Caro afterwards that if dinner with the family was a test, Ted had passed with flying colors. He was nice to everyone, kind to Benjie, interesting to talk to, and fun when Lyle turned on their old jukebox and they danced after dinner.

Ted was a good sport, and he seemed to be crazy about Caro, and never took his eyes off her. It intrigued him too to see how well the partners fit in. The family welcomed them, and then their own charms and talents took over, and they earned their place among the others. They were freely given the chance to show their stuff. Ted really enjoyed talking to Lyle, and Giorgio added a splash of real color, telling outrageous stories about his family, gesticulating enthusiastically, and cooking fabulous pasta. He explained many things about the fashion industry that Ted found interesting. It was a serious business, and his respect for Caro grew as he learned more about it, and how talented she was. Giorgio said she was a genius, and so was her twin. Annabelle said she loved working for them, and hadn't thought she would. She was excited about going back in a month. She was going to stop nursing when she did. Six weeks of intense motherhood was enough. At first, she thought of staying home and nursing him for a year, but changed her mind. At twenty-one, she needed more in her life, although she loved the baby now too, more than she'd ever expected to. Everything about him was a surprise.

Ted had a week's holiday coming to him from his practice, and he flew to San Francisco to see his mother and sister. The relationship with Caro had heated up by then. They were having dinner twice a week, and kissing on the doorstep when they got home, and when he got back from San Francisco, he invited her away to spend a weekend with him. He took her to a little inn he knew on a beautiful beach on Long Island. It was next to a gated community, so the beach wasn't crowded, and he rented a small boat for them to sail. It was a perfect weekend, like a honeymoon. He organized everything. All she had to do was show up with her suitcase and a bathing suit. The rest was a surprise. Caro wasn't used to having anyone take care of her. She always took care of everyone else, at home and in the office. Ted took care of her, and as soon as they got to the hotel on Friday night, they made love, with a view of the ocean, and a splendid lobster dinner afterwards. It was everything she could have hoped for. They lay on the beach in the sun, took the little sailboat out, and sunbathed naked next to each other, at anchor, and then went back to the hotel and made love again. They couldn't get enough of each other.

"If I'd known it would be anything like this, I would have asked you out the first time I laid eyes on you. I wanted to," he said, smiling at her, as they lay in bed and he kissed her, and she stretched out the length of him, pressed against him. She had a beautiful body and he loved watching her.

Making love changed things between them. They felt closer and more at ease, shared the secrets of their youth, and their dreams for the future. They felt like a unit, one bigger whole than two separate parts, when they went back to the city, and she suddenly understood what Charlie felt for Brady. It didn't take away from what they shared as twins, but it added something more, a whole new dimension that she shared with Ted now. The weekend had woven them together, and added something special to both of them. He spent the night with her at the house on Sunday night, and felt mildly uncomfortable the next morning at breakfast, drinking a cup of coffee, when Lyle and Devon walked in, before she left for day camp. She chatted with Ted while Lyle made pancakes for her, and Caro made eggs for Ted. Annabelle came down with the baby, and Benjie wandered in with the dogs and Caro made eggs for him too, as Lyle handed Ted the paper. It was a little bit like living in a hotel, or a boarding school. Once he got over the initial adjustment, he discovered that he liked it.

"Sorry to horn in on your breakfast," Lyle said as he sat down next to him, and Devon chatted with Benjie.

"It's actually kind of fun." Ted grinned at him. It added a dose of reality to their romance.

"It was wonderful when we were growing up. Our mother made every day an adventure. It's hard for outsiders to understand sometimes. My ex-wife hated it. She said it was like enlisting in the Navy. There's a bit of that too."

"My father died when I was sixteen," Ted said. "I grew up alone with my mother and my sister, who's like Benjie. It was always quiet in our house. And lonely. My mother never really recovered from my father's death, and my sister isn't as outgoing as Benjie. This is like a buffet of life and people and experiences. There's always someone to talk to or meet, and you make the 'outsiders,' as you call them, feel so welcome."

"That's because you're a good person and we like you, and you're nice to my sister. If you were an asshole, we'd be mean to you," Lyle said, and Ted laughed, and leaned over and kissed Caro in front of all of them. The weekend together had made them more open about their feelings.

Ted and Caro left the house together. He followed her down the front steps, stopped her when they reached the street, and pulled her into his arms. "In case I forgot to tell you, Caroline Whittier, I love you." He hadn't said those words to her before. "And I love your family too."

"Wow . . . I love you too." She smiled up at him. "I wish you could have met my mom and dad."

"I have," he said, holding her, "through all of you. Now go work your ass off. I'll call you later. See you tonight?" She nodded at him and waved as they got into separate cabs to do what they did every day and loved. Their being together gave new meaning to their lives. And this was only the beginning.

"Good weekend?" Charlie asked her when she got to the office. She couldn't stop smiling, thinking of Ted.

"The best." And then they got to work in earnest, together, doing what they loved most.

Chapter 17

Annabelle came back to work in the last week of August, and hit the ground running. Fashion Week was due to start the day after Labor Day and Caro had a million things for her to do. Their fabrics had come in on time, thanks to Giorgio. He was still on vacation in Sardinia with Gloria. He had a yacht he kept there in Porto Cervo. Caro had spoken to Gloria several times. She said she was in heaven. She and Giorgio were due back in New York right before Labor Day weekend. Their romance seemed to have flourished over the summer.

Annabelle was thrilled to be working again, and to come home to the baby at night. He was sleeping in her bedroom, and she gave him his night feedings since she was gone all day. Frieda and her niece took care of him when she was at work.

Caro offered her a permanent job as soon as she

got back to work, as a personal assistant, at a very respectable salary, and Annabelle looked at her with regret.

"I'd love to do it, but I can't stay. I'm going back to school in January. I'll work for you till then if you want me, but I go back after Christmas for my last semester. But I'd love to come back after I graduate in June, if you'll let me." Caro was relieved to hear it for her sister's sake, and it was the right thing for her to do, and she would be happy to have her back as an assistant after she graduated. Annabelle smiled at Caro. "I'm all yours for now. And I'll only be at school for five months."

"Then get your ass to work," Caro said to her, and she hurried off with her assignments.

Ted got a front-row seat to what Caro's life looked like, preparing for the Fashion Week show. She worked until two A.M. every night, sometimes later, and was back in her office at seven in the morning, sometimes earlier. She worked on designs till the last minute, checked samples, auditioned and chose the models herself. Charlie found the venue, the producer, and the designer to decorate it. And their press office was swamped. "Wow, this is worse than being an OB," Ted said on one of the rare nights she spent with him. She was in his bed for three hours, and then she was gone again. He texted her when he had time, and it took her hours to respond. She wanted this to be the best show of her life, to make Giorgio glad he was in business

with them. They were increasing production, and
hoping for massive orders after the show, as his
participation in the business gave them greater
credibility than before. This was what Charlie and
Caro had been waiting for and had worked toward
for eleven years.

She wanted the show to be perfect.

The night before the show, Caro didn't go to bed
at all. She was on her feet all night, checking samples and doing fittings on models who were up all
night too.

She got a text from Ted around two. He was at
the hospital with a patient in labor. Caro had invited him to the show and he couldn't wait to see it.
The show was set up in a massive auditorium which
had been decorated with walls of flowers. One of
the best set designers from France had flown in to
do it, and Caro had given Ted an actual front-row
seat, between Lyle and Gloria. Her family always
came to the twins' shows. Charlie would be a moving target, troubleshooting and dealing with the
press from all over the world, and Caro would be
backstage checking each model before they came
out. The tension was high as she looked them all
over. And then one by one, like gumballs out of a
machine, the models exploded from backstage onto
the runway in Caro's creations, with fabulous accessories she'd designed to go with them.

Ted had found Lyle in the crowd on the way in,
and they had taken their seats together. Gloria

rushed in at the last minute, as she always did. All six Silvestri brothers had come and were seated across the aisle from her, and Giorgio blew her a kiss. She was wearing a very handsome diamond ring he had bought her in Milan. It wasn't an engagement ring, but it was a promise of a future together and was a stunning piece of jewelry. They hadn't figured out their plans yet, but things were moving forward at a rapid pace. He wanted to buy an apartment for them in New York, since he planned to spend six months a year there.

The house lights went off, the spotlights came on, the music was pounding and sensual as the models strutted down the runway, and more than once the audience applauded for a particularly spectacular dress. Ted was in awe of what Caro had created, and nudged Lyle. Lyle was always blown away by his sister's talent. She darted out from backstage at the end, in jeans and a T-shirt, and took a quick bow, then disappeared again. She hated being in the spotlight herself.

She came out a little while later to find Ted and kissed him.

"It was incredible," he said proudly. "You really are a genius."

"No, just a workhorse." She had to leave him and go backstage quickly. She had promised an interview to *The New York Times*. Ted left the auditorium with Lyle, Gloria went to meet Giorgio, and

Annabelle was backstage to help Caro. Benjie never came to the shows. They wouldn't have interested him, and were too chaotic.

Caro and Charlie didn't stop all day, and they drank champagne with the Silvestris. It was seven o'clock that night when Caro finally took a cab home and took a shower, and Ted showed up to see her. She was lying on her bed, staring at the ceiling, thinking about the show, and the things she should have done differently. But on the whole, she was satisfied. It had been a memorable show.

Ted knocked and walked into her room and found her lying there. She smiled when she saw him, and he came to lie next to her.

"Did you call for a doctor?" he asked, putting an arm around her. "The show was gorgeous."

"I hope the reviews will be good," she said. Charlie had heard rumors through Brady that they were. It had been a magnificent show.

"I don't know how you do it," Ted said. "No sleep and insanity. Is it worth it?" he asked her. He had seen how grueling it was and the toll it had taken on her for the past month.

"Yes," she said, without hesitation. "It is. I love it."

"Then it's worth it." He felt that way about his work too. "Do you want to get something to eat?" he asked her, and she shook her head.

"I can't move, and I have to be at the office early

to see the Silvestris before they leave. We're having breakfast with them. Do you want to spend the night?"

"I'd love to, but I'm on call. I'd better sleep at my place." It was closer to the hospital. They lay side by side for a while, until he saw her eyes start to flutter closed. She couldn't keep them open a minute longer. She had hardly slept in weeks, and she was right. It was an insane way to live. But she loved every minute of it.

A week later, the family met on a quiet Sunday morning. They still hadn't resolved the issue of the house. And as executor, Lyle wanted to see how the wind was blowing on that. There had been important changes in their lives in the last eight months, and he wanted to hear from them.

"Gloria, what's happening with you?" he asked her. She was talking a lot about Milan, and Giorgio was an ever-present feature in her life now. She hesitated before she answered.

"Our plans aren't definite yet. Giorgio wants me to spend more time in Italy with him. I'm planning to leave my job by the end of the year, and help him with his investments in Italy. He'd like to spend six months here, and the other six in Italy, and I want to be with him."

"Are you getting married?" Caro asked her, happy for her. It was a much better life than Gloria had lived in the past, before she met him. She seemed fulfilled now.

"We haven't figured that out yet. We're going to be together, that's all I do know. He'd like to have a baby. I'm not so sure."

"Where do you stand about the house now?" Lyle asked her.

"I still think we should sell it and invest the money." She hadn't changed on that subject, just all the others. And she wasn't living there. Their parents' home was her history, not her present.

Lyle spoke up next. "I love living here with the kids, and so do they. But I think I should get an apartment eventually. I'm not in a hurry. In six months, a year, maybe before that, if I find a place we love. Daphne might come to live with us. That's all I know right now."

Charlie spoke seriously, as he always did. "Brady and I want to buy an apartment together sometime this year, so I'll move out. But I still think we should keep the house for the rest of you, and what it means to us."

"I don't want to move," Annabelle said. "And I want Preston to grow up here, like we did."

"That's a costly business," Gloria reminded her. "It's an expensive house to maintain and run."

"I love it," Annabelle said simply.

Caroline was next. "I'm here, I want to stay here. I don't know what I'm going to do in future. Ted and I are still pretty new. And I think there's a real benefit to our living together. We help each other and give each other strength." Lyle nodded. He agreed. They all did. "And if Charlie buys an apartment with Brady, I want to sell our apartment in SoHo and stay here."

"I just wanted to know your thoughts. Maybe one day we'll sell, or have to, if it gets too expensive. But it doesn't sound like any of us are ready to move yet, except Charlie. The rest of us still want to be here, for a while anyway."

Benjie spoke up then. "I want to stay. Rose and I are going steady," he said seriously. "We love it here." They all smiled. "Caro says I can live with her if we move. And Rose's mom says I can live with them, so I'm okay, and I'll take Duke and Dottie with me if you sell the house." He was no longer afraid of what would happen to him.

They were all accounted for. No one really wanted to sell the house except Gloria. Benjie took a small box out of his pocket then and showed them the ring he was going to give Rose on her birthday. It was a small heart made of pink sapphires. "I bought it myself, with my salary. It's our going steady ring." Her parents let her spend the night there from time to time, and Caro could imagine Rose living with them one day. Maybe when they were a little older. They lived Benjie's life with him day by day.

"It seems like we should keep the house for now," Lyle said. "We're not ready to sell it. As things evolve, we can discuss it again. How does that sound to all of you?"

"It sounds good," they all echoed. The Whittier mansion was still their home, and they hoped it would be for as long as possible. Things could change. Caro and Ted had talked about living together at some point, but they weren't there yet. For the moment, they wanted to savor what they were sharing. Charlie had moved more quickly with Brady than Caro was ready to with Ted, and Brady seemed fine with it, and got along with everyone.

"Thanks for sharing your thoughts," Lyle said, as the meeting broke up and they all stood. It sounded as though he might be the next one to move on, after Charlie, but he was in no hurry, and he loved having his children there, living with the family.

They had a big noisy lunch together afterwards, with everyone talking and laughing and cooking and teasing each other. Benjie showed Ted and Daphne and Giorgio his ring for Rose and they told him how beautiful it was. "I'm going to get her a dog too. She wants one. I put my name on the adoption list at the shelter."

"You should ask her mom if it's okay," Caro reminded him, and he nodded. The house was safe for now. They still wanted to live there together. Caro wondered if they always would. She could see herself living in an apartment with Ted one day, even being married to him, and maybe having children with him. But not yet. Her home was still here with her brothers and sister, and nephews and niece. It was home to all of them. Their parents' legacy to them had lived on.

Chapter 18

All the Whittiers and their partners celebrated Christmas together in their childhood home, with all the familiar traditions. The men went out and bought a Christmas tree, and the women decorated it. They had Christmas Eve dinner formally in the dining room in black tie and evening gowns, as they always did. The siblings had preserved all the memories, the details, and the way of life they had shared with their parents. It was their first Christmas without them. The anniversary of their parents' deaths was in three weeks, and it was still hard to believe that they were gone. They each shed a tear for them over some special memory, or the flaming Christmas pudding, which their mother loved. Lyle carved the turkey the way their father used to. Tommy had just turned eleven and was wearing a blazer, and Caro had bought Devon a black velvet party dress. Gloria had brought a little black velvet romper for Preston from Italy. She loved shopping in Rome and Milan. She and Giorgio were officially engaged now, and planning to get married in the summer, then honeymoon on his yacht in Venice and the Adriatic.

Lyle had bought an apartment a few weeks before. It was exactly what he wanted, and big enough for the children. There was some work to do on it and he was moving in March or April, and Daphne was moving in with them. Amanda was getting married over New Year's in Las Vegas and moving to L.A. with her new husband and his plane. She and Lyle had discussed it and decided the children would be staying in New York with Lyle. It was what they wanted, and so did he. Amanda seemed quite satisfied with a month in the summer with them and alternate school holidays. Her new husband had a great deal of money, and Lyle had been generous with her, so she didn't mind giving up her child support. Brady and Charlie loved their new apartment and looked elegant in their tuxedos at dinner. Their arrangement seemed to be working perfectly.

Annabelle was starting school in three weeks. And after her one remaining semester, she was going to work full-time for her brother and sister at CCW.

Caroline and Ted had been dating for five months. They had talked about the future but weren't ready to act on it. Everything was running smoothly for now. It was all so perfect, they didn't want to rock the boat. Ted was spending more nights at her home than his own and felt totally at ease there now. He and Lyle were good friends, and Caro and Ted enjoyed spending time with Charlie and Brady. Both Brady and Ted had come to understand what it meant to be in love with a twin. There would always be an additional relationship that was precious to them, but there was room in their hearts for both a partner and a twin.

Benjie was wearing a tuxedo that night too. He looked very handsome. He had matured a lot in his relationship with Rose. She was with them, wearing a pink velvet dress Caro had made for her that fit perfectly. There was a little white ball of fluff on her lap at dinner. She was a Maltese puppy that had been abandoned and brought to the shelter. She was three months old when Benjie gave her to Rose for Christmas, and she had named her Snow, short for Snow White. She told everyone that the pink sapphire heart ring Benjie had given her for her birthday matched her dress.

The siblings raised a glass to their parents that night. There were tears in Caro's eyes when she looked at Charlie, and he understood exactly what she felt. He always did. She looked up at Ted, and he put an arm around her and held her. It had been both a hard year and a good one, full of blessings and new faces at their table, and they still had their home. Annabelle had her baby, and had grown up.

"Happy Christmas, everyone!" Lyle said, and they echoed his words, wondering what the next year would bring. Even if they didn't keep the house forever, it had played an important part in their history, and always would, filled with memories of their parents and each other, and the new people who had come into their lives, and their children.

They all hugged each other before they sat down again. Duke, Dottie, and Snow ran around the room barking, not sure what their people were all doing or why they were hugging, and everyone laughed, as they began their Christmas meal and new traditions were born, and old ones were honored. Preston and Connie would have been proud of them.

About the Author

DANIELLE STEEL has been hailed as one of the world's bestselling authors, with a billion copies of her novels sold. Her many international bestsellers include *Happiness, Palazzo, The Wedding Planner, Worthy Opponents, Without a Trace, The Whittiers, The High Notes, The Challenge,* and other highly acclaimed novels. She is also the author of *His Bright Light,* the story of her son Nick Traina's life and death; *A Gift of Hope,* a memoir of her work with the homeless; *Expect a Miracle,* a book of her favorite quotations for inspiration and comfort; *Pure Joy,* about the dogs she and her family have loved; and the children's books *Pretty Minnie in Paris* and *Pretty Minnie in Hollywood.*

daniellesteel.com

Facebook.com/DanielleSteelOfficial

Twitter: @daniellesteel

Instagram: @officialdaniellesteel

Look for

SECOND ACT

Coming soon in hardcover

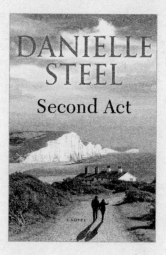

In this gripping novel from
#1 *New York Times* bestselling author
Danielle Steel, a top Hollywood executive
seeks a new beginning when his career
takes an unplanned turn.

Chapter 1

The building that housed Global Studios in Century City was impressive, but going in through the private entrance to the office of the head of the studio, the CEO of Global, was like entering another universe. Or boarding a rocket ship to the moon. A security guard stood at the discreetly set-apart elevator to escort VIPs and use his badge on the inside security panel to give them access to Andy Westfield's office on the forty-fourth floor. No one could reach the CEO's private quarters on the top floor without an invitation. Visitors were checked carefully at the main desk, their IDs examined, their fingerprints and photographs taken, their names verified with the reception desk upstairs. By the time they reached the elevator, they had been thoroughly vetted. No attack had ever been attempted on the CEO at Global, but it had happened to other heads of studios, and security measures were particularly acute and high-tech surrounding Andy.

The private elevator shot up at high speed without a stop. Visitors then found themselves at another reception desk, where they were expected and warmly greeted. The reception area was beautifully decorated with leather couches and priceless contemporary art, and visitors rarely had long to wait. The doors opened automatically into a small anteroom with paintings from Andy's personal collection, and fourteen-foot red lacquered doors led into the inner sanctum where Andy sat in peaceful splendor at an enormous mahogany and steel desk with a view of all of Los Angeles. A long wall to his right spoke of his own history. There was a row of posters of his parents' famous movies. He was the only son of two of Hollywood's beloved legends. His father, the most famous cowboy who had ever lived in films, John Westfield, originally from Montana, had come to Hollywood at eighteen to be an actor, and was a cowboy to his very core. After thirty years as an actor, he fell in love with directing and became one of the great directors of iconic Westerns. He had won four Oscars as an actor and collected three more as a director. He was a man of strong principles and values, which came across to the audience on film. He had set a powerful example for Andy, and been an admirable husband and father. Tall, rugged, and handsome, he was the hero men respected, little boys wanted to be when they grew up, and women dreamed about. His wife, Andy's mother, Eva Lundquist, originally from Sweden, was one of the most glamorous stars in Hollywood in her day. She and John were an unlikely, spectacular, and successful pair. She had two Oscars to her credit as well, and retired young to marry John and have Andy. They had been the most loved couple in Hollywood history, and were a strong role model to their son.

Andy had his father's height and good looks, with blond hair and a chiseled face, which had weathered and aged well in his father's case, and a notable cleft chin. John was an enormous man with a cowboy's frame. His hair was darker than Andy's, who had his Swedish mother's fair Nordic coloring and bright blue eyes. Andy was blessed with his heredity. He was almost as tall as his father, and just as handsome. He had never longed to be an actor. He knew the toll it had taken on his parents, although they did their best to shield their family life from the paparazzi. But they were always there, lingering in the background.

Andy's talent as a screenwriter had become apparent early. He had gone to USC and studied film. He had an undeniable gift. He spent the summers in college working on the sets of his father's movies, and after he graduated from USC he had written two scripts for his father. He'd had a sixteen-year career behind the scenes as a screenwriter, when he got sidetracked into the Hollywood power game. Because of his parents, doors opened to him that wouldn't have otherwise, and the opportunities rapidly became too tempting to turn down. His father had warned him to be careful but seize the opportunities he was given as they came and choose those that would best serve him. Andy had chosen wisely, often with his father's advice.

When AMCO, a major industrial corporation, bought Global Studios to glamorize their image, they sought out Andy and he became the youngest studio head in the business at thirty-eight. It was a heady experience and he handled it well. He put screenwriting behind him and dedicated himself to the business. At fifty-seven, Andy had been head of Global Studios for nineteen years now, and had outlasted all the other heads at rival studios. He was admired and respected and did his job well.

By the time Andy was in his early forties, he was as powerful as any studio head in the business, and little by little he had outstripped them. The qualities he had inherited from his father set him apart from everyone else. Honest, straightforward, hardworking, he was considered a man of integrity and honor. Not only did he have a brilliant mind for the business, he backed it with unfailing honesty. He was a man to be trusted. He had watched others fall in the last nineteen years, but his position only became more solid. The business didn't corrupt him, nor did the vast amounts of money he dealt with, but eventually the volume of his work devoured him. He had grown up with strong family values, which never left him, but the life of a studio head left little or no time for a family or ordinary pursuits. He was always somewhere, checking a film on location, calming a major star who wanted to quit, or making a deal for a new movie. He was the ultimate peacemaker as well as dealmaker, and he had learned from his parents how to coexist with stars and their demands. He had grown up among the biggest stars in the business. Nothing daunted him or frightened him or stopped him.

At forty-five, he had been married for twenty-one years when his wife, Jean, told him she was divorcing him. There was no scandal involved. She told him simply that she had hardly seen him for the past seven years, since he had become a studio head, and it was only going to get worse. He knew she was right. Andy was too good at what he did and loved it too much. Global had tripled its profits in the seven years he'd been the CEO. Andy and Jean's daughter, Wendy, was in college, and he knew he had been an absentee husband and father for some very important years. He had missed every birthday and school event. Jean had had to

be both mother and father to their daughter for all
the times Andy hadn't been there. Jean went to
most social events alone. He didn't have the time.
He loved his wife and daughter, but he loved his job
at least as much. He didn't fight the divorce and
was extremely generous with Jean, and always
spoke highly of her.

In the twelve years since their divorce, Jean had
remarried a cardiac surgeon, lived a suburban life
in Cleveland, and was extremely happy. Wendy had
married in the meantime too. She had always stayed
as far as she could get from the Hollywood world.
She had seen it devour her father's personal life
and destroy her parents' marriage. She was happily
married at thirty-two with a son and a daughter,
Jamie and Lizzie, and lived in Greenwich, Connecticut. She was married to a book publisher and was
an editor herself. Andy had dinner with them when
he had business in New York, but readily admitted he
saw too little of them. Wendy didn't hold it against
him. She understood who he was. He had sacri-
ficed his personal life for his success. She had never
asked him if he thought it was worth it. She assumed he thought it was. It was the life he had
chosen, and he seemed to have no regrets.

Andy had never remarried after the divorce. He
had had a series of relatively long-term girlfriends,
in Hollywood terms. His relationships lasted for
two or three years, often with a major star. He al-

ways had a famous actress on his arm, reminiscent of his own mother. Both of his parents had died by then, and his daughter and grandchildren were his only living relatives. Wendy meant the world to him, no matter how little he saw her, and so did her children. He called her frequently and kept current with her life, but he had little time to see her. He knew she understood the demands of his job, and what it meant to him. He *was* the job by now. It was part of him, like a vital organ.

His current girlfriend was Alana Beal, a truly talented actress who had done several movies with his studio since she had come from England to LA. She was a tall, cool beauty in her forties with stunningly glamorous looks, and she was an intelligent woman. He enjoyed talking to her. He had never abused the perks of his job or his position by seducing young actresses. He was an intelligent man of substance and all the women who had dated him spoke well of him. The relationships always ended because, as generous and kind as he was, he had no intention of marrying again and said so right from the beginning. Sooner or later the women he went out with realized that he meant it, and if they had marriage in mind, they moved on, usually at about the right time. Eventually another woman well-known in some field, usually movies, would take her place. The system worked well for him, and the relationships had usually reached their expiration dates by the time they ended.

Andy Westfield was supremely comfortable in his professional life, in the role of studio head, which was a dream come true for him. He had been one of the most important men in the film industry for exactly one-third of his life, nineteen years out of fifty-seven. He had hit his stride and was sailing along. Being a man of immense power was second nature now, and he never abused it. He didn't need to, and it wasn't his style. He didn't need to show off. He was comfortable with who he was. He never wasted his time looking far to the future. He lived in the now. His future was secure. He didn't need to worry about it. He had made an immense amount of money and invested it well, unlike his parents, who had spent all of theirs by the time they died.

He assumed he would stay where he was until he grew old, and would retire one day. He had improved Global's profits so astronomically that AMCO, their parent company, had no complaints, and there was no reason that would change. AMCO had made numerous acquisitions in the past two decades, and loved the excitement and glamour of owning a major film studio. Andy had never let the company down. He had become a Hollywood legend himself. With Andy running Global, it was a lovefest all around. Tony Bogart, the CEO of AMCO, liked to say they had gotten their money's worth when they hired Andy.

* * *

Frances, Andy's assistant of fifteen years, came into his office through a side door from her own. She had an office right next to his, so she could be at his beck and call constantly. She handled everything for him, including his social engagements. She had a respectful, friendly manner. She had just turned forty, and was twenty-five when she had started working for him. Being his assistant was a vocation almost like a religious calling to her. She worshipped him and lived to make life easier for him in every possible way. She was consummately discreet and reliable, and above all a trustworthy and kind person. She knew everything about his life, and got him out of things he didn't want to do with such grace that no one knew that the excuse wasn't real. Her friends accused her of being in love with him, which she didn't entirely deny, but she knew that nothing would ever come of it. There had never been even a hint of anything inappropriate from him. He was a very proper, respectful man, and she was well paid to do her job. She loved it, and keeping him punctual and organized.

"Just a reminder, Andy. You have to leave in ten minutes. You have to pick up Ms. Beal at four-thirty. Red carpet starts at five. And you should leave your house at four. I gave you an hour in the schedule to dress. Julian will be downstairs in ten minutes to take you home." Julian had been with him for a year. His drivers never stayed long. They were mostly out-of-work actors hoping to be discovered by him, which had never happened.

"Alana will be late anyway. I can have a drink at her place while I wait. She doesn't have you to organize her. Her assistant is more disorganized than she is." He grinned at Frances, who had red hair and freckles and looked like the girl next door, even at forty. She had no film aspirations. She'd gone to Princeton, and had taken the job for a summer and stayed, once Andy discovered how incredibly organized she was. She was from the East, and her family could never understand why she had taken a job as a personal assistant and stayed in it.

She was conservative in her dress, as he was, and wore businesslike suits in dark colors to the office. Andy always wore a suit and tie to work. His daughter Wendy teased him about being "old school," but he was respectful of his job and the people he saw every day. And Frances was too. Dressing the part came with the job, for both of them. Most of Andy's counterparts wore jeans and even T-shirts to the office now, and sneakers, and their assistants looked like they were going to the beach. There was no question that Andy Westfield was a very important man. You could tell just by looking at him.

As she always did, Frances got him out the door on time. He had no appointments that afternoon.

He took the private elevator down. Julian was waiting downstairs and took Andy to the house he'd bought in Bel-Air after the divorce. He had given Jean the house in Beverly Hills where Wendy had grown up, which Jean sold when she remarried and moved to Cleveland. Andy's house in Bel-Air was enormous, with a gigantic pool and patio where he could easily give parties for a hundred, with magnificent, sculpted gardens. The interior was exquisite too, with museum-quality art and more of his parents' movie posters. His job had made him a rich man over the years, and he liked living well and the perks of his success. He had inherited very little from his parents except their Oscars, and the wonderful memories he had of them.

Andy had thoroughly enjoyed his childhood. His parents had taken him everywhere with them. His father had made many of his films in Texas and Arizona, and his mother would take him to visit when they were on location. John had taught Andy to ride when he was four, and he was an excellent rider. He had so many warm memories of them, especially fishing with his father, who loved to fish. They had visited his mother's hometown in Sweden, where she was revered. He had ridden in several parades with his father when he was a little boy, riding his own horse. And they had gone to rodeos. They had visited John's parents in Montana several times before they died. Considering the possibilities in Hollywood, Andy had lived a relatively healthy life, with loving parents.

At times, he regretted not having had more time to spend with Wendy. She didn't have the rich history of memories that he was lucky enough to have, and he was grateful that she never seemed to hold it against him. Jean had wanted more children, but as an only child, he didn't, and they both realized later that it was just as well. He would have had even less time to devote to more children. Andy's father had taught him so many things that he'd never had time to share with Wendy. Andy and Jean lived in a different, faster-moving world. There had been more time, even with movie star parents, when Andy was a boy. The years had flown by until Wendy left for college, and he realized at her high school graduation, and even more so when she graduated from Columbia, that he had missed it all.

She stayed in New York after college and never moved back to LA. Then, two years later, he was walking her down the aisle when she married Peter Jensen. Andy's family life had been in fast-forward for as long as he could remember. For twelve years now since his divorce, he had lived the life of a bachelor in his spectacular home. It was much bigger than he needed, but it went with his image and stature as a studio head, and it was an ideal place to entertain, which he didn't have time to do either.

He hadn't given a party in several years. And he almost never saw old friends. His work dinners came first.

Frances kept his house efficiently staffed. Many of the people she had hired had been there since he bought the house. He had a butler, Timothy, who was English, several people who cleaned the house, a fleet of gardeners. He didn't keep a cook, because his schedule was erratic and he went out a lot, or ordered in from his favorite restaurants when he wanted to eat at home. The housekeeper cooked for the staff.

His dinner jacket had been laid out by the butler, the night of the Academy Awards. He helped Andy dress and did his cufflinks and impeccable bow tie for him.

Two of Global's recent movies had been nominated.

Alana, Andy's current girlfriend, hadn't been nominated this time and had never won an Oscar. His parents' Oscars were displayed in shadow boxes along one wall in the library. Alana was an exceptionally good actress. She and Andy didn't live together but saw each other three or four times a week, including the weekends they spent together when he had time. This would be her third time going to the Academy Awards with him.

Wendy had met Alana a few times but wasn't close to her. She knew her father's women didn't last, so she didn't make any effort to spend time with them. He came alone when he visited Wendy and Peter, and their son, Jamie, and daughter, Lizzie, in their home in Greenwich. Alana wasn't part of Andy's family life and didn't expect to be. She was divorced too, and had no children. Her career was the main focus of her life, just as his was.

Andy left on time and was at Alana's at precisely four-thirty. She lived in a small, elegant house in the Hollywood Hills. She usually stayed at his house when they were together. Andy looked impeccable, his blond hair graying slightly, his vibrant blue eyes, his face alive with interest in whatever he was doing or who he was talking to. His tuxedo had been made by his tailor in London. Every inch of him was perfection. He was as handsome as any actor, his face was lit from within with intelligence and experience, and there was an aura of power about him. It was easy to guess that he was an important man. Alana always dated powerful men or famous actors and had made a career of it.

She rushed into the living room where he was sipping a vodka martini. She was breathless and beautiful. It was five to five, and she was almost half an hour late. She was a tall, very slim woman in her forties, with full breasts pouring out of a white dress that looked like it was wallpapered to her and was vintage Chanel couture. She had borrowed it for the evening, as she did everything she wore to major events. It had been flown in from Paris and fitted to her. She was wearing long diamond earrings that Andy had given her on their first anniversary, with a diamond necklace she had borrowed from Van Cleef. Alana knew just how to do red carpet events, especially the Academy Awards. She and Andy went to the Golden Globe Awards every year too.

"Wow, Ms. Beal!" Andy said, beaming at her. "*You* are a vision! They should give you an Oscar just for the dress." He looked at her appreciatively and she smiled at the compliment and pirouetted for him. Her blond hair was in a sleek French twist and all the diamonds sparkled. A team of makeup artists, hairdressers, and a manicurist had just left.

"They took the dress out of the Chanel exhibit for me. Elizabeth Taylor owned the necklace. Richard Burton gave it to her," she said proudly. The trappings of stardom were all-important to her.

"He would have given you a bigger one," Andy said, smiling as he approached to kiss her. He always enjoyed her company. He wasn't madly in love with her, but they were comfortable with each other, which was all he wanted. She was a bright, interesting woman and a good actress, and he didn't have any illusions about the fact that if he wasn't who he was, she wouldn't have been dating him. But the arrangement worked for both of them, and they were a familiar pair in Hollywood. She loved being in the press with Andy, and he didn't mind. He was used to it, and it was important to Alana. He had never found the kind of relationship his parents had, even with Jean when he was married to her. His parents' relationship really was a love match, but he guessed that his father had been a more attentive husband and had had more time to spend with his wife.

Andy remembered distinctly how his mother's face had lit up when his father walked into the room, and the slow smile on his father's handsome face when he put his arms around his beautiful wife. It had embarrassed Andy as a child, but now he remembered it fondly. He and Jean had always been more matter-of-fact with each other, and playful when they were younger. They had married soon after college. But Jean didn't have a romantic nature, and Andy was shy when he was young.

They became more like friends than lovers as time went on, particularly when he got busy with a big job. Their friendship had carried them through the years, but not all the way to the end. She had admitted to him when they divorced that she had been lonely married to him. Andy thought Jean's new husband was intelligent but dull, although he was supposedly a talented surgeon at the Cleveland Clinic and people came from all over the world to be operated on by him. But Jean said they did everything together when he wasn't working, which was something she and Andy had never done, and she had had no interest in the glamorous side of Andy's life.

Jean had hated going to the Academy Awards and having attention focused on her and Andy. She always felt like she'd worn the wrong dress and felt like a drudge compared to the movie stars. They were impossible for a normal human to compete with. Andy was always very polite and told her she looked lovely, but there was no excitement in his eyes when he said it to her, or in hers. They had fallen out of love with each other and hadn't noticed, while he was running the studio and she was driving Wendy to soccer games and ballet classes. Over the years she had become a soccer mom, and he was surrounded daily by gorgeous movie stars. He had never cheated on her while they were married, but in the last few years of their marriage they hardly ever made love anymore. They had outgrown each other.

The women he dated after the divorce were almost always movie stars. They were readily at hand, and eager to be seen with him. It was easy for him. Alana was a prime example of that. Such women fed his ego, but never touched his heart. He didn't expect to fall in love again, and he hadn't. But it was important to him to be with a woman he could talk to. He had no interest in ingénues and starlets. They looked like paper dolls to him. Alana was intelligent, even if she was ambitious, and constantly aware of what was good for her career. But he was never bored or embarrassed to be with her. She was ladylike, and he enjoyed being with her, whatever her motives. She wasn't interested in marriage either. Just in furthering her career.

When Andy and Alana got to the red carpet, the press rushed toward them, and Alana looked dazzling in the white gown, with the diamonds sparkling on her neck and ears. She posed for the cameras and she and Andy stopped several times, and once inside, the television cameras focused on them constantly. Andy took it in stride. He had lived with it all his life. It was all familiar territory to him.

Both of Global's films won, one for best picture, the other for best actress, and Andy was pleased. He had expected them to win, but it was always gratifying and never got old. He was proud of the studio, and to be the head after all these years.

He and Alana went on to the two most important after-parties when the ceremony was over, and the press crowded them again on the way out. Alana was ready for them, her hand tucked in Andy's arm as they made their way through the crowd, and they talked to an endless stream of people at the parties. Andy was tired of it by the time they got to the second one, but he knew how much Alana enjoyed it, so they stayed, and he chatted with Phil Lieber, an important producer he knew, while Alana stopped for a minute to talk to a friend.

"What do you think of the rumors about AMCO?" Phil Lieber asked him, with a martini in his hand. Andy was tired of talking and drinking by then and looked unimpressed by the question. "I keep hearing they're going to sell Global." It was the kind of thing people said, but it never went far. There was no substance to it, just gossip.

"Nothing new there, Phil. Every time there's a blip in the stock market, someone says they're going to sell. AMCO loves being in the movie business. There have been rumors like that as long as I've been at Global." Andy was visibly bored by the conversation. Lieber was a scaremonger, and Alana caught the tail end of the conversation when she got back.

She brought it up to Andy on the way home in the car. Andy was dropping her off at her place. It was late. He had an early meeting the next morning, and she never stayed with him after the Awards. She would want to gossip on the phone with all her friends the next morning, and he would be in his office long before she woke up.

"What was that Phil Lieber was saying about AMCO selling Global? Someone else said it to me last week. It sounded crazy to me, but is it true?" She looked worried, and she frowned as much as her latest Botox shot would allow.

"I hear that stuff all the time. They're not selling.

I doubt they ever will. They have too much fun being in the movie business. And we make them a ton of money," he said confidently.

"Good, I'm glad you're not worried."

"No, I'm not. Thank you for joining me tonight," he said, as his Bentley came to a stop in front of her house.

"I loved it. I always do, thank you for taking me," she said, and kissed him lightly on the lips. "Do you want to come in?"

"I'd love to, but I'm dead. And I've got a breakfast meeting tomorrow at the crack of dawn." She wasn't bothered by his refusing. She hadn't expected him to spend the night, or even come in for a while. They were both tired, but she thought it best to ask. "I'll see you on Saturday," he said, and kissed her just before she got out, and then he walked her properly to her door and saw her in.

He was back in the car two minutes later, thinking about Global's two films that had won. He was always pleased at their wins. They had at least one Oscar-winning film every year, or several, for best actor or actress or director or best picture. The sweet smell of success was so familiar to him now. He didn't take it for granted, but he was accustomed to it and considered it the norm.

The driver took him home, and when Andy crossed the patio, he noticed how beautiful the pool was, all lit up. It was a balmy night with a star-filled sky, and he sat down for a minute, just to enjoy it. He sat back in one of the lounge chairs and looked up and smiled. He remembered nights when he had gone camping with his father in Wyoming and Montana and how close the stars had seemed, and how full of falling stars the sky was. The memory of it still warmed his heart. As he looked around at his home, he realized again that he was a lucky man, and all was well in his world. He couldn't imagine a better life than the one he had.